DIRTY DEEDS

LAUREN LANDISH

Edited by
VALORIE CLIFTON
Edited by
STACI ETHERIDGE

DIRTY DEEDS

BY LAUREN LANDISH

Join my mailing list (www.laurenlandish.com) and receive 2 FREE ebooks! You'll also be the first to know of new releases, sales, and giveaways. If you're on Facebook, come join my Reader Group!

Other books in the *Get Dirty* Series (Interconnecting standalones):
Dirty Talk
Dirty Laundry

For months, I've watched her. I know she's off-limits, but she's so sweet, so innocent... and so sexy that she haunts my dreams.

Maggie doesn't belong in this world, this seedy underbelly of the city. But there she is, my Angel with her wide eyes behind her nerdy glasses. So, when she needs help, I'm the only one who can protect her.

It didn't even take a single kiss for me to fall in love with her. I know I shouldn't—a man like me doesn't deserve an Angel. I'll hurt her, break her... **ruin** her. Still, I can't help myself.

She's going to regret this later, regret me and probably even hate me. But I'm a selfish man, and if she wants this now, I'll give it to her. I'll give her **everything**.

**For a limited time, this title includes bonus content.

PROLOGUE

SHANE

I lean back, keeping an eye on the club from my position near the wall. On the far side of the club, Marco the bartender is mixing up a pitcher of margaritas for one of the tables while looking cool as a cucumber in his dress shirt and vest, the sleeves on his cranberry-colored shirt rolled up to just below his elbows. Seeing me, he gives a little salute with two fingers. I return it, knowing that within a few minutes, I'll have some refreshment myself.

"Hey, Shane, you want to switch?" Nick, the guy I have working the door right now, asks. "I gotta piss."

"Yeah, I'll cover the door for a bit. Just hurry. I want to do a walk-around."

"No sweat," Nick says, heading toward the back. I take over the door, leaning back in the stance that allows me to keep an eye on the floor while still keeping the door under control.

Nick takes his time. He always does, which is one of the reasons I'm the bouncer in charge here, but I'm not upset as I see a tight, petite blond make her way toward me. "Hey,

1

Shane," she says, handing me a big beer mug filled with Coca Cola. "Marco said you were looking thirsty."

"Thanks, Meghan. You doing okay?" I ask, taking a moment to appreciate the wide-eyed cuteness that is Meghan. She's only been here about a week, but there's something about her that draws my eyes to her again and again, and not because I'm doing my security job. "No troubles with the tables?"

"Of course not," Meghan says, giving me that shy, sweet-girl smile that I've started looking forward to. "Actually, I've got a friend coming in later. Uhm, if a tall knockout chick comes in asking for me, you mind pointing her my way?"

"Sure enough," I promise her, an unfamiliar smile crossing my face. I almost never smile at work, but Meghan seems to pull them out of me without even trying. "You two gonna discuss cookie baking or something?"

For a split second, I see the most beautiful shade of pink as her cheeks blush, but then she ducks her head shyly. "No, she's just having a tough time with a guy she's seeing and wants my advice. I think she mostly needs girl talk, you know?"

"Sure," I lie through my teeth. "I'll keep an eye out. Be safe out there."

Meghan nods, sashaying away. She tosses her hair back over her shoulder, her hips hypnotizing me with each swing left and right. On her, the sexy moves seem unintentional, not a practiced performance like the other girls here. Nick comes back and I drain my Coke before patrolling the floor. It's not really needed, but letting the customers have a silent warning helps stop about ninety percent of the shit that can happen around here before it even starts.

2

As I move around the floor, my eyes tick back to Meghan as she works her tables. It's almost like I'm circling her, edging ever so closer, tempting fire and keeping the best view of her that I can. Her uniform miniskirt hugs her tight ass like it was painted on her, and as she bends down to put a pitcher of beer on a table for six, I swear she's showing off especially for me, popping her ass out in a fantasy-come-to-life move.

Maybe it's just me, or maybe it's Meghan's natural charm, but I can't help watching every move she makes. The way she licks a thumb when she splashes something on it, the way she shows her cleavage as she moves in her uniform bustier corset . . . it's all so damn seductive, and the contrast between the shy girl she is around me and the sex kitten she acts like while working makes me wonder which is more real.

Meghan straightens up, turning and looking over her shoulder at me, adjusting those thick-framed 'nerdy' glasses that push her from cute to hot as fuck. She seems surprised to find me watching, her eyebrows lifting behind the frames, but I catch her biting her lip to hide the little smirk tugging at her mouth. She's fucking with me, she's got to be. I have to hold back a growl as she goes over to her next customer, striking a pose beside the table as she takes their order.

I'd never let any of the fucknuts who frequent this place lay a hand on one of the girls, but I keep a special eye on Meghan. It makes some of the long shifts a bit easier, and stocks my spank bank with plenty of imaginary material . . . Meghan bent over the bar as I take her from behind. Or maybe twirling around a pole in one of the private rooms just for me. The dangerous fantasies are the ones where I picture her in my bed . . . hair a mess with flushed cheeks, wearing nothing but the smile I just put on her full lips.

I alternate door duty with Nick, letting him do the next floor sweep per protocol. A static position sometimes makes me antsy. But for right now, I lean against the doorframe, appreciating the best view of Meghan in the house.

I continue my scan of the room, checking customers, the bar, and the stage, but my eyes always return to the tiny, sweet blonde that is slowly driving me insane. "God damn, what I would do to you if I had a chance," I whisper to myself, knowing the heavy rock music will obliterate the words before anyone can hear them. Still, as if by some form of ESP, Meghan taunts me, crouching down with her ass near her heels to hear a guy's order. He's looking straight down her bustier at her tits and I have to hold myself back from beating the shit out of him just for looking at her. My restraint is rewarded as she rises back up, shifting her skirt back into place and giving me a bigger peek at the curve of her ass. She heads towards the bar to turn in the order, but I see the way she peeks over to check if I'm watching.

Two can play that game, little girl. I casually reach down and adjust my cock, my face hard and stoic as I give her a disapproving look. She squeaks I think. I can't hear it, but the way she jumps a bit and her mouth flies open, I imagine the shocked sound coming from her throat. I laugh to myself, but I'm not sure if she won that round or I did.

Still, I keep my cool, keeping myself under control as the night wears on. Meghan's friend shows up right before closing time, and the two have a long sit-down talk while Marco and I finish up the cleaning.

"Thanks, Shane," Meghan says as they get ready to head out the door. Her friend's gone off to use the ladies' room, and it's just us for a moment. "I always feel . . . good when you're around."

"I just want to make sure you stay safe," I reply, looking down into her adorable face. "After all, this is a gentlemen's club."

Meghan chuckles and looks around. "Not too many gentlemen in this club. But I'm glad there's at least one. Thanks again, Shane."

My name on her lips is a tease that makes me want to taste her mouth as she says it again. But her friend comes out, and the two of them leave. Meghan gives me a little finger wave as the door closes. Oh, my sweet little innocent one . . . if only I were a gentleman.

If only.

I'm anything but, which is why it's safer if you stay away from me.

CHAPTER 1

MAGGIE

"*H*ey, Marco! Can I get a pitcher of Miller Lite for table fifteen, please?" I yell over the throbbing bass of the music in the club . . . and get ignored again. "MARCO!"

He looks over and gives me a half-understanding nod before grabbing one of the plastic pitchers and filling it with . . . well, fudge it, it's beer at least. I roll my eyes, frustrated that I have to drag the bartender's eyes away from the stage. He's been here for years, and you'd think he'd be immune to this after seeing dancers for hours five nights a week.

But he isn't. Obviously, as evidenced by the way he's staring at the stage. He moves a hand, and I think he's going to adjust his crotch, but instead, his hand lifts to his head and he slicks his already meticulously coifed hair into place. In my head, I nag him. Adjust whatever you need to, your crotch or your hair or your suave designer clothes. Just do your dang job so I can do mine. Not too much to ask, is it?

"Here you go, Meghan," he says, sliding the pitcher the last few inches to me. I notice that he doesn't apologize that he's ignored the order I placed on the bar five minutes ago, nor that the delay will likely affect my tip, not his. His eyes still haven't left the show onstage either. Such a butt-nugget.

With a sigh, I turn to see what's got Marco so blasted distracted at the moment. I know from the music that it's Allie's turn on stage. Besides being one of the people I can call a friend around here, she's an amazing dancer, definitely too good to be stripping in a place like this. I watch as she spins around the pole, her legs splayed wide in the splits for several rotations as she flips her head around, making eyes at a guy in the front row.

In a flash, she pulls her legs in smoothly, locking them around the pole and lying back in a death-defying backbend move that puts her eye-level with her prey, although she's upside-down and his eyes are locked on her boobs, not her face. I see her smirk and then kick her legs over, rising to stand tall in her high-heeled red stilettos. It's impressive, even from just an athletic point of view, although I'm sure most of Allie's fans aren't really interested in how much she's had to train and work for her unworldly strength, balance, and flexibility.

The guy picks up a green bill from the stack in front of him, and Allie slithers down to take it, blowing the guy a kiss with her plump, heavily lipsticked lips, knowing she'll have the whole pile before her time onstage is up.

I clap loudly, cheering her on, knowing that the cash will help her out with her debt situation. She's a nice girl, my best friend in this club, and still way too good for this joint.

Still clapping, I don't hear Marco approach. "She's something else, isn't she? Even you can't keep your eyes off her. Can you blame me? Unless . . . that's your thing?"

I laugh, glancing over at him to see a questioning look in his dark eyes. He seems more excited about the idea than I would've expected because he knows me better than that. I shake my head. "You know I don't swing that way, but I can appreciate talent and hard work. Especially in my friends."

"Calm down, Little Miss Goody-Two-Shoes. You know I'm not going near that chick with a ten-foot pole. I like my dick where it is, thank you very much."

I narrow my eyes at him, attempting to appear threatening, but we both know it's not the threat of my tiny little librarian-looking self that has him shaking in his Italian loafers. It's that our boss has taken a rather obvious interest in Allie lately. And no one dares go against Dominick if he's even considering marking some of that territory for himself.

"If you're still interested, your Miller Lite is getting piss-warm and table fifteen is looking mighty thirsty," he says, smirking. "I guess they're not into Allie. They seem to be paying more attention to their beers and their MIA waitress."

Shishkabob! My tip is definitely going to take a hit on this table if I can't turn it around with a little extra sugar. Hoping that maybe they like nerdy girl-next-door types instead of out of this world exotic beauties like Allie, I fluff my girls up in the black bustier that serves as the top half of my uniform and grab the pitcher to walk it over.

"Here you go, fellas. Didn't want to interrupt your view of Allie's special talents," I say, going heavy with the flirty innu-endo as I lean over, confident that while my full cleavage is on display, they're locked solidly in the cups and won't spill out for an unintended nip slip.

Not that anyone would mind. Except me, of course. Petals from Heaven may be the sort of club where the female persuasion exposes their body parts to the spotlights, and my uniform is decidedly sexier than I would choose myself, but I've never felt like I was expected to do more than deliver drinks. Unless I wanted to, which I definitely don't.

The guys' eyes all lock to my chest, same as always, and their eyebrows lift. Gotcha, boys. So Allie isn't their cup of tea, but I am. Well, it takes all types, and it's sort of encouraging to know that a girl like me can be compared to a goddess like Allie and sometimes get the nod. Maybe my tip won't be so bad, after all.

I take a moment to pour each of the four guys a mug, feigning a lack of skill that makes the suds at the top spill over the lip and down my hand, the white foam looking decidedly like something more seductive than beer. I might be kinda innocent, but I'm not as schoolgirl innocent as I look, and I know how to tease.

I give the last guy his drink and then casually lick the bubbles from my fingers, letting my pink tongue curl out before sucking a tip into my mouth. All four guys' jaws drop at my innocent display before the one closest to me grabs my hand.

His blue eyes flick up to me as he holds my hand in a near-crushing grip, grinning drunkenly. "Let me help you with that."

Before I can say yes or no, he moves forward, his blond hair falling into his face as he quickly swipes his tongue against my finger and sucks it into his mouth. *Fudge! Danger, Will Robinson. Need to back this play up without causing a scene.* One of the hallmark rules of working in a club—don't cause a scene unless you really, really need help.

Instead of freaking out, I give my best girly giggle, jerking my hand back and squealing. "Ooh, that tickles!" I laugh as I shake my hand loose. "You shouldn't be so naughty!"

"Honey," Blondie says, half getting up, "if you want to see naughty—"

Out of nowhere, Shane appears behind me. He's part of Petals' security team and the star of too many of my midnight fantasies to admit. I can't see him, but I can feel his presence like a physical force pressing against my body. It's comforting, a little scary, and also frustrating. I can't help it, Shane's just . . . well, he's as sexy as chocolate cake, and probably just as dangerous for my health.

Shane growls, his voice low and dangerous. There's no weakness, no compromising with that voice. Fact is, Shane's not afraid of anyone or anything. He might be the only person in the club not afraid of Dominick. "No touching. Or I'll be the one touching you."

The threat is apparent, and the guy's face shows his fear that Shane will kick his ass. Shane's words have the opposite effect on me, though, and my mind is filled with an image of him touching me, his strong, thick fingers tracing lines along my private silky areas, teasing and tantalizing me before taking me roughly.

Back in reality, finger-sucking guy has his hands up wide, backing down immediately. "No problem, man. Sorry, won't happen again."

Shane lets out one more growl before stalking off. I never even made eye contact with him, but under the slip of dark denim they call my miniskirt, my panties are soaked from being that close to him, having his voice wash over me, and that flash of fantasy.

Needing to save the tip, though, I smile at the forward guy, and he does at least offer an apology to me, a rarity in this place. "No problem, honey. Security is just really protective of us. I'm sure you understand."

"I can certainly understand why," he says as his eyes float down my body, taking an extra moment on my chest, my crotch, and the length of my legs sticking out of the skirt before tracing back up again. Despite my petite height, this slip of a skirt combined with my heels make my legs look a mile long, and it feels like it takes him forever to uncomfortably peruse every inch. "We're good for now, but keep the pitchers coming all night."

He says the last part in a filthy little cadence, emphasizing every word, and I can hear the obvious double-entendre. I nod and giggle, reverting to my innocent girl shtick as I promise to keep them coming.

I walk away, smiling as I hear the guys start loudly talking to each other. Two can play that game, and we're both hoping to get lucky, just not in the same way. Tip me, tip the stage girls, and get out so I can get some fresh meat at my table with another full wallet.

It sounds crass, even to myself, but it's the reality. No one is coming to Petals from Heaven strip club to find love, and really, no one is coming to find sex. Well, I guess some of the guys do come in with the fantasy of having an amazing night with a woman who ticks all their mental boxes, but the odds of that are worse than winning the Powerball.

I don't really get it. Guys crowd in with their other guy friends, pay fart-tons of money for cover, drinks, and tips, then go home to flog their bishop? Why the game? Just watch some porn or something and take care of business.

Unless the guy is paying for a private show, where they're not supposed to whip it out, but according to my dancer friends, they pretty much know they've got a fifty-fifty chance that they're going to be dancing while the patron gets down to business.

Ew. Just gross.

I make another round of my tables, getting refills, flirting, dropping off checks, flirting, collecting cash . . . and more flirting.

As I work, I keep an eye out for any patrons who might be . . . somebody. That's my real job, scouting for celebrities, major or minor, politicians, CEO bigwigs, Instagram-famous people, or anyone else who might be interesting and tends to frequent this particular club.

On one hand, they're usually the best tippers. On the other, they're why I'm really here, working as Meghan, a cocktail waitress at a strip club, undercover for the tabloid gossip rag I work for. Neither job is my dream come true, but since no one is knocking on my door to write for *The New York Times*, online trash talking pays my bills.

I got the assignment to get a second job at Petals two months ago, and to my surprise, they hired me right away. Petals is known for being exclusive and VIP-preferred, so I'd been nervous about their hiring plain Jane me. But I'd been hired as a waitress on the spot based on my resume and my other . . . ahem . . . assets. So far, the undercover gig has paid off in a couple of smaller celebrity-sighting stories, but I feel like there's something bigger here. I just don't know what it is yet.

But Petals from Heaven is sort of the place to go if you're a celebrity who wants a taste of the salacious life but you don't want to get caught out on the town because of your wife, your girlfriend, or just your reputation. There's a sense of discretion at Petals, and Dominick fosters that, making sure the A-listers get what they want, whether it's private rooms or flashy top-notch service. Plus, Petals employs some of the most beautiful dancers I've ever seen in my life. It's almost artistic, just nearly naked too. With this combination, something gossip-worthy has to happen eventually, and I want to be here to report on it.

Ironically, this undercover gig is pretty sweet and is paying more than half my bills now anyway. It was an odd realization that the writing and research I love to do and went to school for are actually less financially rewarding than playing airhead and slinging drinks.

Not sure what that says about our society, but it's not anything complimentary.

I hear the DJ talking loudly over the mic, adding some hype to our last performer of the night and telling everyone in the club to get their last drink and get the fudge out. He doesn't use those words, of course, but I censor them in my head like I sometimes do.

I drop one last pitcher and the check at Finger-Sucking-Guy's table and he clears his throat. "Uhm, hey, so I don't wanna piss off the bouncer or nothing, but what are you doing tonight? Wanna party?"

I forcefully contain my eye roll, choosing to twirl my hair around my finger and kicking my voice up an octave. I deal with this at least once a week. Can't get the dancer, go for the waitress. "Oh, no. Sorry, honey, I can't. I've got school in the morning, so I'd better be a good girl and get home."

The reality is, I've been out of school for over three years, but they always believe this excuse because I look a lot younger than my twenty-five years. I still get carded when I buy wine.

Luckily, he takes the refusal gracefully, or maybe he's worried about Shane showing up again. "Mmm. Yes, you should be a good girl. Get right to bed."

It's still flirty and slightly sleazy, but at least he's not arguing with me. I give a wink and turn, flouncing off to close out my other tables.

Once everyone's gone and the club is cleaned up, I head backstage to change. Pulling on sweats and a long-sleeve T-shirt, I'm thinking of only a few things. Mainly getting home, taking a good long shower to get the leftover smell of the club off me, and then collapsing into bed. After all, I've got to be ready for work at ten . . . and my boss hates it if I'm late.

CHAPTER 2

SHANE

*R*eaching down, I wrap my hand around the handles of each keg, lifting one with each arm. Marco needs the help restocking or else he's going to be here until sunrise, so I normally help him out by carrying the kegs up from downstairs while he brings up the bottles he needs and sends in our orders for the suppliers.

My arms are a little tired by the time I get the two kegs up the stairs, and it's with a grunt of relief that I set them down. Marco's working the register, checking his money against the Point of Sale system. "You have a good night tonight?"

Marco nods, smirking a little. "Yeah, pretty solid. Decent tips, and with the eye candy from Allie's new routine, I can't really complain."

He waggles his eyes at me, like he expects to chatter on about Allie's tits or something. It feels like a test. I'm just not sure if it's a bro one or seeing if I'm aware that Dominick has marked her as off-limits.

Doesn't really matter either way. I'm a fucking professional

LAUREN LANDISH

and I know that I *do not* get involved with any of the girls here, whether they've been tabbed by Dominick or not. So Marco's going to be disappointed in my answer. "Yeah, she's good. She's been working hard and it's paying off."

A couple of the girls come into the club from backstage, and I'm thankful for the break from Marco's slick vibe. Time to do my actual job and not just help out. "Ladies, let me walk you out."

They murmur their thanks but basically ignore me, especially Tina, who's already gabbing away on her phone, telling her babysitter that she's on the way home. I get it. They've got men talking to them all fucking night, and ninety-nine percent of it more or less leads to 'I wanna fuck.' They just tune it all out. It's a survival instinct.

I don't mind. Walking the girls out is one of my usual duties and the one I take the most seriously. There's always a chance that some 'fan' might not be able to check their fantasy at the heavy door, and I'm here to ensure that doesn't become a problem. I make sure they get in their cars safely and then watch from the doorway to make sure they pull out alone.

It's a little sad, really. I can't imagine any of them as little girls thinking, 'Hey, when I grow up, I wanna be a stripper.' But life sometimes doesn't go according to plan, and we do what we need to so we can get by. So when these girls are under my supervision, they deserve respect and safety, and I'm gonna give that to them, even if no one else in their lives does.

After the girls are gone, I head back inside, seeing Meghan swinging through the saloon-style doors from backstage. She looks young, even more so than usual in her sweats and oversized T-shirt. She could pass as a college freshman on any campus in the US.

She's 'just' a waitress, but in my opinion—not that anyone asks me. I'm not paid to have an opinion—she's the best-looking girl working here. She's absolutely gorgeous when she's done up for a shift, all poufy blonde hair, big doe eyes with fake lashes, puffy, kissable pink lips, and a sexy rack atop a tiny body. She usually favors a sort of 'naughty innocent' look, and there's a reason she's getting more tips than any other waitress.

But my favorite is her 'after shift' style, when she's fresh-faced with her hair pulled up, wearing her big owlish glasses and jeans or sweats. She looks cute and sweet, and small enough I could pick her up and put her in my pocket . . . or over my shoulder. She's almost shy, walking into the main room like she's making sure she's allowed to come in before committing to the movement. She sees me and smiles, walking with more confidence.

That smile feels like a secret view not many people get, like it's a lazy morning at home with a lover look, even though it's damn near three in the morning and we're at a strip club. It makes me . . . Shaking my head to let that train of thought go, I call out to her. "Meg, you ready to go?"

She nods, giving me a little wave and a thumbs-up. "Yep. G'night, Marco. See you tomorrow night."

I have the urge to stick my elbow out for her, gentleman style, but the no-touching rule extends to staff. Unless asked, don't. And I'm the enforcer of the rules, so there's no way in hell I'm going to let myself break them. So I clamp down on that urge and have to be satisfied with opening the door for her. Still, I do let myself take a moment to admire her pert ass as she walks through. I can't help it.

Outside, I ask her the same generic question I asked Marco, but I hope for a better answer from Meghan. "You have a good night tonight?"

Meghan gives me a nod, adjusting her glasses and giving me a tired smile. "It was okay. Good tips, even from that one table," she says, and we both know exactly what she's talking about. "Thank you for that, by the way. I didn't even have a chance to react before you swooped right in."

I shrug, not letting Meg know that when she's on shift, I always keep an extra eye out for her. She's just so . . . innocent. "That's my job. Already had my eye on that table anyway. They were giving bad vibes."

She nods in understanding. She's been here long enough to get those gut feelings too. "Well, I appreciate your being the bad guy so I could be the good girl."

I tease her, knowing it's a bad idea but unable to stop myself. "And *are* you a good girl?"

My voice has dropped a little, low and gravelly. Meg always makes me feel this way, like a caveman on the verge of dragging her off to have my way with her. She makes me yearn to control the situation, control her, but I have to settle for controlling myself.

She giggles, but it's not the false one she gives guys in the club. She sounds nervous and . . . flirty, maybe? "I try to be, but sometimes, it's hard to be good."

There's a hint of sex to her voice, but it feels like there's more truth to what she said than a casual coy response. It's maddening, the way we seem to dance around each other, half innuendos and comments that just toe the line between 'playful banter' and 'outright suggestion,' but I can't go further. It's too dangerous, and not because of her.

Before I can think on it too much, we reach her car and the silence of the early morning dark is broken. "Hey, honey! You ready to go?"

I'm instantly on alert, shoving Meghan behind me as I turn to see the finger sucking asshole who was putting the moves on her earlier. Considering that it's now a good hour after the last patron was out the damn door, we're way, way past the bounds of appropriate behavior.

He's leaning up against the car next to hers like he's waiting for her. While it's against the official rules, some of the girls will do date-nights with patrons on the side, almost sugar daddy style. But Meghan isn't the kind to do that sort of thing, and I don't consider for a second that she told him anything but a polite version of "fuck off".

Even if she did, I'm not letting her leave with him. Not her. Not with a guy like him.

Instead, I shift my left foot forward while covering Meghan with my body. "You need to leave, asshole. The no-touching policy extends to when we're closed too. So get in your car and take a fucking hike."

Blondie pushes off the car, facing me fully, and I do a quick assessment. He's big, at least six feet, but I've got a few inches on him, and though he looks muscled, it's in a gym rat way. Not the look of someone who's surprisingly strong because of real manual labor.

Most importantly, he doesn't have that air of 'I'll fuck you up.' He seems on the verge of drunk and a bit prissy, like he's used to getting his way.

Well, not tonight. Instead, Blondie talks about Meghan like she's not even here, and as she almost shivers behind me, I know that if a line needs to be crossed, I'm going to cross it. "We're partying tonight. She told me to wait for her."

"No," I declare, bringing my right hand slightly up while tilting my hips to protect against a bitch move kick to the balls. "Leave now."

I see the fire flash in Blondie's eyes as he steps closer, and Meghan steps forward a bit too, leaning around me and setting me on edge because she's too close to this jerk.

"I can't," she says sweetly, trying to de-escalate things before I put this asshole on the ground right here in the parking lot. "I've got early school tomorrow, remember? Sorry, baby."

I tense just a little as I hear the code word all the girls have for trouble. They'll call patrons just about anything—honey, daddy, sugar, sweetie—but the rule at Petals is that 'baby' is the safe word that'll get security on a patron like white on rice.

I already knew he was full of shit, but Meghan just let me know for certain. I shift a little more, knowing that the beating is about to commence. I just have to make sure Meg's safely out of the way before I start.

Blondie's either too drunk, or probably too stupid, to notice. "C'mon, baby. Just a quickie. We don't even have to leave. I've got some goodies in my car so we can party right here. Big Guy won't mind, right? I can slip him a few bills."

He reaches for Meghan's wrist and it's automatic from there. In a move that's so fast that most people don't even realize what's happening, I deflect his hand, directing it down and back while grabbing his wrist in a sweeping motion as I twist it up behind his back. In less than half a second, he's fully hammer locked, and in the next half second, he's pivoted away from Meg and toward his own car.

I slam him face down on the hood, lifting his wrist while twisting his hand to maximize the controlling pressure on his shoulder, finding that edge where the pain is balancing on the razor's edge right before his arm dislocates. "She said no, asshole."

Blondie yells out in alarm, struggling from pure instinct. "Hey! Hey! Ow! Fuck, man."

I press him into his hood some more, using my booted foot to kick his legs out from under him, holding him in place easily even as he struggles.

"Meghan?" I chance a quick glance behind me to see she's frozen, her face a mask of shock. I raise my voice a bit, knowing she needs a bit of command. "Meghan."

She shakes her head, her vision clearing as her eyes meet mine, wider than usual behind her frames. "Yeah . . . yeah?"

My voice is clipped, all business. Right now, I don't have time for emotions. "Get his wallet out of his pocket. Read his license for me."

She's shaking but does as I order, coming close and with delicate fingers, reaching into Blondie's back pocket and withdrawing a brown leather wallet.

"What the fuck, dude? You're robbing me now? I just wanted to talk to her."

He has another burst of energy and thrashes underneath me,

making Meghan jump back. I grab his neck with my free hand, thumping him head first into his hood, not hard enough that he can't drive out of here . . . yet. "Shut up, asshole. Meg?"

She opens the wallet, finding his license inside, and starts to read out loud. "Miles Jacobson, 3654 Sidewinder Trail. He lives here in East Robinsville."

I nod, giving her a professional smile. "Good girl. Now put it back, carefully. And Miles, if you so much as fucking move, I'm going to break your arm."

I emphasize my point with a little yank on his shoulder, encouraging him to be still while Meg puts his wallet back.

Waiting until Meghan's stepped back and is safe, I yank him off the car to growl in his ear. "Miles Jacobson of 3654 Sidewinder Trail, you are banned from Petals from Heaven. If I ever see you even close to this block again, I'll take special care of you. It won't be over quickly, and you will not enjoy it, I promise you."

"But—"

"*If* you ever see my girl here anywhere at all," I interrupt him, "you'd best run the other fucking way because if you so much as lay an eye on her, I'll fuck you up so badly, your own mother won't be able to identify the body. *If* they find it. Clear?"

He nods jerkily, weeping softly and sober as a judge at the turn of events. I don't feel sorry for him at all. He probably thought a little more forceful asking in the deserted parking lot would lead to Meghan partying with him, willingly or not.

Fucking pricks like him, thinking they're entitled to whatever they want just because they want it.

Still, I don't have time for a philosophy lesson. "Meghan, open the car door."

She moves from behind me, and I keep an eye on her movements, making sure no other threats pop out of hiding in the dark lot. I pull up a bit on Miles's arm, the pressure forcing him to stand in front of me. I prisoner-walk him to the side of the car and push him in, where he clumsily falls into the driver's seat, yelping as his shoulder gives him a warning twinge at the release of the hammerlock. "Fuck, man, I'm gonna—"

I lean down, keeping eye contact as I cage him in with one hand on the roof and one hand on the door. "Think about your next words and where you're making your threat. Goodbye, Miles Jacobson. I don't want to ever see you again."

I give him a hard stare, memorizing every detail of his face and his car, down to the company parking garage badge hanging from the rearview mirror.

Stepping back carefully, I slam his door and then give it a swift and solid back-kick with my hard-soled boots, denting the panel. It's not enough. I'd rather break his jaw or the glass out of every window of his fancy car, but it'll have to do.

I stand, stoic and solid, still threatening as Meghan hides behind me again. He peels out of the lot, but I catch the 'Fuck you!' he yells out the open window.

Not worrying about his need for the last word, I turn to Meghan, gently putting my hands on her shoulders. She's trembling for real this time, and so tiny I have to be careful not to accidentally hurt or scare her with my roughness. It's more difficult than I thought. I'm still on edge, and this is the first time I've touched Meg other than to shake her hand the first night we met.

"Are you okay?" I ask. "It's all over now."

Her eyes are glassy, but she nods, biting her lip. My thumbs are tracing circles on her arms, soothing her and soothing me too. This could've been bad, really bad, and I'm glad I was here to keep her safe.

"You're okay. He's gone, and you're safe," I murmur softly. "I'll always do my best to keep you safe."

She suddenly collapses forward, all the energy keeping her upright whooshing out as she falls against me, shaking and rambling. "Holy fracking . . . he could've . . . fluffernutter . . ."

She says some of the words like she's cussing, even though she's decidedly not, and even in the midst of the insanity, it makes the corners of my lips tilt up. I've noticed it before, and in some ways, Meg sounds a lot like someone's church-going cousin.

She's sweet, an innocent little darling who doesn't belong in a rough life like this. She's way too much of a good girl for someone like me. I gather her closer, wrapping one arm around her shoulders, and lead her back inside the club.

"Marco. Hey, man!" I call out as the door closes. "Get your ass out here!"

Marco pops up from below the bar after a few seconds, already teasing. "Took you long enough. I need your help grabbing another case of—"

His words cut off when he sees Meghan, and he rushes out to get on the other side of her. Despite his player tendencies, he's got a decent heart and knows a girl in need when he sees one.

I squeeze off the growl of 'Don't Touch' that threatens to pass my lips when he grabs her hand, but together, we get her sitting at the bar.

"You got a pen and paper?" I ask as Meghan shivers, putting her head in her hands.

Marco rushes behind the bar again, grabbing a tumbler and filling it with ice and water before setting it in front of Meghan. "Yeah, yeah. Here you go." He grabs a notepad and pen from beside the register, and I write down Miles's information and description, along with his vehicle description and license plate.

I push it back toward Marco, who looks the information over. "This guy. He's banned from the club, from the whole damn block, and definitely from Meghan. Pass the word."

Marco reads the note and nods, knowing that my request isn't directly to him, but to Dominick. His club, his rules, but for something like this, Dominick will definitely agree with my assessment of the appropriate response.

Pocketing my note, Marco turns to Meghan. "You okay, sweetheart? You look pale. Need something a little more than just ice water?"

She shakes her head, then seems to reconsider. "Can I have a scotch? Just a little sip to settle my nerves?"

It's part of Meghan's magic. Here she is, scared out of her mind, and I swear she sounds like little girl who's asking to have a sip and not get in trouble for it. Marco smirks, turning to grab a shot glass that he fills to the brim with the amber liquid before setting it in front of her.

"Don't sip it. Just shoot it down so it can work its magic, warm you back up."

She picks the shot up with delicate fingers, and for a moment, I wonder if this girl has ever even done a shot. If not, she's about to be in for a rude awakening.

But she tilts it back, opening her throat and swallowing it down with ease before slamming it back to the bar top. Wiping her lips, she offers Marco a hint of a smile. "Thanks. I needed that."

All on its own, my cock jumps right to attention in my pants, wondering if she'd swallow something of mine down her pretty little throat, and if I could put a bigger smile on her face than what the scotch has.

Fuck, I've gotta get my head on straight. Now is definitely not the time for me to be thinking dirty thoughts. Hell, there's never going to be a time for me to think that about Meghan. Even if she wasn't too damn good for someone like me, I'd break a sweet little thing like her.

Still, I can't help but put my arm around her, mindlessly patting and rubbing her back, even though I'm treading dangerous territory for us both. "You gonna be okay? We can hang out here as long as you need," I reassure her. "Whenever you're ready, I'll walk you out to your car again. Make sure you're safe. 'Kay?"

She sighs, looking up at me, her pupils black and large behind her glasses. "Actually, do you think you could drive me home? I'm not much of a drinker, and I have a feeling that scotch is going to knock me out in three, two, one . . ."

She smiles a tiny smile, but it sounds like she's telling the truth. This is a girl who can sling drinks like a certified pro, but one shot knocks her out for the rest of the night. And no, my dirty fucking thoughts don't avoid the innuendo there either.

"Yeah, I can do that," I reply, even as part of me says this is a bad move. I've wanted her for weeks, and my instincts are going apeshit. *Bad move, Shane. Bad move.*

Doesn't matter. The smile she gives me is more than enough to overcome whatever my mind is saying. I turn to Marco, who's cleaning the shot glass carefully. "Will you let Dominick know I'm leaving my truck here overnight? I'll drive Meghan's car to her house and cab it home."

Marco gives me an evaluating look, and I again appreciate that for all his slick player persona, he's actually a pretty solid guy and is making sure that I'm not running some game on Meghan when she's shaken up.

I must have passed his test because he nods and sets the glass aside. "Yeah, I'll let the boss know. Take care of her."

With a nod, I help Meghan up. I walk her back outside, head on a swivel as I look for any threats, any sign that Miles Jacobson got a shock of courage and came back, but all seems to be quiet and dark. We make it to her car, a nondescript little thing that looks like it sort of hangs together by sheer force of will.

Meghan digs in her bag for her keys and hands them to me. I do a slight double-take as I see her keyring has a fucking pompom on it. A puffy fluff of soft fur that's white like a rabbit's tail. It suits her.

I hold the passenger door for her and make sure she's buckled in before I go around. "You ready?"

"Yeah. And thanks, Shane," she says, giving me a smile that

could melt Ebenezer Scrooge's heart. I pull out, still keeping watch for anyone who might be following us, and head away from the club, toward the main road.

"Where to?" I ask, and Meghan gives me directions to her apartment from there. As we drive, I have to admit I'm interested to see where she lives.

A tiny piece of me is disappointed when I pull up outside a regular apartment complex, just one like a hundred others around town and not some special, secret hideaway with unicorns in the driveway befitting the fairy-princess sparkle of this girl. I walk her to her door, planning to get her safely inside and then call a cab . . . from the parking lot, not wanting her to feel weird about being alone in her apartment with the huge, scary guy from work.

Hey, I know what I look like, and yeah, I use it around work to my advantage. I'm surprised when I turn to go and she calls out, "Shane!"

I turn, hearing the fear returning to her voice. "Yeah?"

She's clutching the door, the toe of her Ugg boot digging in the carpet, looking for all intents and purposes like the scared little girl she is. My heart melts even as another side of me growls possessively, wanting to claim her as mine.

She takes a deep breath, biting her lip, but her voice is surprisingly strong when she speaks again. "Do you want to come in? Have a cup of coffee or something?"

I pause, most of me wanting to say no. This has bad idea written all over it. We're pushing four in the morning, I'm with a girl who's had a scare and might be slightly drunk, and for the past two months, she's jumped to the top of my fantasy list as she ticks boxes on my mental fuck list I didn't even know I had.

But I can man up, be the security she needs, and not let on that she's slowly driving me insane every time she looks up at me in those glasses. That half of me wants to comfort and soothe her, to tell her she'll never be hurt . . . while the other half of me wants to rip her clothes off and make her hurt so damn good she screams in blissful agony before I empty my balls deep inside her body.

"Are you sure?" I ask, keeping my voice calm. "You're home, and you're safe. I can just call a cab."

She doesn't answer, just gestures with her hand into the apartment, inviting me in. I walk past her, careful not to touch her or crowd her so she doesn't spook again. Keeping my steps casual, I feel dirty as my heavy boots cross the threshold into her apartment, and I feel an intense, sudden need to just take them off and not pollute her space.

Her apartment is cute, just like her. Her living room is full of soft furniture, with fuzzy blankets thrown over the arm of an old, overstuffed sofa and a floral coffee mug sitting on the table. The room is white and beige and all the other shades of . . . white. With a few highlights of pink.

I'm nervous to sit on her furniture. I think of the places my pants have been, and I'm afraid I'll sully it up just with my presence. But she motions for me to sit, so I do. "Uhm . . . thanks. It's a nice place you've got here."

"Thanks. Just hold on a moment, would ya?" she asks, bustling off to the kitchen. Moments later, she's making coffee, by the sound of the clinks I hear.

I look around and see a huge bookcase filled with books. I

don't recognize any of the titles, but whatever type of books she reads, she's got a shitton of them. "You're a reader, huh? Lots of books in here."

Her laugh from the kitchen is slightly self-conscious, and I hear the click-thunk of a knob being turned through the open doorway. "Yeah, I read . . . a lot. Little bit of everything. Non-fiction, like historical stuff and biographies, and fiction too, romance, drama, mystery. You read much?"

I grin, even though she can't see me. Romance, drama, and mystery? *God, you're fucking perfect, Meghan.* "No, can't say I'm much of a reader," I reply. "I'm more of a dumb jock type."

A minute later, she appears with a tray, holding two cups of steamy coffee and the fixings. "I wasn't sure how you take it."

She sets the tray down, and I lean forward to grab a cup. "Black is fine. Sugar at this time of night gets me jittery."

She scrunches her nose and adjusts her glasses again. "Ew, too bitter for me. I like lots and lots of cream."

Oh, for fuck's sake, she's really testing me here. If it were any other girl, I'd think it was intentional. But Meghan seems completely oblivious to the effect she's having on me.

She sits down next to me, and I watch as she adds enough creamer and sugar to her cup to make it basically coffee-flavored ice cream before taking a sip and sighing happily. I sip my own coffee, and I have to add another mark on this girl's list of accomplishments. I haven't had coffee this good since a vacation to Chile two years ago.

There's a comfortable silence as we both sip before she breaks it, looking at me earnestly. "Shane, thanks again. That was some scary intense stuff tonight. I'm glad you were there."

I nod, setting my cup down on the tray. "It was no problem, Meghan. I'm glad I was there too."

She flinches a little, and I'm afraid she's having a bit of a flashback, so I slip my arm across the back of the couch, not touching her, but she scoots closer, curling into my side, so I place a light hand on her shoulder. "I usually think of myself as capable of handling whatever comes my way, and I've dealt with some handsy customers, but if I'd been alone in that parking lot tonight . . ."

Her voice trails off, and I know she's imagining all the ugly things that could've happened. "It's okay," I reassure her. "You're safe now."

CHAPTER 3

MAGGIE

I wake slowly, feeling warm and fuzzy-headed and safe. It's funny, because normally, I have to be yanked out of sleep by the harsh braying of my alarm clock just to make sure that I can get to work on time. But a quick glance to my left confirms that it's only eight o'clock, and I've got time. So I curl tighter into a ball before stopping because my pillow feels harder than usual.

The thought makes me stop and actually wakes me up, because I'm not in my bed. I'm on my couch underneath one of my throw blankets, the clock I saw was my microwave, and I'm curling up to a hard body . . . the very hard body of Shane.

His breathing is even and slow, still asleep, so I take stock. He's lying half reclined on one end, his boots hanging off my couch and his muscular left arm lying across the back of the couch in a protective position, like he wanted to hold me but didn't. Meanwhile, I've got my cheek pressed against one nearly iron-hard but delightfully warm pectoral and my left leg's half draped over his like the world's biggest body pillow. It feels . . . good. Safe.

I hum softly, and Shane stretches slightly in his sleep, his muscled arm descending slowly to lie on top of the blanket, almost instinctively cupping my butt.

I have a momentary freakout as my body thrills and *fully* wakes up in a lot more ways than just shaking off the last cobwebs of sleep. Did we? No, no. We're both fully dressed, and I'd definitely remember that. I have no doubt that having sex with Shane would be something a girl would never forget. Considering I've had a few fantasies about him over the past two months . . . yeah, I wouldn't forget it.

At that thought, my core fills with warmth, making me squirm slightly. The leg I have thrown over his lifts, and I feel the hard fullness of his dick. Sweet mama's fairy tales, he's . . . I don't think I could even fantasize about someone this amazingly put together.

Shane moans lightly in his sleep from my pressure, pulling me to him and grinding against me ever so slightly, and I gasp as electricity shoots through me. Unfortunately, the sound seems to wake him and he stirs beneath me. He rubs my butt, pressing into me again as he stretches and groans. The sound alone turns me on, and I bite my lip, lifting my head to look at his face.

Shane blinks and smiles sleepily back at me before I get a close-up view of the second his face goes from smiling 'good morning, sweetheart' to frowning 'oh, shit.'

Sigh. I never should've even pretended he'd be happy to wake up here with me, even if we didn't do anything. I mean, I'm just a nerdy girl next door, and he's so far out of my league it's not even funny. He's the sort of guy who has girls like Allie and the other dancers drooling over him.

It's only because Shane's so nice, and that I basically begged him to stay like a little girl last night, that he's here. But I was truly scared after the parking lot incident.

I can feel the blush rushing across my cheeks, and I do my best to try and smooth all this over before I die of embarrassment. "G'morning. Guess we fell asleep?"

Smooth one there, Maggie. State the dang obvious, why don't ya?

Shane smiles back softly, though, lifting an eyebrow. "Guess so." Suddenly, he notices his hand on my ass and maybe the feeling of his morning wood against my thigh, and his smile disappears in an instant. "Oh, uh . . . sorry."

He lifts his hand off my butt, and I lift up, trying to disentangle myself from our compromising position before my heart fails. "Thanks for staying last night. I was pretty freaked out after everything. Think that guy will stay away?"

Shane's face hardens, and it's reassuring to see absolutely no doubt in his eyes. "He'll stay away, or he'll wish he had. But you're safe, okay?"

I dip my chin, feeling silly that he's still reassuring me, and deciding I need to act a bit more blasé about the whole thing, put it in my past and move forward. I'm supposed to be a tough girl, not a scaredy cat.

Decision made, I stand and straighten my back, rolling my shoulders back to look as tall as I can, which isn't much considering my petite five-foot-nothing self. "Let me put on a fresh pot of coffee—"

Shane interrupts, straightening up himself. "Thanks, but I'd better get going. Need to get my truck before tonight's shift starts."

A tough ball of disappointment forms in my gut, but I plaster a fake smile on my face anyway. I mean, I was pathetic enough to almost beg him to stay last night. I shouldn't keep the streak going. "Sure, of course. Want me to give you a ride back to the club?"

"No, thanks, I'll grab a cab. I'm sure you've got plans today," Shane says, getting up. I do have plans. I mean, I have to go to my other job, but he doesn't know that. And there's something about the way he says it that sounds like a dismissal, not like he's fishing for me to hang out with him.

"Yeah, busy." He folds the blanket and lays it on the arm of the couch, and something about that strikes me as so domestic, so tame considering he's a wild beast of man who didn't hesitate to put the beat-down on that guy last night.

The contrast makes me feel dizzy, or maybe that's just him and how he makes me feel inside. I walk him to door, one hand on the doorknob as I turn and look at him again. "Thanks for last night."

Shit, that sounds like I mean something else, something decidedly more vulgar, and I can feel the blush warming my cheeks. Even Shane smiles a little, and I quickly try to get myself out of this quicksand I've stuck myself in. "I mean with the guy at the club. And bringing me home."

I know I look like a total fool, and Shane seems amused by my awkwardness. He gives me a little grin that leaves my heart hammering even more in my chest and chuckles. "You're welcome. Just doing my job. Well, mostly," he says with a pointed look at the couch. "But I'm glad I was here."

I think he's trying to make me blush more, and to be honest, he's succeeding. "Uh . . . me too."

Shane clears his throat, and I have a half-second to wonder if he's serious that he liked being here. "I'll see you tonight?"

I nod, thinking that I wouldn't miss a shift at Petals for the world right now. "Yeah, I'm working dinner to close tonight, so I'll see you later."

There's a moment where it seems neither of us knows what to do, so I finally lean in for a hug.

I mean, heck. I slept draped over the guy like he was a body pillow last night. A hug doesn't seem all that intimate, right? And we're colleagues, work buddies even. And work buddies will sometimes give each other a hug.

Except when I reach up and wrap my arms around him and press my chest toward his, all I can think about is how good he feels. My breasts tingle as they smoosh against his hard chest muscles, and my body feels every bit of his hand splayed on my back. I can almost read the way his fingers adjust their pressures, his thumb pressing against one of my 'dimples' for a moment before his fingers take over, alternating like he's playing a piano before he pulls me tighter and his musky-manly scent fills my senses. I have to bite back the moan in my throat.

"You be good," Shane says with a tantalizing ghost of huskiness in his voice that makes me think maybe he liked the hug as much as me. With one last full, white smile and a little two-finger wave, he steps out. "And take it easy."

As soon as he's gone, I melt back to the couch, a wistful sigh mixing with the floomp of my cushions as I flop.

"Damn, that man is hot with a capital *Oh, yeah*!" I sigh,

knowing that he's also incredibly off-limits, for so many reasons. First, there's my waitress job where the no fraternizing rule is strictly enforced.

Second, there's the fact that I'm undercover for the tabloid and he doesn't even know my real name. He thinks I'm Meghan, not Maggie. Major buzzkill to be mid-flagrante delicto and for him to cry out your name, except it's not yours but rather the alias you gave him.

I won't even touch on the third reason, considering that contemplating how out of my league he is won't do my self-esteem any favors. I know I'm a catch, and I'm picky because I can be, but Shane is in a whole other dimension of gorgeousness.

Shaking my head, I rally and grab a cup of last night's coffee, nuking it in the microwave and dropping in three sugars and a lot of milk, just the way I like. The caffeine and sugar are just what I need to get dressed and into the office for my check-in and assignment update.

Yeah, big plans, that's me. Get off work and go to work. If I'm lucky, I might be able to squeeze in a workout at the gym to try and keep up my girlish figure.

Living the dream, baby.

THE BIG OPEN 'BULLPEN' OF *THE DAILY SPOT* IS HUMMING when I get in. Of course it is. A lot of my coworkers have been here for a couple of hours already, trying to make the noon update deadline. We may be a gossip rag, but that doesn't mean we don't have a schedule. Seven in the morning for the pre-work and water cooler crowd, noon to catch the lunch-timers, and then at six to give everyone a late-night update.

As soon as I log into the computer, my instant messenger box opens in the corner of the screen. It's my new boss, Jeanine. *Hi, Maggie! Come to my office ASAP.*

Shoot, wonder what she wants. She's definitely better than my old boss, who was a skeevy jerk. Actually, he was worse than that, but he went out in a blaze of glory . . . publicly. *The Daily Spot*'s reputation took a hit, but at the same time, website traffic is up. I guess it's true—controversy creates cash.

Jeanine's been here a little over a month now, but I don't have a good read on her yet. She always seems serious and cold, and she communicates in snippets of sentences rather than in full, embellished diatribes. I'd bet money she's never so much as cracked the spine of a book of poetry. No time for that prosaic nonsense.

So a tabloid full of gossipy blurbs is probably right up her alley. Actually, I read her biography when she took the editor's job, and she's worked in some legit journalism too, but still, the woman communicates by the five Ws—who, what, when, where, and why—almost exclusively. She doesn't even bother with how. That's my job, I guess.

I don't waste her time by responding to the message. I just lock my computer and head her way as quickly as possible. Knocking on her doorframe, Jeanine doesn't even look away from her computer, although she does wave me in with a quick little flutter of her fingers.

Ah, well. I sit in one of the chairs, waiting for her to finish whatever she's working on and speak first.

Jeanine hits her *Enter* key with a flourish that's sure to break her keyboard before too much longer and looks up, giving me a professional smile. "Maggie, how are things? What have you got for me?"

I swallow, knowing she won't like my answer. "Honestly, not a lot right now. There hasn't been even a pseudo-celeb in the club in over a week. I wrote that one up for last Saturday's edition, remember? The headline was *Bad Boy of Soaps Gets Glitter Bombed.*"

Jeanine is silent, but she nods so I think she at least remembers the story. I'll admit, it wasn't that big of a story. I mean, sure, the guy's made a few housewives fan themselves, but ever since he came over from New Zealand, he's been getting himself in so much trouble the biggest story is whether the INS is going to let him renew his work visa.

Jeanine's grey eyes narrow at me as she purses her blood-red lips, her expression making her look even harsher than usual. "Glitter. Oh, yes."

She says it with a sneer, like the sparkly confetti is unwelcome contagious merriment. But that's what it was, if you count getting smacked in the face with a dancer's glitter-covered hiney a 'bomb.' But he's single, not dating anyone, and most fans don't really mind if a guy like that gets up to no good.

With a shake of the head, she continues. "I've received word that a certain All-Star basketball player will be clubbing sans the missus at a rather high-end venue tonight. I need you to go in, look the part, and see if he's up to anything devious. If so, get pics and write up his delinquency. If he's being a good boy, take pics of the sketchiest thing you see and write it up as supposition for why he's out alone. Trouble in paradise type story. Got it?"

I fidget and tug at the sleeve of my blouse. "I'd love to, but I'm already working tonight. I can probably get someone to cover the later part of my shift and catch up with him after the liquor kicks in though. He'd be more likely to behave badly then, anyway."

I've agreed, but only partially, and Jeanine definitely catches the difference. Her face goes hard, a mask of iron determination. "Maggie, my dear. Are you a waitress or are you a reporter? Because it sounds as though you're turning down a sure-bet reporting assignment to sling beer to drool-mouthed drunks. If you'd rather wait tables, by all means, feel free to do so. However, if you'd like to be a reporter, I'll need you at Club Noir all night in case Jimmy Keys shows up."

The threat is obvious, and while I only took the waitressing job as a means to get sordid stories, it is a big part of my life now. I have friends who work there, and the money is great. Dominick is tough, but he's a good boss, and I won't lose the waitressing job for calling out on one shift.

But missing this assignment from Jeanine will definitely cost me the reporting gig, so with a sigh of resolve, I plaster a saccharine-sweet smile on my face. "Of course, I want to be a reporter, Jeanine," I reply, while inwardly wondering if working for this gossip rag can really be called reporting. "I'll get my shift covered so I can be at the club well before the target arrives and will have a story submitted by tomorrow."

Jeanine doesn't compliment me, just smiles shrewdly, knowing her intimidation worked and I'm solidly ensconced in my place once again. 'My place,' of course is at least one notch lower than her, as everyone in the office has quickly learned that Jeanine carries her job with a superiority like a cape that swishes along behind her like a pissed off queen. And everyone knows that in her right hand is her scepter, which she'll beat over your head if you push her far enough.

She doesn't even bother answering as she turns back to her computer, just waving me off as her attention goes back to whatever it is that she's focusing on now that her favorite little petite social wallflower knows what to do.

Summarily dismissed, I head out to my desk, digging my phone out of my purse. I think and text one of the other girls at the club. She's a dancer, but considering she's new and nowhere near as good as Allie, her paychecks could use the help.

Hey, Sarah, can you cover my shift tonight, please? Last-minute thing came up.

She replies quickly, happy to cover.

Sure! I'd love a bonus Friday shift.

Thanks! I owe you one. Anytime you need me.

With a sigh, I set my phone back down and get to work, scanning Instagram accounts for celeb news, checking Twitter feeds for vague posts, and although Jeanine would never admit it, searching other tabloid sites for their stories to see if we can do a story better justice. Twice, that's hit for me, being able to read between the lines and get a juicy tidbit that someone else left behind.

It's a hard knock life for me.

CHAPTER 4

SHANE

J know it's not quite professional as I scan the room, but when eight o'clock comes and goes and I don't see the petite figure of Meghan working the tables, I get worried. I've been looking forward to seeing her all day, ever since waking up with her snuggled against me, and to not see her . . . well, it just feels weird.

Especially after we both said we'd see each other tonight. Marco won't know anything. He sleeps most of the day, and if it wasn't for his slight tan, I'd swear he's a vampire, and most of the dancers are the same. Instead, I find Sarah, a newbie dancer who's wearing a lot more clothing than normal as she carries a pitcher of margaritas through the club. "Hey, where's Meghan?"

Sarah delivers her pitcher, earning her 'tip' with a little flirt and a shake of her curvy hip before giving me a smile. "Oh, I'm covering her shift. She texted saying something came up."

"I see. What happened?"

Sarah shrugs, already walking away as another table waves for her attention. "I don't know what though. Sorry."

I grit my teeth, knowing Meghan was fine when I left this morning. I thought she was even looking forward to seeing me when she came to work, and I'll admit that I've spent a decent amount of time today with some extra pep in my step at the thought. Sure, something innocent could've come up, but after the incident last night, I hope she's okay.

But the question, the doubt creates a tension in my gut that twists and gnaws at me. What's worse is that I can't even do anything about it. I've got a job to do here, and it's not like Sarah could cover *my* job.

"Hey, Shane."

I look over from my perch by the door to see Marco waving at me. We're in between dances, so he doesn't have to yell or use the walkie-talkie system we have. Getting up, I walk over, still keeping my eyes on the patrons. "Yo, Marco."

"That was Dominick on the phone," he says. "Asked to see you in the office."

I nod, walking over to Logan, the other guy working security tonight, and ask him to cover the door for a minute while I talk to the boss. Logan's a MMA fighter who works here part-time to help cover costs. With his bald head and trimmed goatee, he's intimidating enough that I don't have to worry.

Comfortable the floor is secure, I head upstairs to Dominick's office and give two quick raps on the door. A moment later, a deep voice inside calls out. "Enter."

Even though I was invited in, I open the door slowly, both to give anyone inside time to get decent and so that I can make sure some goon isn't going to grab me as I enter.

Dominick isn't a guy you mess with, and while I never have, I don't want to be caught unaware. But all seems chill as I enter, Dominick sitting behind his large mirrored desk.

The whole room is done in contemporary modern lines, mirrors here, low-slung leather chairs there, all surrounded by sleek black shiny walls. Of course, those are one-way mirrors that look onto the dance floor and audience area downstairs, but they're good quality so the noise in here is barely noticeable unless Dom turns on the speakers. Dominick is watching, always watching what happens in Petals since it's his club, his territory.

I sit in one of the white leather chairs, although I don't dare get comfortable and familiar in his office, not with the Desert Eagle I know he keeps under his desktop. Instead, I lean forward, appearing poised and ready for anything. "What can I do for you, sir?"

Dom's the only man I call sir, and while I don't like it, it makes my life a lot easier. He drums his fingers on the top of his desk, looking at me with those perceptive eyes of his. If I ever needed a reminder that my life is perilous, those eyes are a perfect one. "Shane, Marco tells me there was trouble last night. Explain."

It's an order, and one I know to obey. I give Dominick the full-detailed version of last night's incident, knowing withholding anything would be seen as a betrayal, finishing with Miles's name and information being posted behind the bar for Marco and shared with the rest of the security team.

As I speak, Dominick spins the gold pinky ring he wears. It's filigreed but has been passed down in his family for a long time, so the decorations are nearly worn as smooth as a new wedding ring. It should look stupid, my upbringing telling me that real men don't wear rings, especially pinky rings. But Dominick pulls it off with style, the ring fitting in perfectly with his custom-made deep navy suit and silver tie.

He radiates wealth and power, and though he's a few years older than me and about twenty pounds lighter, I'm pretty sure that if he and I ever threw down, it'd be one hell of a scrap. And that doesn't count if Dom fought dirty, in which case all bets are off.

Dom knows my evaluation of him, and in some ways, that helps me. He knows that I view him not with fear but with the respect of one warrior to another, and because of that, he gives me respect back. He nods and folds his fingers together. "And after the incident?"

I nod, knowing what he's talking about and that honesty is the best policy here. Marco would have told him that I left my truck here and drove Meghan home, and that I didn't come back to pick up my truck at all.

Better he hears the story from me than find out later from someone else, and he will find out because he has an uncanny way of always knowing things.

"Meghan was in shock, asked me to drive her home, which I did. I offered to call a cab from the porch, but she asked me to come in for coffee. We talked, and she calmed down. At some point, we fell asleep on her couch. I left her apartment this morning and she seemed fine."

Dominick's fingers tighten a little before he unlaces them, setting them almost casually on the arms of his office chair. I'd be fooled too if it wasn't that I know his right hand's about six inches from that Desert Eagle of his. "You slept with her?"

I nod, speaking quickly but calmly. "I feel like that's a trick question, asking one thing but meaning another. We slept on the couch, fully clothed. If you're asking if I had sex with her, the answer is no."

Dominick nods, his hands relaxing and going back to turning his ring. "Well answered. I do feel the need to remind you of our no-dating policy, both the dancers and waitresses being strictly off limits."

"I'm aware."

Dom nods, smiling tightly. "Beyond my policy and its enforcement, although I don't know Meghan well, I sense that a man like you would break a girl like her. And then I would be called upon to break you for the misstep. Am I clear?"

Like that exact thought hasn't been running through my head since I felt the flawless curve of her ass in my hand and the soft pressure of her thigh against my cock this morning. I tilt my chin in deference, blinking once. "Crystal clear," I answer. "No worries."

I pause, taking a moment to let Dom know that I'm not just spouting some fear-inspired bullshit, then continue. "Well, actually, I am concerned. But not about that. It's Meghan."

"What about Meghan?" Dom asks. "Do you feel she is under threat still?"

I shrug, tenting my fingers in my lap. "Not sure. When I left, she seemed fine, even said she'd see me tonight because she was scheduled to work dinner to close. But she got Sarah to cover her shift. I'm sure it's nothing, but I wanted you to be aware."

Dominick's eyes flick to the black walls, seeing through them to the dance floor below where the familiar but faint bass beat is telling me Allie is on stage. "I'll have Allie call Meghan," Dom finally says. "They're close, so she can see what's up and why she ditched her shift. Tell Allie to come up after her performance, please."

Hearing the dismissal, I rise and walk out of Dominick's office, feeling like I just received a pardon from the firing squad. Even knowing I'd done nothing wrong, Dominick is one of the few men I legitimately fear. Even now, leaving his office, there's one percent of my brain that expects to hear the *snick* of him drawing the hammer back on his pistol.

The fact is, Dominick is ice-cold and all business, willing to do whatever is necessary, regardless of where the law or public opinion lies on his actions. This time, though, I'm safe, and I get downstairs to wait behind the curtain backstage for Allie to finish her set.

As she comes though, her costume is wadded up in her hands, and she jumps slightly, not expecting me to be standing there, and she squeaks a little. "Jesus fuck, Shane! You scared the hell out of me!"

"Sorry, didn't mean to startle you. Dominick wants to see you for a second."

She bites her lip, and I can see she's nervous, but there's something else in her eyes too, but it's gone too fast for me to identify it.

She lays her costume down, grabbing a towel and patting herself off so she removes the beads of sweat without disturbing the waterproof makeup and glitter too much. She's got a couple more dances coming up tonight, and Allie's a girl who absolutely hates to do touch-up work once she's got her 'costume' on. It's interesting the things you learn working in a strip club. Girls' makeup habits being one of them.

Thinking of girls' makeup makes my brain flash to Meghan and the way she can go from sultry to fresh-faced in a flash, and in my jeans, my cock twitches. Thankfully, I prepared for tonight, and I'm wearing my tighter compression briefs, and my semi-chub goes unnoticed.

"Thanks, I'll head up now."

I hold the back-stairwell door open for her, giving her a nod as she walks by before I head back out to the floor to resume my door duty. Yeah, Dominick might have Allie call her, but I'm going to have to check on Meghan tonight to satisfy my own questions.

I just need to make sure she's okay after last night's incident, and maybe moreso after this morning's awkward wakeup.

CHAPTER 5

MAGGIE

"*W*hat a freakin' waste of time," I mutter to myself as I look around the club, wishing I wasn't here. As ordered, I've gotten dolled up, paid the rip-off twenty-dollar cover charge to get into the fancy-schmancy Club Noir, supposedly the hottest night club this side of New York. I've sat here at a table, nursing two weak girly drinks for the past four hours, tipping the waitress generously as she gives me looks.

I've spent since eight o'clock tonight looking like the world's biggest club loser, hanging onto my seat and turning down the guys who have approached simply because this chair has the best view of the door, the dance floor, and the stairs up to the VIP section.

And did Mr. Basketball Star, Jimmy Keys, make an appearance in said VIP section? Did his twenty points and eleven rebounds a game ass even show up?

Of course not. The closest thing I've seen is a guy who's

about six four and looks like he might make a good basket-ball player.

So now, as people start to pair off and head out to continue the night in private, I'm almost fifty bucks in the hole for the night. I have no story, and based on my last text to Jeanine, my boss is somehow pissed off at me for the whole thing.

Not to mention that by giving up my shift, I've lost out on a couple of hundred dollars in tips. Grabbing my purse, I head home and flop into bed, growling the whole time.

THE MORNING ISN'T MUCH BETTER, AND I SPEND MOST OF THE day Saturday just stewing and trying to get Jeanine to unclench her sphincter.

Pulling up in front of Petals, I'm just hoping that we've got a big crowd. The parking lot looks good, so Hello, Dolly! I've got a shot of not ending the week on a bad note . . . if I'm lucky.

I slip through the door without anyone noticing me, a plain-ish girl in oversized sweats and a hoodie that hides my face, helping me be invisible. Except to Logan, who's on door security and does his job, giving me a quick once-over to make sure I'm allowed entry. I give him a small smile, but he returns his attention to the door, dismissing me without a word.

Backstage, I change, putting the last touches on my makeup and giving my hair and my girls one last poof as I cross my fingers for a good night. "Here's to hoping we've got high-rollers who like fifties over fives."

Looking over, I see Allie slipping into lingerie for her performance tonight and giving me a cockeyed grin. If you'd told me a few months ago that hanging around a bunch of half-naked, or sometimes fully naked, women wouldn't make me bat an eye, I'd have laughed my butt off. I'm no prude, but it's not like my real life has offered many opportunities for in-depth analysis of panty styles, grooming habits, and ways to highlight your best assets.

But these girls, the ones I call friends, are real and open. They've given me a lot of insight into men, some good and some bad, and most will be the first to give you a Cosmo-worthy tip when you have an unfortunate pimple or need a hair plucked from a spot you can't quite reach.

"Hey, Allie, sorry I missed your call last night," I reply, glad I get to wear real underwear as Allie fiddles with her four ounces of 'stage costume.' "Everything okay?"

"Yeah, I heard about what happened Thursday night from Dominick," Allie says, straightening up. "I just wanted to make sure you were okay. You are, aren't you?"

She looks at me, her brown eyes warm with concern, and I blush, nodding. "Yeah, totally fine. Just had to take care of something unexpectedly for a friend, so Sarah covered for me. I think it's almost time for her next school loan payment, so she seemed glad to get the weekend shift."

I feel guilty for not being completely honest, but I can't exactly explain that I was working my other job as a reporter, no matter how good of friends we are. Allie's too close to Dominick, and I've got to keep that screen between us. It sucks too, because honestly, I'd count Allie as one of my closest girlfriends. And she doesn't even know my real name.

"Marco said Shane took you home."

It's a statement, not a question, but I treat it as one anyway. "Yeah, I was pretty shook up, so he drove me home. It was nice of him."

I purposefully leave out that he spent the night and the awkward morning departure. Allie grins, shaking her bouncy curls and boobs at the same time. "Nice? I'm sure Shane would love to hear you describe him as nice. Because trust me, there isn't a single nice thing about that man. He is bad . . . in the best way."

Her voice goes all breathy at the end, and I'm struck with a twinge of jealousy. I cover that with a smirk and zing her back. "Hmm, sounds like someone has a crush. Better not let Dominick hear you talking like that."

Allie flushes instantly, stammering and shaking her head. "No, no, no. Listen, Shane's got the whole bad boy persona going on. Hard body, tattoos, you know."

"He's got tats?" I ask, surprised. I mean, I'm not that surprised, but I've never seen Shane in anything but his normal long-sleeved shirt. It makes me wonder when Allie saw him.

"Yeah, and before you ask, there was a night right before you started where Shane had to deal with three drunken frat boys. One of them got a handful of Shane's shirt, and we all got an eyeful of some pretty impressive eye candy. Actually, that was the only damage Shane took."

My pulse is hammering in my chest and I can't help it. "Wish I could have seen that."

Allie grins. "But you also know Shane. He's a badass, to be sure, but he's got that golden core to him. There's a deep-seated decent streak about him. Dominick's a different creature altogether. It's not a façade with him. He actually is a bad guy."

She says 'bad guy' like most folks say yummy cake, and I wonder exactly what is going on between the two of them. Part of me hopes it's not what I think. Allie's the kind to let her heart get broken in a futile quest to redeem the bad guy.

Before I can question her further, she gives her boobs a little shake and blows me an air kiss. "Anyway, off for my first set. Make sure you clap for my back walk-over move."

I smile. "You know I will. It's really a brilliant hook for your routine. I've seen guys' eyes just about bug out of their heads when you do it. Well done!"

She gives me a high-five and sashays out to wait backstage for her music cue. I quickly join her out on the floor while she's just getting her hips rolling for the crowd, immediately realizing that my section is already nearing capacity. Tossing a quick wave to Marco, I hustle over, jumping into the routine of getting orders and drinks.

As I work, I scan the room, sensing a vibe of tension for some reason. Usually by now, there's an ambiance of wicked abandon, wild chaos barely restrained. Too many guys are looking around the room too, ignoring Allie even as she hits her sexiest moves.

But instead, everyone is on edge, sitting up and looking over to the right, even as Allie comes off stage and the new girl takes over. Her approach is a different style from Allie's elegant grace, but the confidence and sex appeal are all there and should be garnering the crowd's attention.

Hmm, something's got to be up. I wonder what's over there? I try to look surreptitiously, especially since it's not my section and I don't want to be seen as a table poacher, but I just have to know.

Holy Mama Llama! That's Jimmy Keys, all six-foot-eight inches of millionaire himself, here at Petals, not at Club Noir like he was rumored to be last night. He's sitting back, two girls already hanging out with him, a bottle of very expensive bubbly sitting on the table.

The devil on my shoulder wants to tell Jeanine to suck it because this waitressing cover just might pan out after all. Mr. Basketball getting his drink and dance on at a regular club without his wife is one thing. Getting his jollies off at a strip club with a table full of what totally looks like his boys is another.

I can definitely use this for a story in *The Daily Spot*, but I need pictures as proof. I move to the far end of the bar, calling out an order to Marco and staying back to wait while he makes my drinks.

I pull out my phone, which is against the rules, but I need to take the risk. Acting like I'm checking my messages on my phone—*yep, nothing to see here, folks*—I quickly pull up my camera and fire off a burst of pics rapid-fire style. Score! Knowing when to cut and run, I don't even check the pics before shoving my phone back in my apron pocket. If they're fuzzy, well, it's not the first time we've run with unfocused photos, and these aren't even of UFOs or Bigfoot.

I'm just in time as Marco sets my drinks down. "One JB on the rocks and one draft beer for table nine," he says, grinning. "Good times tonight, huh?"

"I'm guessing you mean the bar tab?" I ask, and Marco nods. "Yeah. Good times."

I deliver my drinks and check in with my tables, my eyes flashing back to Jimmy every few minutes. I hear some guys cheering and laughing and look over to see his boys all riled up as Jimmy stands from his seat. He's grinning but not seeing a damn thing as his eyes read one thing and one thing only. Lust.

I can easily see why as Sasha, a stunning blonde from Russia, takes his hand and leads him straight into the back hallway where the private rooms are.

Not just a score, this could be a jackpot! Family man basketball star getting a private lap dance. I can see the headline now.

Once upon a time, I'd have been ashamed of peddling gossip like this. I would have been even more ashamed that a public person like this is acting so . . . dishonorably, but after a few years of tabloid work, you get numb. It feels like there's a sense of justice to it sometimes, at least. Jimmy trades and exploits his image as a family man, banking millions on his mantra of 'being a real man who treats his woman like a queen,' with endorsements, speaking fees . . . heck, the man spoke in front of a ten-thousand-seat church once. But something tells me his wife won't be too happy with her husband getting a private, one-on-one show from another woman.

Before I can even question more deeply, I follow them down the hallway, staying back and acting casual so no one suspects anything. They go to the big room that is used for private lap dances, and Jimmy sprawls out while Sasha saunters over to pick out whatever music she's going to use, temporarily leaving the door open.

I pause, leaning against the hallway wall, and take out my

phone, clicking on the screen as though I'm texting but silently taking shot after shot. You can only see a bit of Jimmy from the side, but with the shots I got earlier being of his face, the clothing and his height instantly identify the faceless image as Jimmy.

I slip my phone back into my apron again before Sasha turns to close the door, knowing this will be a job well done and a hit story. I'm about to turn back onto the floor when I hear an angry voice behind me. "What the fuck are you doing, Meghan?"

I jump, startled and fearful as I look around. Shane steps forward from the end of the hallway, where he was standing in a dark corner. Considering he's wearing black pants and a smoke gray silk shirt, he's damn near a ninja.

His face is hard, his jaw clenched as he grabs my hand and drags me over to his hideaway corner, standing in front of me to block me in. "Shane, I—"

He shakes his head, looking down at me with iron-hard eyes. "Spill it."

Thinking fast, I pull out my airhead act, letting my voice rise girlishly. "Oh my gosh, Shane. You scared the poop outta me. Are you just skulking over here in the dark?"

Put the attention back on him. Good job, Maggie. I can play young, dumb, and broke all night long. But he's not having it at all. "One more time, Meg. What the fuck are you doing back here?"

I look into his dark eyes, which are boring into mine, and I can't help it, my gaze drops to the floor submissively. I try to work my way back up, letting my eyes trace the multitude of tattoos visible on his forearms where his sleeves are rolled up. I've never seen them before, and they're fascinating.

As I get higher, I follow where the tanned skin peeks out, and I can't help but wonder how much of his shirt I'd need to unbutton in order to see the tats on his chest.

But my gaze stops at his mouth, not able to meet his eyes again.

Deciding that a speck of truth will work better than my airhead act, especially since he's seen it with patrons before, I swallow my fear and let out a whisper. "Look, I'm a huge fan, okay? I just wanted to get a better look at him."

Shane grins, cocky and obviously holding back his laughter. "You're a basketball fan?"

I manage to look him in the eye, seeing his disbelief. "Well, maybe more of a Jimmy Keys fan than the whole sport. I always liked his wholesome family guy image. Seems that's not real, though, considering he's got Sasha grinding in his lap right this second. I just . . . I wanted to know for sure."

Shane tilts his head. "I've been around here longer than you. Even good guys are bad sometimes, and bad guys are good sometimes. No one is a simple character all the time. People are more complex than that."

I swallow, more of a gulp, honestly, and my eyes dip down again, intent on studying the buttons of his shirt and wondering about what's underneath the thin, dark fabric in front of my eyes. "So, which one are you, a good guy or a bad guy?"

From my peripheral vision, I see Shane's hand move, but I still freeze when he cups my chin, tilting my head back and forcing me to look up at him. There's heat in his eyes, a tension in his body as he leans forward, basically looming over me due to our height differences.

"Weren't you listening, Angel? I'm both good and bad. I suspect you are too."

The throaty, deep challenging purr of his voice drives the breath from my lungs as my pussy clenches, moisture almost immediately wetting the cotton of the good girl undies I'm wearing. Yeah, I am a good girl . . . but I so want to be naughty with him.

I suddenly realize my jaw is hanging open in his hand, and I force my mouth shut, my teeth clacking together. "I don't know what you're talking about."

Shane's thumb traces along my jawline, sending another thrill down my spine to stoke the heat inside me. "Pity," Shane softly growls, looking both amused and disappointed. "You looked so pretty with your mouth wide-open and waiting. Waiting for something . . . to suck on."

A shudder racks through my body, unbidden and uncontrollable at the image that brings to mind, and it takes every ounce of willpower I have to stay standing and not drop to my knees to immerse myself in obedience just to feel the intensity of what he's promising.

There's a moment of tense quiet where I think he's waiting to see what I'll do, and I wonder if he actually thinks I'll give him a blowjob right here in the hallway.

While the thought might be hot, it's definitely not something I'd actually do, even though my body's saying something very, very different.

Finally, he stands to his full imposing height, no longer angling over me, and he crosses his arms, his feet splayed wide. The mood has changed, seemingly at his whim, going from heated sexiness to all-business in a flash.

His chin dips as he lowers his gaze to look me in the eyes again, and his voice loses the growl, becoming softer but at the same time less intimate. "I was worried about you last night when you gave your shift away. Everything okay?"

I get the sense he was disappointed, and maybe a bit worried I wasn't here, either because now he thinks I'm some wilted flower who can't handle a jerk customer or maybe because he just wanted to see me.

Maybe both, to some degree? my mind asks, the hope mixed with the arousal that is pulsing its way through my body. I try not to let that hope plant too deeply and tell my hormones to calm the fudge down.

"Everything's fine," I finally reply. "Something just came up with a friend and she needed my help."

That's true, or as close as I can get to it. Jeanine isn't exactly a friend, but she did require my help.

Shane doesn't look convinced, his eyebrows lifting as he studies me closely. "A friend needed help? That's . . . vague."

Dang it, every time I try to play him, even a little bit, he calls me on it. He's giving me a little wiggle room here, maybe because he wants to find out more or maybe because he's just being nice, but he knows something's up.

Stuck, I shrug, hoping to play the one trump card most women have. "She thought her guy was stepping out on her, so she wanted me to do a little recon, see if he was being honest about where he was. He actually no-showed, so I gave up my shift to slowly drink in another bar for no good reason. I'm a bit bitter about the loss of tips, honestly. I'm out fifty bucks for the night."

It's just enough of the truth that it rings honest, and Shane's eyes soften as he accepts the expanded version of my story. Giving me a slight nod, he smiles, his white teeth flashing in the dim light. "Okay, just wanted to make sure you didn't have a freakout after I left. And next time, before you go drinking alone at some random club, call me and I'll be your cover story so you don't get caught spying on some friend's dude."

I nod, too stunned at his casual offer to say anything. Is he serious? If he were drinking at a club with me, watching my surroundings would be the last thing on my mind as I got lost in his brown eyes and powerful presence. Although last night would have been a lot more fun if I could have taken Shane out on the dance floor and shown him that I might not be on Allie's level, but I can work it myself a little . . . with the right guy.

"I'd better get back to my tables, see if they need anything," I say, clearing my throat and my mind. "Gotta make up for yesterday to pay the bills."

Shane chuckles. "Sure. And stay out of the private room area, Meghan. It's no place for a good girl like you."

I almost tease him about being a bit bad too, throwing his own words back at him, but something about his calling me a good girl feels nice, and instead, I just bask in the compliment as I hit the floor again.

CHAPTER 6

SHANE

For the next week, I keep an extra eye out on Meghan. It's not that hard, honestly. I keep an eye on the entire club anyway, and I've been paying attention to Meghan for at least the past month regardless. She's just so tempting that I can't help myself.

But now I find myself making sure that her area is even better behaved, that nobody gives her any grief even as I keep my distance physically. My attention never wavers from her tiny body as she swishes around the tables, leaning over provocatively to flash the fullness of her lush tits as she flirts harmlessly, giggling her little girl laugh and playing her airhead act every night. The guys love it, and the few girls who come in love it too. They just see her as the totally relatable girl next door.

Every flirt, every move, every time she makes eyes with a customer, it feels like she's taunting me. But deep down, I know it's her usual schtick as a waitress.

Every girl has one, dancer or waitress alike. They have to in order to survive in a place like this. They find a mask, a mantle of fakeness they put on like a Halloween costume when they hit the floor. For some, they become sweet or sarcastic, and for some it's femme fatale flirty or bitchy snippy. They find the personality type that attracts the customers, and the best girls know how to read their customers and behave accordingly to get the big tips.

For Meghan, that's her natural innocent bubbliness. It's disarming, enchanting, and very effective camouflage. I've watched her for long enough to see how smart she really is, and that while she's innocent and maybe even naturally flirty, she's no airhead despite her act. It's in the flow of her words, the way she shoots guys down even as she compliments them, and how she can subtly manipulate every table into falling in love with her. She's quickly gotten a small group of regulars who come not to see the dancers, but to get their beer and liquor with a side of her sweetness.

They see her as the girl they always wanted in high school, the good girl whose sparkling eyes and smile say she'll be honest and pure ... but that underneath is a kitten waiting to be unlocked if she can find someone able to teach her.

Although, I'm not entirely sure that part is an act. I remember the way she blushed at my tawdry comments, her eyes dropping even as her breathing quickened, and her awkwardness the morning after we'd slept on her couch.

I don't think the innocence is all that fake, and though it shouldn't, that just ramps up my interest in my little angel Meghan all the more. Because I know, deep down in my guts where the good and bad sides of me swirl in constant tension, that I could unlock that sex kitten.

All I'd need is one opportunity. Much like the thought I had in her apartment about sullying her white couch with my griminess, I can picture dirtying Meghan up—lipstick smeared across her face by my lips, long blonde hair a mess from my hands tugging and pulling her at my will, my cum all over her tits in her black bustier uniform as she sags, spent from spasming helplessly around my cock before I marked her as mine.

Suppressing a groan, I shake my head, trying to clear it. Meghan's taken up so much real estate in my damn mind, I'm having to wear my compression shorts every time she's on shift, or else I walk around with a tent in my trousers.

Needing something more, I head over to the bar for a cold drink. No booze. That's unprofessional . . . but the bar has more than liquor. "Hey, Marco. Can I get a Coke when you get a chance?"

Marco doesn't look my way, too far in the weeds with orders to talk, but he flashes me a thumbs-up so I know he heard me. While I wait, I lean against the bar, surveying the room. Meghan and two other waitresses are hustling about, Sasha is on stage crawling on all fours toward a front-row guy in a nice suit who looks like he's going to have a stroke with as red as his face is getting, and every table is full. Best of all, the patrons are behaving themselves. It's a good, easy night at Petals.

My eyes are drawn back to Meghan, and before I know it, Marco clears his throat from right beside me. Shit. I never even heard him approach. And in my job, letting myself get that distracted is dangerous.

"How's she doing?" Marco asks as he hands me a Coke, no ice, just like I always have it when I'm on duty. "Any problems after the parking lot guy?"

I shake my head, taking a swig of the cold Coke. "No, she's been fine. Seems to have moved on."

Marco wipes the bar beside me with his towel, even though it's already spotless. He's a neat freak and compulsive in keeping up appearances both on the bar and in his personal habits, so I know it's not just for show. I wait, knowing he'll speak when he's ready.

"So if she's all good after the incident," he says, flipping his towel over in a quick quarter-fold before tucking it in the strings of his work apron, "why are you staring at her like you expect her to need you to run in like a knight in shiny fucking armor to slay the dragon?"

"Maybe because some people attract the dragons?" I ask. "She's different, you know? The other girls in here, they're more experienced and harder than she is. They can handle their shit and not blink twice about it. But Meghan has a softness to her. Dragons are attracted to that and would burn her to ash without a second thought just to ruin her tenderness."

Marco laughs a big belly laugh, his smile flashy. "That was some fucking panty-dropping poetry, man. Hold on, I gotta write that down."

He actually grabs a pen and paper from behind the bar, scribbling chicken scratch notes that only he can read. That's Marco, a dapper, fastidious dresser, a decent bartender with a neat freak fetish, but his handwriting is so messy I doubt even an expert can decipher what he puts down.

Marco tucks the paper away and looks up at me. "Shane, you said she attracts these types that can burn her up, right?"

"Yeah."

Marco nods. "One question then. What color dragon are you?" His laugh is gone, his tone serious and his eyes intense, reminding me that behind the affable exterior, there's the soul of an alpha male. "Oh, make that two. Who's protecting her from you?"

It's a question I've asked myself for the past week, but instead of answering, I take a drink from my Coke and lift it in salute to Marco. "Thanks for the drink. Better get back to the door."

I give Thomas, one of my fellow security guys, a nod, which he acknowledges, and we rotate positions. I resume my relaxed but ready, arms crossed front door stance, scanning the room.

As I do, something catches my eye. There's a patron at a side table, far from the stage, in a hoodie with a ball cap on. Not too unusual, since not everyone wants to be recognized at Petals, but something about him sets me on edge, like he's trying to not be noticed or seen. Every time the waitress in his zone comes by, he slinks down, turning his face even farther away from her.

I press the button in my ear, triggering the walkie talkie. "Hey, did you catch a sight of the hoodie guy at table twenty-eight coming in? I don't like the way he looks."

Thomas's voice comes back in my ear, and I see he's on the other side of the club, easing his way over. "He came in while you were taking a break. Had sunglasses on but took them off once he sat down. No clear visual, but no red flags."

Thomas is okay. He knows how to handle himself, but he's not the best at faces or at spotting fake IDs. Twice, I've cleaned up behind him when he's let in underage kids. "Thomas, man . . . sorry, but can you come back and cover the door for a second? I wanna get a closer look."

Thomas is quick on the reply, which I appreciate. "Sure, no problem. On my way."

I see Thomas coming and then look back at the hoodie guy to see Meghan has approached the table. Twenty-eight is just on the edge of her zone, and obviously, the girl working that area has given up on Mr. Hoodie.

Meg seems fine, her usual smile on her face as she greets him to take his order, but then I see her face fall as she steps back. Before I can even take two steps, the guy's hand shoots out to grab her wrist, and I'm reacting, sprinting for her.

I sweep between them, my hip forcing the guy's hand free as I use my left arm to sweep Meghan behind me, and I'm struck with déjà vu as I realize hoodie guy is actually the parking lot fucker.

"Miles Jacobson," I growl, my right fist clenching, "I told you that you were banned. In fact, I told you that your own mother wouldn't even be able to recognize your body if you showed up here, but yet, here you are."

He looks at me, clear-eyed and sober and spoiling for a fight after the beatdown I gave him. "I just wanted to apologize, but this stuck-up bitch wouldn't even let me."

He leans to the side, trying to make eye contact with Meghan, spitting out words quickly. "Sorry I scared you the other day. I was drunk. Just didn't want to be banned. I bring clients here, you know."

He sounds like that should mean something. It's almost comical. I resist the temptation to bend down to his level—it would compromise both Meghan's security and mine—and instead grab him by the front of his hoodie, pulling him to his feet. "Correction. You *used* to bring clients here."

Before he can react, I twist his arm up behind his back at the same time I shove him belly-first into his table, bending him over and knocking the wind out of him. "Agh!"

"Exactly," I growl as I yank him up, applying a half-nelson to his other arm to walk him toward the back. I'm trying to not make a scene on the floor, but a few people are applauding already, and I just have to trust that Thomas will have already activated our standard protocol for unruly guests. I know I'm right when Logan meets me by the door to the back.

"Boss will be down any second. What's the plan?"

I don't bother answering him, knowing I'll have to explain again when Dominick arrives. Speak of the devil. Just as I push Miles through the doors, Dom emerges from the private staircase he has to his office.

"Shane, what seems to be the problem with our guest?"

Meghan, who's been nearly glued to my back, answers before I can even open my mouth. "It's him. The parking lot guy."

Dominick looks to me for confirmation, and I nod, jerking Miles's head up to face Dominick. "You fucking assholes! I'm going to call my lawyer!"

Wrong fucking answer. Instead of laughing, Dominick's voice drops to a silky, amused tone, his cadence slow and clear. If you don't know any better, he sounds civilized, maybe even casual. But if you pay attention, you can hear the coldness, the lack of fucks he gives about whatever shit Miles is spouting "Ah, Mr. Jacobson. Yes, I do know your name, as well as your address and vehicle information. Since I don't take my girls being accosted in the parking lot of my place of business lightly, I took it upon myself to get to know your

71

business too. By the way, how is your hedge fund going? You seem to have hit a rough patch, isn't that right? It'd be a shame if your whole deck of cards came falling . . . falling . . . down."

Dominick's creepy menace permeates the room, and I can feel Miles's skin getting clammy under my hold as he begins to realize just who and what he's messing with. He stammers, and I swear he sounds like he's on the edge of crying. "Look, I'm sorry. I just wanted to apologize and hoped to not be banned because of a misunderstanding. I can see that was a mistake. I'll just go."

Dominick strokes his chin, but there's no doubt or softness in his eyes. "Yes, I do think we should go . . . out the back, perhaps?"

Dominick's eyes meet mine with his judgment and sentencing of Miles complete. I nod, understanding, but gesture behind me with a lift of my chin. We've got company, and he doesn't want to say more.

Dominick follows my gesture, his face softening instantly as he spies Meg's blonde locks. "Oh, Meghan, I'm afraid Shane casts such a huge shadow I lost sight of you for a moment. Are you okay, honey?"

She seems more angry than fearful, her voice tight. "Fine. Thank you."

Dom smiles, charming as ever as he comes around, taking her hand and patting her on the shoulder. "Very well, then head back to the floor and resume covering your tables. We'll escort Mr. Jacobson out."

Her eyes dip to the floor, but she lifts them instantly. "Uhm, Dominick? Can I ask you a favor?"

He's a dangerous man to ask that question, but I'm curious what she's going to ask. He inclines his head, the curiosity on his face too. "You may ask."

"Can I have a word with Mr. Jacobson before you throw him out?"

I can see the smile on Dominick's face as he motions with a wide sweep of his hand for her to proceed. She steps in front of Miles, all five foot nothing of her puffed up and standing tall. Curious to see what she'll say, I lean my head to the side, making sure that my grip is still strong. She meets Miles's eyes with no problem, and I'm damn proud of her.

"I wish I'd had the chance to do this before," she says before her right fist flashes out pretty damn quickly in a straight punch that smashes perfectly into Miles's nose. I might be able to dodge it, but most people would have no chance, especially since no one would see it coming from an angel like Meghan. The crack is unmistakable as Miles squirms in my arms, cursing a blue streak as blood streams from his ruined nostrils. "Fucking bitch. You'll pay for that. Let me go!"

Dominick puts a gentle arm around Meghan's shoulders, guiding her again toward the door to the club. "Well done, I must say. And quite surprising, which is a rare occurrence for me. We'll take it from here."

She nods, shaking her hand a little as she heads back to the floor. As soon as the door swings closed, Dominick turns back to me, all the polite softness gone from his face. "Now, shall we go outside? I hate to get blood on the tile back here. The cleaning staff tends to gets rather upset."

Logan opens the door, and we scan for any cars in the dark

rear parking area, knowing that there won't be any but always checking to be safe.

I heave Miles through the doorway and out into the dirty backlot. It's closed in on three sides between the building and two sides of chain link fence. It's perfect for what I need to do, especially when Logan stands sentry at the backlot entrance, ensuring our privacy.

"Now. I was polite inside," Dominick says as he unbuttons his jacket, "but let's be clear now. You're not going to forget this fucking lesson. You will not come here. You will not come to this neighborhood. Shane, make sure those lessons stick."

I step forward, my boot flicking out to catch Miles just above the kneecap. His leg hyperextends, and he gasps in pain, dropping his hands so that I can punch him in the temple.

"How dare you fucking touch her? You're not good enough to even lick the floor she walks on, asshole," I growl as I follow up with a big uppercut that catches Miles right in the teeth. I feel my knuckle split, but I don't give a shit as he rockets nearly straight, his hands blindly flying out.

"Excuse me, Shane," Dominick says as he steps forward. He's rolled up his sleeves, his sinewy forearms rippling as he grabs Miles by the ears and drives him backward. Dominick's not as formally schooled as I am. He learned his techniques from the streets, and he fights dirty.

"Shane's nice," Dominick says as he knees Miles in the balls. "Sometimes, too nice. So let me continue. If I hear that you've been within a half-mile of this club, or within a half-mile of Meghan, this is going to seem like a walk in the fucking park. *If* I decide to let you live, you won't leave the hospital for a long fucking time. Do you understand me?"

By this point, Miles is sobbing. "Y–y–yes," he blubbers, tears mixing with his blood. "Please."

I'm disgusted by this piece of shit. Begging for what? Mercy? Like he would've given any to Meghan if he'd gotten her alone in his car? He's weak, preying on a woman when she's defenseless. Although, after that jab to Miles's nose, maybe she wouldn't have been quite the meek mouse he expected. The thought gives me a hint of satisfaction.

Miles continues to cry, his pleas to stop peppered with threats of lawsuits, still not understanding that we don't handle things like that at Petals. Dominick looks offended at Miles's breakdown and winds up, kicking him in the stomach hard enough that I'm pretty sure Dom missed his calling as a field goal kicker. "Shane, before Miles leaves us, make sure he'll be jacking off left-handed for the next two to three months."

"Certainly, sir," I reply, stepping forward again. Miles tries to fend me off weakly, but I grab his right hand without a problem, goose necking it before punching him in the ribs just for fun. "This way, asshole."

It's harder to lead Miles out to his car, mainly because he's taken so much of a beating his legs can't really support him. It takes both me and Logan to get him across the lot.

Finally, we reach his car, and I twist Miles's wrist a little more, making him whimper. "Keys."

Using his right hand, Miles finds his keys, holding them out to me. "Unlock your door."

He pushes a button, and I open the door, looking into his teary, fear-streaked eyes. "I'm not a bad guy," he whines. "I just wanted to say sorry."

"I'm sure. But you know what?" I ask, lowering my voice. "Now you understand fear. Now you understand what she felt when you grabbed her wrist tonight. How she felt when you came at her in this parking lot. Now you understand that for all your macho bullshit, you're just five seconds away from being someone's little bitch. Put your hand in the door."

The realization of what's about to happen clears away some of the haze in his eyes, and he starts shaking his head, a whine coming from deep in his chest. "No! Please, no—"

I force his arm out, slamming the door on his fist. There's a crack, and he cries out, dropping to his knees. "My hand!"

"You have until I count to twenty to be out of the parking lot . . . or else, your neck is next," I say, picking him up and heaving him into the driver's seat of his car. "One. Two. Three."

I'm bluffing about the neck part, but it does the job. He leaves as quickly as he can, running over the curb as he pulls out just as I reach twenty.

Turning, I head around to the back door of the club to report to Dominick. As I walk, I know that on some level, I should be bothered by what I did tonight.

A two-on-one beating that left a man broken, bleeding, and with only fate to decide if he lives through the night should give me pause.

But the fucker deserved it for what he did to Meghan the first time. And the fact that he showed back up to intimidate her again?

A part of me hopes he does die, all snug in his fucking bed tonight, choking on his own blood. And if he doesn't die, he spends the next week pissing dark brown and looking like he picked a fight with a steamroller, because if he shows his face near the club again, I will kill the son of a bitch. Consequences be damned.

Whatever it takes, because Meghan deserves to be treated with respect.

CHAPTER 7

MAGGIE

Stretching on my sofa, I lean back, sighing. Thank goodness I'm off today from *both* of my jobs. After last night's craziness, I need a day to recover, unwind, and settle my mind. My hand is sore from where I punched Miles, and typing this afternoon might be a bit of a challenge, but I'm not the least bit sorry.

The light throb is a reminder that I'm a strong beast of girl who can put those killer cardio-kickboxing class and elementary school Tae Kwon Do moves to good use when needed. Getting up, I doctor a cup of coffee and plop back down on the couch, turning on old gameshow reruns as background noise as I curl up with my laptop. For some reason, listening to Richard Dawson asking what the survey said gets my creative juices flowing.

I click around, checking my emails, Instagram, and Twitter to see if there's anything I can cull into a story for the tabloid. There isn't much. An Instagram girl famous for her booty seems to be stiffing her video editor, both literally and financially. I also cobble together a quick hundred-word blurb about a celebutante dining at the fanciest restaurant in town with her brother, noting that they're rarely seen together in public. It isn't much, but it'll keep Jeanine happy enough to not bug me on my day off.

Nothing's really smashing ground-breaking journalism, but it's what I've got. Fortunately, I'm still riding high on the Jimmy Keys expose story I was able to write based on his appearance in the club. Jeanine ate that up like candy, just like I knew she would.

I'd even written a couple of follow-up pieces about the fallout when his wife found out, and then when he admitted to having a sex addiction and was seeking treatment.

I think his reaction's a bit overblown and probably more to save his reputation, considering he was just getting a lap dance. There's no need for the melodrama, but the cynical side of me wasn't surprised to see the pedestal-living pseudo-hero fall to Earth with a crash.

After a few more minutes of clicking around, I find myself staring at the TV screen mindlessly rather than digging for more juicy stories. Sure, it's a waste of time, but it feels good to laugh as a bunch of pseudo-celebrities swap one-liners and give double-entendres for answers to ridiculous questions. It's light and bright. Nothing they're saying really matters, but that's what makes it fun.

Setting my laptop aside, I give in to the draw of the show, but after a few minutes, my phone rings. I mute Charles Nelson Reilly, circa 1978, to grab it, seeing it's Allie.

"Hey, Allie. What's kickin'?"

"Are you serious right now?" Allie asks, sounding outraged and amused at the same time. "You punch an asshole customer out last night, and today, you're all casual, 'Hey, Allie, what's kickin'?' Bitch, you'd better start spilling the story."

I grin, loving how she's blunt and straight to the point. She also shows that she cares that way. The more direct she gets, the more she likes you. "It wasn't that big of a deal."

Allie guffaws. "Actually, pause right there because I need to see your face when you tell this story. I gotta see how much of your bullshit you actually believe. What are you doing right now?"

I look around my apartment, at the muted show I'm watching, the nest of blankets wrapped around me on my couch, and me still in my pajamas. "Literally, nothing. Why?"

"Perfect. I'm picking you up in fifteen minutes and we're going for mani-pedis so I can hear it all. Okay?"

"That sounds great, actually," I admit, grinning. When Allie makes me offers like this, she always insists on picking up the tab. "I'll be ready."

We hang up, and I hurry to get ready, pulling on shorts, a T-shirt, and flip flops before retying my ponytail and swiping some mascara and lipgloss on. It's not fancy, but it's what I've got on short notice. I'm just making sure my mouthwash is doing its job when I hear a knock, and I know I'm out of time.

Of course, when I open the door, Allie looks like a million bucks. Her chocolate hair is hanging straight down her back, her makeup is impeccable but perfect for daytime, and while she's also wearing shorts and a T-shirt, she manages to look like a Pinterest pin while I look like a fashion don't list victim.

"Are you planning on handing out heart attacks today?" I ask, and Allie grins.

"Nope, that's your job. You look gorgeous," she says.

I smooth the wrinkles out of my T-shirt and laugh. "You must be high! Come on, let's go. Who's driving?"

"Like you have to ask," Allie says, dangling her keys. "Come on, I'll drive."

Forty minutes later, we're sitting in matching pedicure chairs, my feet already feeling softer as they soak in eucalyptus-scented water. "Mmm . . . nice."

"So, what color do you think?" Allie says, flipping through the color guide. "I'm thinking dark navy blue, something that'll stand out."

"Yeah . . . I don't think so," I reply, flipping through my own copy. "Hey, what do you think?"

I hold up my card, a pinkish light lavender that just caught my attention. Allie grins, giving me a thumbs-up. "Totally you. It's so sweet I need to check myself for diabetes."

I stick out my tongue, and Allie laughs. A few minutes later, our technicians take our choices and get to work, buffing and smoothing our feet until they tingle.

As the ladies really get into their work, Allie looks over at me, leaning back in her chair. "Okay, now spill it."

"Well, I was working the floor," I begin before giving her an edited play-by-play of last night's events. Of course, I have to leave out names. We're in public, and I know that name dropping could bring unwanted attention. "So, anyway, I socked him in the nose."

"You caught that motherfucker in the nose?" Allie asks, barely containing a fist pump. "How'd the boys react?"

I think back to the shocked looks on Dominick and Shane's faces, and I grin. "I surprised them pretty good, I think. I'm sure they thought I didn't have it in me. Honestly, I didn't think I had it in me either, but watching the way he was trying to weasel, I just knew I had to fight back. Or else."

"Or else what?"

"Or else I was going to be afraid of jerks like that my whole life," I reply. "And you know what? It felt really good to stand up to him that way. I think the guys probably scared the bejesus out of him more though. Hopefully, he won't try coming around again."

Allie gives me an odd look, like I must be having the sillies or something. "Uhm, he definitely won't come around again if he knows what's good for him. I'm sure they beat the shit out of him. Did you see the guys again last night?"

I think back, then shake my head. "No, Bossman came in and told me I could take off early, considering everything. He even comped me the missed tips—reached into his pocket and slipped two Bennies in my hand like it was nothing. I was so surprised, I went straight home and slept like the dead till late this morning. Why?"

Allie seems uncertain if she should say more but finally hums to herself and makes a decision. "Well, I saw the boss's hands later. He had a few scrapes, and his right shoe was scuffed. And I'm thinking your knight had more of an axe to grind."

"How so?"

Allie bites her lip before replying. "Later, when he was walking us out, I noticed that one of his hands was bandaged.

I asked, and he said he was fine, but . . . if I could give you a guess, I'd say your knight laid a major asswhipping on your motherfucker."

I let that sink in.

Dom and Shane beat Miles up . . . for me. I should be horrified at the caveman-like behavior, disgusted that they sank that low instead of . . . what? Using their words? Not saying pretty please and calling the cops?

I scoff at my own line of thinking. It's not like this is kindergarten, and I know Dominick protects the club and his girls fiercely. They used brute force because they're able to and that's what the situation called for, especially after Shane gave Miles a threatening talk the first time around.

I mean, even I got a shot in, so their beating him up isn't all that different from what I did, right? Maybe more aggressive, taken further, but I know that deep inside, I'm not upset at what they did.

I'm thankful they defended me that way, made me and all the other women Miles has likely tried to intimidate safer with their actions.

"Well, I'm glad then. If I never see that poohead again, it'll be too soon."

Allie chuckles, shaking her head. "Poohead. I swear the universe missed out on one of the greatest jokes in history when you weren't named Pollyanna. Then again, you don't seem upset by the news."

"I'm not, honestly. It was . . . I guess you could say it was noble. From a certain point of view."

Story complete, our conversation turns to other matters.

Allie chats about what she's been up to, mostly sticking to some new clothes she picked up online the other day before grinning. "And guess what?" she says, not even giving me a chance to guess before she rattles on excitedly, "I got another job!"

She's giddy, almost dancing in her seat, making the lady working on her nails look at her sharply. "Miss, I cannot do the contours correctly if you keep moving."

"Sorry," Allie apologizes, turning back to me. "So, yeah, new job!"

"Oh, my gosh, are you quitting?" I ask, worried. Allie's my best friend. I couldn't imagine what work at Petals would be like without her.

She laughs, shaking her head. "Of course not. Nothing pays like the club. But this is a shot at some classical ballet. Two classes a week to adults who want to stretch and tone and feel graceful. It's not much, but it's a start, and I can use my training for more than splits and spins on a pole."

"That's so awesome, Allie," I reply honestly, grinning. "If I could hug you or high-five you right now, I so would!"

Even though we don't move, the nail tech by Allie gives us a shrewd look. It's just that I know Allie's been busting her butt to make some sort of inroad on her dream of working in the ballet world. She trained for years, even to the point of injuring herself to try and get more turn-out on her feet before an eating disorder put her in the hospital.

Even just her dancing in a strip club is a step for her. I think it shows that she's at least a little confident in her body again. Sure, she's got bills a mile high, but in almost every other way, I think she's almost a role model for me.

LAUREN LANDISH

Finally, when our nails are done, I'm able to give Allie a congratulatory hug, both of us keeping our nails away from each other in a weird forearm patting embrace.

I'm truly happy for her to get this job because I know she misses ballet. She has an empty room in her apartment lined with mirrors so she can dance and improve. I'd teased her about her voyeuristic sexcapades the first time I'd seen the mirrors, but when she turned on some music and began swaying and leaping through the small space, I knew exactly what that room was for her.

It's her sanctuary. I guess we all need one.

"Come on, let me buy you a cupcake to congratulate you on your new gig!"

Allie grins but refuses. "Thank you, and maybe later, but I should get going. I work tonight and need to get ready. You working?"

I glance at my watch, surprised at how late it is already. "Yeah, I'm only doing a partial shift tonight though. I'll be in at ten 'till close. But come on, one cupcake? I'll make it double-fudge red velvet."

Allie glowers at me, then grins. "You're buying."

CHAPTER 8

SHANE

"*R*oom check," I say quietly into my ear mic, notifying Nick, the guy working the door. It's just another Sunday night at Petals. You'd think Sunday would be the lightest night of the week. I mean, East Robinsville has a lot more churches than strip clubs, but it's not. It's not quite as busy as Saturday night, but Sundays aren't slack either.

There are quite a few patrons. Maybe it's a carryover from their Sunday morning activities, or maybe it's the fact that they're not looking forward to Monday, but the customers seem pretty chill.

But tonight just doesn't seem the same. Instead of the shit-load of things I should be watching for, including but not limited to making sure the customers behave, that the dancers are comfortable, and that Marco's not getting stiffed at the bar, I find myself waiting for Meghan. I even know her schedule, and she's not supposed to be in for a little bit, but that's not stopping me from anticipating her arrival.

Trying to rein my attentions in, I scan the floor. The new girl

LAUREN LANDISH

on stage seems to be doing all right, although I can't remember her name. Candy? Caramel? Something with a C that's definitely fake.

Most of the patrons are watching her with rapt attention, except for the bachelor party that seems more intent on roasting the groom-to-be, leading to some raucous laughter from their table. They haven't gotten to their lap dances yet, but from what I see, I'd say the bride-to-be has nothing to worry about. Her beau's got a look on his face that says he's enjoying himself, but he's just putting up with his buddies' antics and he's going to behave.

Still, I scan each face for a moment, making sure it's just good ol' boy fun and not going to be an issue before continuing my threat assessment of the room. It's a normal Sunday crowd, with guys in just about every age bracket, wealth bracket, and confidence bracket . . . and three girls, two of whom are having 'nights out' with their guy friends.

Petals is a decent place, more high-class than most country clubs, so we don't get too many low-life types. Still, there's always a mix of folks to keep an eye on, especially in Dominick's place where he rules with an iron fist. The inherent combination of guys full of liquid courage and sexy women flirting with them is a dangerous equation, like sparks near dynamite . . . unless the rules are strictly followed.

So I keep my eyes open. From my perch, I can angle to the side and see behind the curtains on the far side of the stage. I see when the backdoor opens and Meghan walks in, a backpack thrown over her shoulder, her sweats and tank outfit in place but with full fuck-me hair and makeup going, probably done at her apartment. It's an oddly endearing combination, the sweet and the sexy all mixed up.

Giving Nick a nod to keep an eye, I step away from my station, needing to make sure Meghan is okay after the shit-storm last night. I'd driven by her apartment after I got off shift, hours after Dominick let her go home early, and I barely managed to keep from banging on her door.

But the single glowing light in the living room told me she was home, and I let that be enough to soothe the beast inside me. Besides, my hand was still pretty busted up, and it would have freaked her out to see my knuckles that way.

Backstage, I lean against the doorframe and watch for a second like the pervert that I am, enjoying the way she gently moves to the music pumping through her earphones as she touches up her makeup in front of the big light-up mirror. Her eyes meet mine in the glass, and she smiles, turning around to face me.

"Let me see it."

For a heart-stuttering moment, my filthy mind thinks she wants to see my cock, and it instantly hardens, liking that idea a lot. But as she walks toward me, it's not my crotch she grabs, it's my hand, lifting it to see the bruises and scrapes along my knuckles.

"I'm fine, nothing that won't heal in a day or two," I reply softly. Thankfully, I patched up my hand last night—hydrogen peroxide to clean it out, and then NuSkin does a lot to cover the damage.

She runs a feather-light fingertip over the roughly crinkled skin, her voice soft. "You did this for me?"

In my pants, my cock surges again, and my compression shorts are not up to the job this time. Instead, I'm resisting the urge to take her hand and press it into the wall above her head before taking her mouth in a strong kiss. "Of course. Asshole had it coming. That's no way to treat a lady, especially not you."

She blushes a bit, her cheeks pink with pleasure. "Thank you. That's sweet."

Before I can reply, she bends down, laying little butterfly presses of her lips along my knuckles, like she can kiss my injuries away. "Meg—"

"I'm nothing special, just . . . me," she says, looking up at me with emotion in her eyes that makes me want her all the more. "And no one has ever done anything like that for me before. Thank you."

I growl, wrapping a hand around the back of her neck as I step closer to her, our bodies a mere whisper away from touching. "Don't say that. You are beautiful. You can haunt a man's dreams, his fantasies, filled with your laughter, your sighs . . . and your screaming his name in pleasure. You're special, Meghan."

A small whimper escapes her lips as she looks up at me, her lips parting, almost begging for me to take them in a kiss. I shouldn't. I can't . . . for so many reasons.

But she's irresistible. I need to know what she tastes like. I have to experience the taste of her skin, whether it's the sparkle vanilla cupcakes she makes me think of, all sugar and sweetness. Or if there's the musky undertone that has haunted my dreams, the sexual essence of a woman that I sense burning just beneath the surface.

Instead of tasting her lips the way I want to, I trace my free hand down her arm, slowly and steadily to take hold of her hand. Bringing it up, I inspect her knuckles too, noting that they're looking a little bruised even in the dim light of the hallway. "Are you okay? That was quite a punch you landed."

She nods, her eyes so wide as I kiss her knuckles, one by one, letting my tongue slip out to lick at her as I caress her skin. She's even more thrilling than I thought, electric vanilla fireworks that make my head spin.

As I heal her not-at-all-injured hand with my ministrations, I look up to meet her eyes. "Not sure any of us saw that coming from such a sweet, innocent thing."

She smirks, a fire sparking deep in her eyes as she gathers herself for a sassy reply. "Who says I'm sweet and innocent?"

I chuckle, flipping her hand to kiss her fingertips and palm. They're silky soft, and in my mind, I can imagine this hand holding my cock in front of her open mouth for me to fill. "Angel, everything about you says sweet and innocent. That's what's so fucking dangerous. You don't know what you're playing with. You make me want to dirty you up, shock you with the filthy things I want to do your body, and tease at that sweetness until I can drink up every drop of you like candy."

My words galvanize Meghan's body, leaving her panting, her breath smelling like sugar with a faint hint of coffee, making me want to sip the flavor from her lips. I don't think she means to say it out loud, but a soft hiss escapes her pink lips unbidden anyway. "Yesss."

I cup her jaw in both hands, forcing her eyes to meet mine and lock. The next words are the hardest words I've ever spoken, tearing from the depths of my stomach like coughing up nails. "But we can't. You know the rules. Dominick would kill me. Literally, most likely. And you deserve better than me. You see me as a dangerous thrill, but I'd ruin you. A night with me would leave your pretty pink pussy in tatters from fucking you so rough because I'm not a gentle lover. I'd take you hard, wringing your orgasms out of you until you passed out in exhaustion. I'd give you so much cum, your pussy couldn't even hold it all and it would run down your legs."

Her eyes are dilated, wide and soft as if I'm whispering sweet nothings in her ear. I thought she'd be shocked, maybe even offended by my crude words. Some of me hoped she would be, that she'd be repelled and maybe we could end this dance between us. But it seems this angel has a bit more devil in her body than I thought.

Every bit of me wants to make good on my words, toss her on the chair in the corner and earn the first cries of her orgasm with my tongue between her legs. With the way her skin tasted, death by Dominick's hand might be worth it.

As much as I don't want to, I have to tell her the rest, leaning in to smell her hair before whispering in her ear. "As much as that excites you—and yes, my cock is throbbing at the idea too—I'll break your heart, Angel. I'll take what I need, make you a dirty mess, and leave. It's what I do. I'm a bastard, a motherfucker who only hurts those who let me in. You deserve better than me."

I pull back from her ear, letting her see the truth of my words in my eyes, on my face, knowing that even if I wanted to, I can't keep her. That's not who I am. It's . . . impossible.

The spell is broken, my words sinking into her head, her heart. I can see the moment her desire and arousal turn to hurt, then anger. She pulls back, putting space between us, and I hate it instantly, missing the feel of her so close.

"I see," she says, turning on a heel and heading toward the lockers. I want to chase her, push her to the ground, and take her like the predator I am. I want to bury myself inside her, feel her spasm as I stake my claim on her body, mind, and soul. *Mine.*

But this is the right thing to do. Let her push me away for her own sanity and safety. I can take it, even if it hurts. And right now, it does hurt, both in my gut and in my balls.

Just before reaching the curtain to the changing area, Meghan turns back, her eyes flashing dangerously. "You say I deserve more. That's for me to decide. Don't act like you get to make decisions for me. Is this just a game to you? Get me all riled up and then squash me with some lame justification that sounds more like a carrot on a stick enticement than a real warning? Well, fu–forget you."

She pushes the curtain aside, and I feel like I just got punched in the gut. She almost cursed at me. If I needed any more proof, that tells me how hurt she really is. Fucking hell. That was the last thing I wanted to do. I just couldn't help myself. She calls to me without even meaning to, and I'm barely holding back, for her sake.

She leaves the curtain open, stomping her little body over to her locker and ripping her scrap of a miniskirt out. She glares at me over her shoulder and then pulls it on over her sweats, only dropping them once she has the scrap in place.

I don't bother telling her that when she bends over to grab the sweats from the floor, I can see the bottom of her ass cheeks, so grabbable and biteable. And the peek of her good girl panties, white with lace trim against her tan flesh, does more for my fantasies than any fancy lingerie ever has.

She snatches her black lace bustier off the hook, holding it to her front like a shield even though she still has her tank top on.

She makes a shooing motion with her hand, swatting the air at me like I'm an annoyance. "Weren't you just saying you would leave me? Well, go ahead. I've got to get ready for my shift."

I should, I absolutely should. But I can't walk away when she's so mad at me. Instead, I assume my security guard stance, my feet planted firmly on the floor with my arms crossed over my chest, eyes daring her to test me. With a huff, she turns back to face her locker and rips her tank over her head.

The expanse of her back beckons me, and I want to trace the line of her spine with my tongue, make her arch beneath me as I fuck her from behind. She quickly fastens the bustier, not needing any help, and then leans forward, shimmying slightly and doing something to her tits, but my eyes are fastened on the flash of her ass again.

It's delectable, just enough that I could massage, knead . . . and spank it until it's bright red. It's taut, perfect, the type of ass that could grip my cock until we're both crying out. That peek is going to taunt me all night and for a long time to come. After slipping her heels and apron on, Meghan struts toward me looking like a fucking Valkyrie in petite-fairy form.

I hold my position, expecting her to either stop in front of me for another scathing dismissal or maybe push me out of her way. But she does neither.

Instead, she turns her body to step around me, not even brushing me with a faint touch of her skin. That stabs my heart more than anger or violence somehow. It's a dismissal. It's her saying that she understands and isn't going to waste her time on me any longer.

The scent of her lingers in her wake, and with a deep breath, I draw it in, knowing it might be my last chance to savor it. I let it sear its way into my brain for the upcoming lonely nights and empty beds, when the weaker side of me gnaws at my mind and tells me I could have had the most beautiful, flawless woman I've ever seen next to me. Even if only for a moment.

It takes me a while to settle my nerves, and I wipe at my cheeks and forehead, dismissing the moisture on my fingers as just sweat from the heat back here.

It's gonna be a long fucking night.

CHAPTER 9

MAGGIE

How dare he? I fume to myself as I move around the tables, catching as many orders as I can. *That arrogant son of a biscuit!*

Shane had me all fired up and ready to break the rules. He talked about Dominick, but I know that rule too.

The first day I worked here, before I'd even met Shane, Dominick had gone over his employee rules. Number one of which, and the one that seems the most pertinent right now, considering my wet panties, was no fraternizing between staff.

Considering what I now know about the way his eyes follow Allie's every move, it seems a bit hypocritical. But he's the boss, and if he wants to break his own rules, I guess he's allowed. Although, maybe he really does just watch her from afar. Allie has never said otherwise.

At the time of my sit-down with Dominick, I'd just been concerned about getting the undercover job without his being suspicious, and the rule seemed reasonable. I totally understood, but now I'm frustrated. Shane has me so . . . darn it, all I can do is try and avoid him. But he's a dang moving target all night, working the door, working the floor, and with those dark clothes of his, he's like a ninja when he wants to be.

At one point, he settled into a position on the far wall, so I asked Sarah to switch sections with me, and she did, albeit with a questioning look.

I had a few moments of glee at getting away until Shane switched stations too, glaring at me as he took up his new perch. Ugh, fine. Play your games, but I'm not playing.

Even as I tell myself that, I know it's not true. I'm pissed, I'm disappointed, but if he told me right now 'one-time ride . . . get on', I'd hop on his dick so fast he would see stars.

I sigh, shaking my head. Why do bad boys have to be so hot?

How is that even fair to us mere mortal girls? I mean, I know that I shouldn't be looking at guys like Shane.

I should try to find a nice guy. One who'll take care of himself and his family, who might not be perfect but will love me and any children we have. I need a guy who wants that too, a simple, happy life. That's what good girls are supposed to do.

But with Shane, I feel such a connection. And I'm no fool. Chemistry like that is rare, and if once was all I got, I'd go for it and pay the emotional price later.

So I spend the night alternating between ignoring him and glaring daggers at him.

Marco doesn't slow down, though. He's got drinks to get ready and customers to serve. Still, he's not heartless. "Hey,

Meghan, here's your pitcher for table forty-five, but what's up with you tonight? You okay?"

I huff, trying to make my voice light and bubbly but failing miserably. Still, I gotta try. "Yeah, I'm fine. You?"

Marco laughs, shaking his head. Good bartenders are half-baked shrinks, and Marco's no different. "Nice try, sweetheart. Last night hit you harder than you thought?"

"No, it's not that," I reply, hoping he doesn't push the issue. What Shane and I did in the back was probably close enough to being over the line, and as pissed as I am at Shane and his sexy bad self, I don't want him to get in trouble. "Just one of those nights, I guess."

"I can dig that," Marco says with a chuckle. "We all get them. By the way, I heard you put the smackdown on Mr. Creepazoid last night. That right?"

I grin a little, showing Marco my knuckles. "Yeah, I got one good punch in before Dominick sent me home."

Marco takes my hand and looks it over, giving a small whistle. "Sweet. Glad that Shane and Dom took care of the rest though. You mad at that?"

He looks at me questioningly, and I know that he's giving me an evaluating question, one that might have multiple layers to it. But regardless of the legality of the beating, my reply is quick and honest. "Oh, heck no, definitely not mad at that. I appreciate their having my back. Tonight's just a weird night."

Before I can stop it, I glance over my shoulder at Shane, who is watching my exchange with Marco with eagle eyes, even from across the room.

99

Marco follows my eyes and sees Shane looking our way. "Hmm, not really my business to get involved in. But Meghan?" He waits for me to look back at him before continuing, "Don't go barking up that tree. He might've saved you a couple of times, but he's no Prince Charming. And you know the rules."

Marco's eyes pointedly flick up to the camera at the corner of the bar. I understand. Dominick's always watching. You just never know when. "Best to stay in your own lane, especially around here. I wouldn't rat you to Dom, but I'm also not going to lie to the man if he asks."

I sigh, nodding. "I would never ask you to. Not trying to court trouble. Just . . . a weird night."

I know I'm repeating myself, but I don't want to take the risk of exposing what happened backstage. At least I can be assured that Dom didn't see that. He's never put a camera back there to give the girls some privacy. Or that's what we've been told. "Okay," Marco says, giving me a shrug. "Just be careful."

"I will, thanks. Thanks for listening," I reply. "Anyway, back to work."

I grab the pitcher Marco poured for me and deliver it to table of what looks like personal trainers, who seem to be out for more work talk than to watch the performances on stage. At least, while they remark on Tina's dance on stage, they're peppering their comments with remarks about her 'intercostals' and 'core stability' as much as her boobies.

After another hour, I've managed to push Shane from my mind, too busy slinging drinks to see if his eyes are still following my every move.

At least he's not positioned in my section anymore, the security team's rotation putting him on the other side of the room now. Thank goodness for small favors. Besides, I'm nearing the end of my shift, and I can't wait to go home, slam a Nytol to put me out quick, and dream of a tomorrow without a certain bad boy both frustrating and arousing me.

I come back around, checking on one of my loner tables, a single guy. He's my age, maybe, but his eyes look wiser than my twenty-five years and his suit easily costs more than my car. He has a worldliness to him, watching the performances almost as though they are artistic displays, not tawdry fantasies of the flesh.

As I come nearer, he raises a manicured hand. "Can I get another Macallan, miss? Actually, I'm headed back for a private dance with Allie. Can you bring the bottle back, Rare Cask Single Malt?"

I nod, surprised. Allie's very particular about her private dances, and her rates are pretty exorbitant. "Of course, sir. I'll keep your table reserved for after?"

He dips his head, rising to stride confidently to the back, and I head back to Marco to order the bottle service. With the bottle and a fresh glass on my tray, I head back to Allie's usual private dance room, the one closest to Dominick. It's the best room in the back too, mirrored and with a pole, but with a luxury feel to the supple leather seating and soft lighting.

I give one sharp rap as warning and then slowly and invisibly enter, pouring the scotch for the customer as Allie selects her music from the playlist in the corner. I give her a wink as I turn to leave, and she winks back. Considering that he just ordered a three-hundred-dollar bottle of scotch, it's gonna rain in here.

As I head down the hallway, I see a large guy striding toward me. He's wide, and the black of his jeans and T-shirt blend with the dimness of the hallway, although the moving laser lights bounce off him. He looks cold and calculating to a degree that seems to almost chill the very air around him. Our security guys are pretty badass themselves, but there's something raw about this guy, a missing element to his soul.

He's ugly as sin too, with a bald head that gleams lightly in the dim light and squinty eyes. His left ear's all types of screwed up, what I think some people call cauliflowered, like an alley cat that's had one too many scraps over the garbage cans.

I walk past him, hugging the wall and drawing myself in tight to seem as small and unimportant as possible, knowing that I'll have to tell security to keep an eye on him. Even still, my back ripples in goosebumps as I slide by.

This guy zings my red flags as a definite potential problem. I'm almost to the corner when I hear a fast ra-tat-tat sound, but it's barely audible over the loud bass-thumping music on the main floor. My brain takes a split second to register the sound as gunfire, but it's not until I hear Allie scream that I turn and run toward her. It's stupid. I shouldn't be running *toward* gunfire, but all my brain is telling me is that my best friend may have just been shot, and I have to help her.

I see the guy in black running out the other end of the hallway as I stop in the doorway of Allie's room. She's crouched in the corner and covered in blood splatter but seems to be uninjured. She's just frozen in shock, her eyes wide as she stares at what used to be a human being slumped on the couch.

My brain seems to shift, taking all of this in, not in panic, but in still-frame shots like my eyes have turned into a camera. I see the scotch-drinking suit guy, obviously dead since he's got three bullet holes in his chest, slumped over on the couch, blood pooling brightly across his white shirt.

I see the other holes in the wall and can only assume that Allie's alive because she was near the wall when the attack happened. Maybe she hadn't fully gotten into her routine, or maybe she was getting ready to drop her bra. Whatever the case, there's a bullet hole in the wall just about a foot from where she's cowering, and it's by luck or fate that she's not wounded too.

"Allie—" I start before Dominick blasts through the door that leads to his office, charging down the hall like a raging bull.

"What happened?" he yells, his face taut. "Allie?"

Dominick pushes me out of the way, rushing in the room and gathering Allie in his arms, blood and all, as he checks her over. I somehow find my voice, pointing down the hall. "He went that way. Big guy, in all black, black and cold eyes. Had a screwed-up ear."

As I speak, the security guys surround me, so fast and quiet I didn't even realize. Nick turns, his voice hot with anger. "On it, Boss."

He races down the hallway, following the direction I pointed. Shane grabs me, turning my face to his chest, where I burrow in without hesitation, needing something solid to hang on to because this is all too surreal. "I've got Meghan."

Dominick never takes his eyes off Allie, but he talks over his shoulder to Logan, the last of the security guys. "Take care of that."

Logan nods, moving closer to the suit, and Allie flinches. Dominick picks Allie up, heading toward his office, and Shane moves me quickly and steadily to the dressing room, dragging me to my locker and pulling out my backpack.

His voice is urgent but quiet in my ear. "What do you need outta your locker? Anything?"

He's shoving my wallet, my phone, my makeup, and clothes into my backpack. "What? What do you mean?"

He glances back once but then returns his attention to my locker, giving it one last scan before closing the door. It's nearly empty, except for maybe that chocolate chip muffin I brought in last week and had sort of forgotten until now.

He slides the backpack onto one shoulder before turning and looking into my eyes. "Meg, we have to go. You can't have seen what you just saw. They won't allow it. We gotta go. Now."

CHAPTER 10

SHANE

My heart's hammering in my chest as I peek out the back door of the club, scanning the lot carefully. It's nearly deserted. The soundproofing is good and nobody heard the shots. If it wasn't for Dominick getting on the radio, nobody on security would have known.

So there isn't a panicked rush of customers running for their cars. Part of me wishes there was. It'd help cover what I'm about to do. Instead, I'm forced to lead Meghan across the parking lot by her arm in a quick walk, looking more like I'm escorting a drunk customer than helping her flee for her life.

I aim for my truck. It's closer than Meghan's car, and a lot more secure. Hitting the unlock button on my remote, I shove her in the rear seat of the crew cab from the driver's door, hopping in behind her and yanking my door closed. I'd like to be gentle, but right now isn't the time for gentleness. It's the time for action.

"Buckle up," I instruct her, and thank fuck, she listens and sits up, reaching for the belt as I start the truck. It takes all of my willpower to pull out of the lot calmly and not put the pedal to the floorboard and peel out. I know that Nick's still out here somewhere, and Logan might be around too. I can't take the risk that two guys, one of whom I trained, might react.

Right now, eyes on us is the last thing we want. The parking lot cameras are bad enough. I know Dominick's going to check the tapes when he notices that Meghan and I are gone, but hopefully, he'll be so distracted with Allie that we're far away before he does.

It's not that I don't care about Allie. She's a nice girl who I hope is fine, but I know Dom cares about her. He'd never touch a hair on her head. Meghan, though . . . I have to protect her.

Meghan is quiet, curled in on herself, with her feet in the seat and knees hugged tightly, obviously in shock as we hit the highway.

As my truck growls its way up to eighty, chewing up pavement and spitting out miles and minutes between us and what she saw, she finally settles. I watch her out of the corner of my eye, never taking my awareness off the road in front of us or the cars behind us to make sure we're not being followed. Can't be too safe.

I can see Meghan willing her mind to focus, taking deep breaths that she holds for a two-count before letting them out slowly. Still, after five miles, her body is still shaking, her hands trembling as she reaches up to adjust where the shoulder belt is rubbing against her bare neck. And when I meet her eyes in the rearview mirror, they're wide, but with a turn of my head, I can see that they're at least clear as she starts processing things. "What are we doing? Where are we going?"

I nod, shifting my eyes back to the road. "Those are great questions. And I promise to answer them, but what you really need to know right now is that I'll keep you safe. I'm taking you somewhere secure until all this blows over."

She opens her mouth to ask more questions, always inquisitive, but right now, we don't have time for her to be curious. I hold up my right hand, silencing her. "Angel, I promise. Just give me a minute to get us where we need to be."

The nickname subdues her, even as her eyebrows perk up. She's so smart. Her mind ticks along in a way that's impressed me since I first met her. But she closes her mouth, looking around as I exit the highway and head to a deserted lot on the outskirts of town, just before we get to the truck stops that mark the way west.

I pull in next to a covered car, knowing that underneath is a four-door sedan that looks like a million others on the road. That's the point. I want us to look like any other car that might be out right now, and as 'un-Shane-like' as I can get.

Grabbing her backpack from the floor, I rifle through and grab her cellphone, leaning forward to drop it to the floorboard. I do the same with mine and then grab a duffle bag from behind the seat. "Okay, when I say go, open your door calmly, get out, and get in the car next to you. I'm doing the same."

"What about our phones?" she asks, reaching forward. "Why did you put them in the floorboard? I need that."

I place a hand on her forearm, the touch electric as I feel the tremble of her muscles underneath my fingertips. "Nope.

They're traceable, like my truck, and we've got to be ghosts until we figure out what's going on."

She sputters, looking at me with renewed fear in her eyes. "Traceable? Ghosts? What the heck are you talking about?"

"Go," I order. "There's time for answers later. I promise you that, but for now . . . go."

I open my door, snatching the corner of the dust cover on the sedan and pulling it back, revealing a ten-year-old Ford before grabbing the spare key from the magnetic box hidden in the rear wheel well and climbing into the driver's seat. I hit the unlock button, relieved when Meghan opens her door and buckles up, her eyes full of questions, but she keeps her silence as I start up the Ford.

Thank fuck.

With a turn of the key, we're back on the road, heading way out of East Robinsville. As we drive, the reality of the situation hits me.

Fuck. This has gone so damn sideways.

How much do I tell Meghan? There are secrets piled on top of secrets around her, and the layers go so deep that sometimes even I don't quite remember which way is up.

How much does she already know? It's common knowledge not to cross Dominick, but just how much does she understand?

She's quiet in the seat next to me, scanning around us occasionally but mostly watching the scenery blur by, but I know her silence won't last long. She's just too curious.

"Your truck?" she says after a bit, and I shrug. "What's that mean?"

"I mean that if it gets stolen, it gets stolen," I reply. "That lot's pretty out of the way. Decent chance it might be unnoticed."

"And this thing?"

"Just an old car. I promise to explain. Just wait a bit longer."

My answer silences her for a bit, and it's almost dawn when we pull over at a no-tell motel in the middle of nowhere. I know where half a dozen of these places are around the area, places that are desperate enough to take cash without too many questions but not so rundown as to become crack houses that'll attract the attention of the police.

I run inside and rent a room under a fake name, paying cash before parking and shepherding Meghan inside. Closing the door behind us, I lock it and peek out the window. We're clear.

But as I look back to see Meghan perched on the edge of the bed, so tiny but her eyes sparking with anger, I know the grace period of time I asked for is over. Hell, considering the worn-out carpet, dingy walls, and patched bed cover, I'd be pissed too, even if I was clueless about the rest.

"Okay," I start before she can say anything. "Where do we start?"

CHAPTER 11

MAGGIE

I stare at Shane, who's looking for the first time since I've met him less than a hundred percent sure of himself. If anything, he looks frightened, which scares the schnitzel out of me. "Okay, so we're wherever this is," I start.

I look around us, my nose upturned at the dingy motel room, noting the large crawly thing underneath the table in the corner and reminding myself not to go to sleep without covering every pore of my skin. "And seemingly safe-ish, wildlife notwithstanding. Now what the frick is going on? Why aren't we at the police station reporting a murder? Shane!"

He sighs, running a hand through his hair, and steps away from the door to sit down on the edge of the bed, still watching me with those eyes of his. "No matter how I spin this, you're likely to freak the fuck out, but you're in the middle of it now, so I'll dive in as delicately as I can."

I nod, just wanting him to tell me already. "Delicate, not delicate. Just get to the truth, Shane. I'm not following you one more step without it."

He nods and strokes his chin. "Deal. So, do you know who that was back at the club?"

I shake my head, turning to face him and criss-cross apple-sauceing my legs between us, needing the space to keep a clear head for this conversation. "The suit or the shooter?"

He eyes sharpen, and he sits forward, his voice immediately hardening. "Either."

I shrug, refusing to break his gaze as I stare back at his face, making sure he understands me clearly. "No idea. The suit was drinking Maclellan in my section for a bit, the expensive stuff, and he took Allie back for a lap dance. I took the scotch in and Allie was picking music in the corner. She gave me a thumbs-up, and I silently wished her luck."

"And the other guy?"

I take a deep breath, hating the fact that I have to try and relive those few moments but somehow knowing that it's important. "I saw him coming down the hallway. That guy chilled me just with this . . . I don't know . . . aura. Next thing I know, big man was shooting up the place and Allie is screaming bloody murder. You were there for the rest."

He nods, letting that sink in. "Okay, the shooter is a hired gun. Hitman. Assassin. Maybe if you tell me more, I might be able to tell you who he was. The list of men with the skills and either the guts or insanity to make a hit inside Petals is pretty small. The suit was Carlos Rivaldi, bastard son of Sal Rivaldi. Names mean anything to you?"

I shake my head, and he scoffs lightly, smiling a little. "So fucking innocent. Let's rewind. Meghan, you know Petals is a money laundering front for the mob and Dominick is The Boss, right?"

I squint, making sure I heard right. "Wait, Boss? Money laundering?"

Shane nods. "Boss. As in, Boss of the Angeline family."

I shake my head vehemently, but after a moment, my brain whirls. I think back to some of the customers, the business meetings in Dominick's office, and the large security team that has always made me feel safe. Petals is a small club. There should be no reason they always have three and some-times four guys working security. I thought it was because of the clientele, a sense of fancy-schmancy to make the celebs feel like VIPs.

I gasp, looking at Shane. I knew Dominick was a shrewd businessman, but the level of what I've walked into . . . did my former boss, Donnie, know when he came up with this idea for me to work undercover? Does Jeanine know? Do they even care that I'm covering stupid celeb gossip in a freaking mob club? Oh, my God, everything I've been doing suddenly seems so much more dangerous. My reporter senses felt like there was more to Petals, but something like this never even occurred to me. How could it have? It's crazy. "Dominick is The Boss? Holy frack. But . . ." My words stut-ter, another thought jumping forward. "Oh, no! Allie!"

Shane shakes his head. "Allie is fine. She's Dominick's. Well, she isn't, but she might as well be by the way he looks at her and I suspect feels about her. He wouldn't touch a hair on her head unless she directly betrayed him. That's why I'm confused."

"Confused about what?" I ask, the reporter in my head pushing back the fear. It's not hard. Right now, I'm pretty sure that information means life, and Shane's about my only source of more information.

"Dominick is the head of the Angeline family, who are basically mortal enemies of the Rivaldi family, even though there's been peace for years. It's been a Cold War in the area, two sides that posture and talk a lot of shit, but nobody's been willing to actually draw blood. Still, it's not like Carlos Rivaldi was welcome inside Petals. So why was Carlos in Dominick's club? The Rivaldis have their own bars, their own club. So why would he be at Petals?"

He looks to be thinking for a moment, but my mind has already begun rolling, considering angles and strategies and manipulations. It's what's given me my best stories, being able to see all the possible motivations and consequences of people's actions. "Maybe he was a spy? Or you said he's the bastard son. Maybe he's pissed at that label and wanting to stir stuff up? Or maybe someone just invited him to come check out the show and have a drink? It could be anything."

Shane rubs his jaw, his words coming slowly as he considers my comment. "You're right. Carlos could've been spying for his daddy, in which case Dominick would be pissed as fuck and could've hired the hit. There's another option though."

"What's that?" I ask, nodding when I understand a moment later. "Dominick invited Carlos."

Shane nods. "If he thought he could bring Carlos on board, it'd have changed the entire game in this part of the country. The Angelines are the big dogs by far, but it wasn't always that way, and the Rivaldis do have some pockets of power. Sal Rivaldi's getting up there in years. The issues between the two families started with Dom's daddy. If Dom and Carlos thought they might be able to forge an undercover alliance and get Sal to retire quicker, either voluntarily or the hard way . . . Daddy Sal might have heard about it, and he's not the kind to forgive treason, even from his own blood."

I swallow, feeling like I want to throw up. Down the rabbit hole, and I'm still not sure how deep I've gotten. "He'd kill his own son?"

Shane nods once, chuckling darkly. "Carlos is his bastard son. He just found out about him a few years ago and there's no love lost. Apparently, Sal had a one-night stand when he was trying to make inroads with the Colombians, and he left Carlos's mom with a souvenir."

"And he never knew?" I ask, and Shane nods.

"I don't know the full story, but apparently, Carlos just showed up, wanting his birthright and being pretty fucking aggressive about it, from what I hear. Sal ran the DNA, but not much else he could do about it."

"So either Dominick killed his arch nemesis's son, in which case, I'm guessing Sal will be pretty POed, even if he didn't like the kid. Or someone, maybe even Sal himself, sent Carlos to his death on Dominick's turf. It sounds like the beginning of a mob war," I comment and shake my head. "And I got a look at the ugly mug who did it. Great."

Shane's face pales as he looks at me. "You might be the only one who did, too. Allie was near the edge of the sofa, right? And she had blood on her chest and face, so she couldn't have seen from that angle. She'd have been facing Carlos, her back to the door. But you saw the hitman face-to-face. Could you identify him?"

I nod, biting my lip. "I feel like that's a question you should automatically say no to when you're talking mob hitmen, but yeah, I'd recognize him anywhere. That face, the squinty eyes and cauliflowered left ear . . . I could probably sketch him for you, if that's helpful. I'm not an artist, but it'd be close enough."

"Yeah, we'll see if we can get a pencil and some paper because we need to know who the hitman is so we can figure out who hired him," Shane says, sighing. "I can't believe we're talking about your sketching a hitman."

"But why can't we go to the police? They could help us," I ask, almost pleading with him, and Shane laughs harshly. "What? That's their job!"

Shane looks at me with pity in his eyes and smiles bitterly. "Both families have the police in their pockets. The only way to be a cop above Desk Sergeant in East Robinsville is to be friendly with one family or the other. If we go to the cops, we'll likely never be seen again because they'll turn us over to whoever wants us the most."

"As in?" I ask, fearing the answer even before Shane says it.

"Meaning whoever's willing to pay more for our silence. Knowing some of the cops in this town, they'd do the job for the families and might even try to collect from both of them if there's money in it."

Hating that answer and needing more, I run through the whole evening again in my head, something wiggling at me, but it's not until I see the blood spatter on Allie's favorite costume that I realize what it is.

"Hey! What about the cameras? The security? How'd the hitman even get inside without being seen? He should be on cameras all over the place. There should be all sorts of images of him, not just my memory."

Shane nods but gets up to pace the carpet. "Yeah, but that's only helpful if it's Sal's guys fucking with Dominick. If Dominick did this, he'd erase the recordings. All it takes is a single button push on his system. That'd leave him just one last loose end to clean up."

Shane gives me a pointed look, and I realize he's telling me that if Dominick is behind this, he'll want me killed. If Sal did it, Dominick won't hurt me, but Sal probably will. I'm messed up either way. "So, where does that leave us? You're Dominick's guy."

I leave the question as to whether he'll hurt me unasked, but he knows that's what I need to know. Shane walks to the curtained window and glances out before turning to me, looking at me from across the room with intense eyes that burn with . . . something.

"It's more complicated than that, but I swear to you, Meghan, I would never, ever hurt you. I work at Petals for Dominick, but I'm not in the mob, not one of his guys. I promise with my very last breath to keep you safe."

"And how do you plan to do that?" I ask, my heart pounding as the intensity of Shane's words hit me. In another light, another situation, they'd be the most romantic thing a man has ever said to me. I feel the sting of tears in the corners of my eyes, but refuse to let them loose, even though this is all so overwhelming.

Shane doesn't have the magic answer I was hoping for, instead being a bit vague. "We'll figure it all out."

For a moment, I think about telling him that it's even more complicated than he realizes because I'm not just a cocktail waitress at Petals, but an undercover reporter using the job to get stories for a celebrity tabloid. Part of me wants to tell him everything, because deep down inside, I feel this almost instinctual need to be totally honest with him.

We've danced around each other for two months to the point that earlier tonight ,we nearly kissed, despite knowing the rules. We both know that we want the other, and that the only reason he'd gotten me so angry at him earlier tonight is that he's under my skin.

But that seems minor in comparison to mob hits, and honestly, I don't think telling Shane that I've been lying to him is going to ingratiate me to him.

And I need him right now, to stay safe, to stay alive.

So I let the truth die on my lips, keeping that secret.

For now. I only pray that before this is all over, there's a chance that I can tell him the truth. Because just once, I'd like to hear him call me Maggie instead of Meghan.

CHAPTER 12

SHANE

For a moment, Meghan looks like she's got something to say, maybe something important that dances on the tip of her tongue, but with a sigh, she deflates, biting the words back, and I'm curious what she was going to tell me.

Maybe something about the shooter? Big guy, cauliflower ear. I can think of a few suspects, but I'd need more to be sure since the ear doesn't ring a bell at the moment.

Still, the look on Meghan's face. I have to know what she's thinking. Unable to stop myself, I cross the room, crouching in front of her and tilting her chin up, forcing her to look me in the eye.

"You're safe. We're okay right now."

She bites her lip, and I can see the sheen of fear in her eyes. Tears form on her lower eyelids, and I pull her to me, hugging her close. She lays her head on my shoulder as I rub up and down her back.

I hear her sobbing gently, her sniffles breaking my cold heart wide open. "I . . . I never . . ."

Nothing should make something as sweet as her cry. Ever. I lean down, bringing my lips close to one perfect shell-pink curve of an ear, and breathe deeply of her scent, which is undercut with the acrid stench of fear that still can't overwhelm how beautiful she is. "Shh, let it out. I've got you."

She quakes a few more times, burying her face in my chest as she clutches at me for a moment before taking a steadying breath, but even that sounds a bit shaky. She might have pulled herself together by sheer will, sealing over the cracks in her worldview with Scotch tape, but she's still fragile, and that tugs at every heart string I have.

As she pushes back from me, a watery smile on her face, she's trying so hard to be brave. "I'm not sure why I'm even crying. It's just a lot to take in, you know? Guess I'm a bit over-whelmed. And mad! I'm mad I didn't see what was going on when it was right there in front of my face. I feel stupid, and I'm definitely not. I was just focused on the wrong things and didn't see the forest for the trees."

Her voice is stronger by the end of her rant, her fire making me reevaluate just how fragile she is. I think she's made of stronger stuff than I gave her credit for, and the momentary breakdown was the anomaly, not her usual default when things get tough. It's an odd reassurance that her sweetness is tempered with some iron, like pretty cotton candy on a steel core.

I lay a light kiss to her forehead, comforting her, but the touch of her skin to my lips is like fire in my veins and blood rushes to my cock. "Meghan."

The heat in my voice is evident, and she looks up at me, her eyes flickering too. "Yes."

I don't need another word as I drop to my knees on the carpet, and Meghan spreads her legs as wide as her skirt will go, letting me between her thighs. I press the growing bulge in my jeans against the side of the bed, looking for any relief as I get closer to her while trying my damndest to be respect-ful. She just saw a shooting, had a breakdown . . . the last thing she needs is my intensity. I force myself to sit back, making my jeans tighter to the point that my cock and balls are painful, but I take a deep breath, regaining a modicum of my unraveling control. "I think Dominick does a good job of hiding the truth from those he doesn't want to see it. He's cultivated an image of being a high-class businessman, and only those who need to know the truth do. Hell, some of the guys in his organization probably don't even realize he's The Boss at the very top. That's the way he likes it. Low-key and calculated. But Meghan, I'm not lying when I call you an angel. You have no place in this mess, and I'm sorry you got caught up in it."

I didn't realize it, but I've been rubbing small circles on her thighs with my thumbs, soft and gentle but getting higher and higher.

Her breath hitches, and I can smell her arousal, like vanilla and sugar, as her muscles contract beneath my fingertips. She leans back, her shoulders thumping lightly against the wall as she bites her lip, looking down at me. "Shane?"

I force my hands to stop moving, instead grabbing hold of her thighs and squeezing her flesh with a tight grip. "Yes, Angel?"

"What are you doing to me?"

I clear my throat, but my voice still feels gravelly, rich with lust and need as I look up at her. "What I want to do is run my hands up higher, take your panties down, and bury my tongue so deep in your pussy that you scream my name the way I've been dreaming for weeks."

She lets out a mewl, her hips fighting against my hold to lift toward me. "Oh, God. I've wanted that too."

I squeeze one last time, forcing myself to let go as I roll back, my cock screaming in pain as my jeans nearly become a goddamn tourniquet. "But you already said you're over-whelmed. I will never take advantage of you. That's not how I do things. You're not ready for this, for me. Not now."

With all my willpower, I get to my knees and push to stand up, pressing a palm against my throbbing cock, hoping the attention will relieve the pressure, but it just makes me want to arch against my hand.

Meghan's mouth opens when she sees the bulge in my jeans and a little squeak sounds out from her throat. "You're . . . big."

I force myself to stay still, not giving in to the urge to release the pressure of my zipper and show her exactly how big I am, but my cock jumps anyway, desperately wanting to be closer to her mouth as she sits forward, just inches away from my crotch. She watches me, the tip of her tongue coming out to trace one plump lip, and I have to turn away. "Fuck, Angel. Don't look at me like that, all wide-eyed and open-mouthed. All I can think of right now is how much I want to slide my cock past those full, pink lips and into your hot mouth. I wonder if you could swallow me to the hilt?"

I tilt my head, watching her throat work as she swallows. "I wonder that too."

Her voice is breathy, a sex siren so damn close to making me crash on her shores.

I rub my cock through the denim once more before balling my hands at my sides, wrangling control back of my lust-addled body before I need to punch myself in the thighs. "I need—"

Meghan interrupts, her voice soft as she looks up at me. "Yes."

I smirk, wishing I could finish that sentence the way I want but knowing that I'm right, and fucking Meghan right now will only make her regret it more later.

A deep part of me says to do it anyway, fuck her and take what I want while she's willing to give it. But I'm not an animal, and if I'm going to be between her thighs, I don't want her to hate me for it tomorrow.

She'll hate me enough from all this mess. I don't need to add to my karmic bad shit list, so I hedge, turning away and squeezing my eyes shut. "I need you to take a shower, get cleaned up while I make some calls to see what the word on the street is. Then we'll sleep for a few hours. I want to be back on the road by sunset. This place . . . it won't be safe for more than twenty-four hours."

My words don't register for a split second, but when they do, her mouth closes hard enough that I hear her lips smack together, and I glance back to see her blushing, looking down and embarrassed by my denial. "Shane, this is maddening. One minute, you make me feel like the sexiest woman in the world and then you turn—"

I lift her chin again, meeting her blue eyes. "Angel, don't do that. Never, ever doubt yourself. Fuck knows, I want you, but

I'm trying real fucking hard to be a good guy here and keep my promise. You . . . you deserve a good man. Not me."

She stands to study my face, her body so close to mine that my cock is straining for her. Her eyes soften, then sparkle, and I can see the sass in them before she even speaks. "Fine. I'm getting in the shower. But Shane?" She pauses dramatically, lifting to her tip toes and leaning toward me. "Nobody asked you to be a good man. And I happen to have some fantasies involving you . . . and a shower."

With that parting shot, she bites at my jawline, the stinging flash of her tiny teeth on me making my blood boil. She turns to swish to the bathroom, but I reach out, smacking her ass through the denim miniskirt.

The pop is loud in the silent room, but her cry is one of pleasure, not of pain. She glares at me over her shoulder, but I can see the spark of interest in her eyes and make a mental note of that. *Oh, Angel. You do have a little devil inside you, and those wings might not be the purest white either. Fuck me, but it makes you even sexier.*

But as the bathroom door shuts behind her, I know I can't go there with her, no matter how much we keep crashing into each other. The whisper of the shower through the door is pure torture, but with this sword of Damocles hanging over our heads on a single silken thread, I can't let myself get any more distracted by the pleasures that she offers me or the ones I could readily give to her. I can't, because I have to keep her safe. I have to get us both out of this mess. That's all this can be, or we'll both end up dead.

The fact is, even at my best, I might still end up getting us both killed, but I have to try. And I need a clear head for this. The dire thought is enough to calm my raging desires and let my brain focus on the tasks ahead. Taking a moment to at least undo my zipper and let my cock have a little bit of relief , I dig in my duffle to pull out a burner phone.

I dial Chucky, a guy who's more a tool than a friend, but someone good to have on your side. He's gotten in trouble a few times with the law and walks in that gray area where what he does can be legal or illegal simply based on whose computers he's doing it to and who he's working for. The line connects, but it's silent, as always, because he waits for you to speak. "Chucky, it's Shane. Ran into some issues at work."

His voice, high-pitched and wheezy, comes through the line like it always does. "Shane. Good to hear from you, man. Heard there was some carnage."

Chucky speaks like everything is a video game come to life, and I doubt he's ever seen actual carnage or he wouldn't throw that word around so carelessly.

"What have you heard?" I ask, not only for curiosity's sake but to know how fast and far the word's getting out. I can judge the heat on me and the severity from that.

"Heard a legacy man went down on enemy soil," Chucky replies. "That true?"

I consider how much to tell him, but I need his help, and getting information comes at a price, usually telling or confirming information. And this isn't too bad. Chucky can't use it to hamstring me. "True. Professional hit on Dominick's turf. Carlos Rivaldi."

Chucky whistles low and long, knowing that there's always a ticking time bomb between the Rivaldi and Angeline families, just waiting on the spark of ignition, which this could be. "That is a problem, isn't it, Shane? You do it?"

"No," I growl, wanting him to understand this one hundred percent. "Did you forget who the fuck I am? I had nothing to do with it. Hitman came in and out clean, and we were all chasing our tails to catch him, deal with Carlos, and get the girls out."

"Girls? What girls?" Chucky asks, and I can hear the excitement in his voice.

Shit. He didn't know about the girls yet. "Girl was in the room when the show went down, uninjured. Another was in the hallway, also uninjured. Come on, man, it's Dom's club. What did you expect?"

"Hmm, either girl see the hitman?"

Trying to appeal to his nature, I use his vocabulary. "Maybe. That's why I'm calling, Chucky. I got an innocent that needs protection, needs to disappear for a while, maybe long-term respawn."

Chucky laughs in my ear, not harshly but he's not buying it yet. "Good one, but don't bother, Shane. Just tell me."

I try again, knowing I don't have a lot of time. "Look, Dominick's keeping the dancer safe. She's his. But this other girl, she's mine. Not like *that*, but I promised her I'd keep her safe. Also, right now, other than the camera, she's the primary witness who can identify the hitman and help figure out who's behind the whole thing. I need you to see what you can find out. Let me know how much shit we're in here and if we should be hiding from Dominick or Sal or both of them. I don't fucking know."

Chucky huffs, sarcasm dripping from each wheezy exhalation. "Oh, sure, just all that. No problem. Would you like for me to get into the IRS D-base while I'm at it?"

"Please, Chucky," I beg, wondering how much more horse trading this guy's going to need. For Meghan, I'd be willing to bargain away every chip I've got, and maybe promise a few more down the line. "This is important."

Thankfully, Chucky lets me off the hook, humming for a second as I hear his keyboard clacking away in the background.

"All right, Shane," Chucky says finally. "I'll see what I can find out. But this is a big ask and a big owe. I won't forget."

I nod, even though he can't see me, relieved that he's not going into details. "I know, Chucky. Thanks."

CHAPTER 13

MAGGIE

*W*hen I come out of the shower, Shane is lying back on the bed with his eyes closed. For a moment, I let my eyes trace over him, noting the flops of dark hair he's obviously been running his fingers through, his long lashes, the soft part of his full lips, and his strong jawline. Before I can continue my perusal any lower, his eyes pop open and he catches me leering at him like a creeper. Without a word, he stands and disappears into the bathroom to clean up, giving me time to change clothes. My body's exhausted after all the stress of the night, the fear, and then having a couple of heaping doses of arousal thrown in there with it.

Still, slipping into my after work tank top and some fresh panties helps me regain some sense of normality, and despite my earlier worries, the sheets on the bed are fresh and smell like fabric softener. I promise myself that I'm going to stay awake for Shane, but I'm just so worn out, my eyelids are drooping almost immediately, and the darkness seems so inviting and unavoidable after everything that's happened.

Sometime after I fell asleep, Shane must have decided to join me in bed because when a bad dream wakes me with a barely suppressed gasp, I find myself waking up in his arms.

The dream was horrible. I was back at Petals, but this time, I was in the room ready to dance, and instead of it being Carlos in his thousand-dollar suit, it was Shane watching me with lustful eyes when the door burst open and suddenly, Shane's body exploded in bullet holes.

Still, the feeling of him holding me melts the dream away in an instant, and I relax. His bare chest is warm on my back, the big spoon to my little spoon, one arm wrapped high around my shoulders and one low around my hips. The fingertips of his left hand are just above my panty line, in that small space where my tank top always seems to ride up, but it feels good and reassures me that my dream was just that—a dream.

I wiggle slightly, pleased and comfortable in his arms. When I press my hips back, I can feel him, thick and hard against my peachy bottom, barely contained in his boxer briefs.

I bite my lip to suppress my moan, knowing I'm already wet between my legs. This fire he keeps stoking in my core had cooled to embers while we slept, but it lights to an inferno instantly as I feel him grow even larger against me.

I grind my hips back again, stroking his length between my cheeks, mimicking the lap dances I've seen the girls at the club give. It's amazing, electric to my very core, and my panties feel soaked as I part my thighs a little, still making little movements against him with my butt. But Shane stays still, sleeping through my attempt at seduction. Frack, I'm so turned on, already on the edge.

Maybe I could . . . no, not with Shane right behind me. He

begins snoring softly, his breath warm against my hair. He's passed out, deep in sleep and would never know. I'll just have to be super quiet so he doesn't wake up. I know it's a risk, but maybe a quick release will help me deal with him today?

Decision made, I slowly let my fingers trace up my thigh to my center. My panties are soaked through, my clit already pulsing in need.

I rub slowly, circling clockwise and then counterclockwise, teasing myself through the cotton as I chase my own touch.

Slipping my hand inside my panties, I cup myself, sliding a thin finger inside to spread my juices up to my clit. I find a rhythm, trying to stay still, but my hips are circling against Shane, the feel of him against my ass giving me that extra spark, taking me higher.

I bite my lip, stifling my moans, already so close to coming.

Suddenly, Shane's hands tighten around me, his hips pressing forward to squeeze his cock between us. I have a split second of hope that he's still asleep, reflexively pressing against me like he did when we slept on the couch.

That hope is dashed, mortified horror taking its place as he moans, obviously awake, and his hand comes up to cup my breast, pinching my nipple. I don't know what to do, but then he growls in my ear. "Don't you fucking stop, Angel. You started this and we're fucking gonna finish it. Touch that pussy for me. Get yourself off and let me hear you come."

He grabs my wrist, pressing my palm flat against my core with his. I'm still frozen, but as he moves my hand, his fingers rub with mine against my clit in strong, hard circles. He arches against my back, stroking himself along my ass, and I give in, too far gone to stop.

"Shane, oh, my God . . . so good."

"That's it, Angel. Show me how dirty you are, rubbing your hot little pussy while you think I'm sleeping behind you. So fucking innocent. So fucking sexy." Shane grunts, his hips grinding against me in time with his finger, guiding me to his rhythm.

I gasp, thrumming at my clit faster, bucking my hips to get closer to my own touch and then to massage along his length. "Oh, Shane, I'm gonna come."

"Do it," he gasps, his cock throbbing against my ass. "Come for me. Come for me, and I'll give you the same. Get those fingers coated in your honey so I can lick them clean. Fuck, I need to see if you taste as sweet as you smell."

Every muscle in my body tenses, riding the knife-edge of pleasure, and with one more brush across my clit, I cry out, feeling myself release intensely. Shane pinches my nipple hard again, pulling on it as I cry out once more. My body shudders, riding the waves of bliss as they roll through my body.

Behind me, I hear Shane grunt, his body jerking as he pulls me tight against his hips, his cum warm through the cotton separating us. I circle my hips one last time, trying to wring out the last drops of pleasure from us both, but Shane has other ideas. He rolls me to my back, half pinning me as he props himself up on an elbow, looking in my eyes. "Give me your hand."

His fingers encircle my wrist, holding my wet fingers up for his savoring. With a smirking grin, he licks a long line up my index finger before taking it into his mouth and sucking the whole thing deeply. It makes me think of what I could do to him, and my soaked pussy quivers again. I whimper, "Shane."

He hums in appreciation and repeats the sexy move on my other fingers, his eyes gleaming with appreciation. "You do taste like sugar and vanilla, so sweet, but there's more, sexy undertones of a dirty girl. Isn't that right? Maybe you're not so innocent after all, considering you just used me to get yourself off."

My jaw drops, indignant anger racing through me. I press my leg to the side. "You did too!"

Shane smirks down at me, and I realize he's teasing as he gives my fingers a final lick before bending down to murmur in my ear. "Yeah, but you took advantage of a sleeping man, rubbing that tight ass of yours along my cock and touching your little pussy so soft and quiet, like you didn't want to wake me up. But you can wake me up like that any fucking time, Meghan."

I cringe inside, keeping my face steady. Meghan. Not Maggie. I can't believe I just basically had sex with Shane and he doesn't even know my real name. Is that weird? I've never had sex on an undercover job, and I don't know the moral code for that. Actually, we've never even had a date, and that's a new one for me too.

But Shane must see the flash of thoughts on my face because he lets go of my hand where he's been licking and suckling along my fingertips to cup my cheek. "What's going on in that head of yours, Angel? Talk to me."

I bite my lip, mentally racing through potential reactions and outcomes to telling him the truth, and still not sure if this is the best course of action. But I can't do this any longer. He's risking his life to protect me. The least I can do is tell him my real name, especially considering the rest of the lies I've told.

Apparently, there's a big web of lies and deception around us, considering the things I didn't know about Petals. But this is within my control. If it ruins me, if it ruins what I've felt building with Shane for the past few months . . . I'll have to live with the consequences. If it risks my life, that he won't want to protect me . . . I'll walk out the door and do my best to figure out what to do. At least then he'll know my real name, and if he reacts poorly, then I'll know better than to ever tell the rest of the truth.

I look down, unable to meet his eyes. "Shane, my name . . . it's Maggie, not Meghan. I didn't want to use my real name at a strip club. I'm sorry for not telling you before."

I can feel the heat radiating from his body, hear his teeth grinding, but I don't lift my eyes, flinching as he growls. "What the fuck? Maggie? You'd let me fuck you and call out a name that's not even yours?"

I gasp, looking up at him in pain. "We didn't . . . I mean, kinda, but not really."

He jumps up from the bed, his eyes flashing as he paces back and forth before turning to me, legitimately angry and hurt. "Not really? Not sure of your definition, Angel, but what we did is riding a pretty fine line of fucking. Maybe you make a habit of telling guys fake names or not caring what theirs might be, but I fucking don't."

He runs his hands through his hair, growling in frustration. I'm mad too, and flustered by his reaction as I sit up in the bed holding the sheet to my body. I'm not yelling, but I'm dang close as I form my reply. "I'm sorry, Shane. It's just been my work name for so long that I answer to it too. But I wanted you to know in case . . . well, because I don't go around having sex with guys who don't know my name."

Shane grabs his jeans from the chair, sitting down and

yanking them up his legs. "Get dressed. We need to hit the road."

Feeling the shift in the room, I'm embarrassed again by his easy dismissal of me. How does he always seem to do that?

"Yes, sir!" I say with all the sarcasm I have, which is admittedly not much. It's childish, but I can't help needling him for his bossiness, the sudden urge to get out of here coming out of nowhere to escape the discomfort of the argument.

He freezes, his voice cold and commanding as he looks at me with eyes that are flashing with warning. "Don't call me that, Angel. Don't mess with things you don't understand."

I know what he's talking about. I'm innocent, not stupid, and a curiosity whips across my mind and through my body. The spanking. The promises. Now this? On the heels of my revelation is another ripple of desire.

There's still plenty of sass in my voice, though, and fiery anger sparking between us as I press him. "Sir? You don't want me to call you 'Sir'? Are you sure about that? Because you seem to like it . . . a lot."

I look down pointedly at the reawakening bulge in his boxer briefs, the dark stain of his cum making him look even bigger and sexier. He moves to stand in front of me, grabbing my hair in his hands and tilting my head up to lock eyes. "You think you want to play? Push me and see where my limits are? Trust me, girl. You'll break long before I will."

I can see the lust in his eyes mixed with wariness as he tests me, but I want to test him back, challenge his assessment that I'm some fragile, dainty little thing. I can take him. Heck, I want to feel him wild and rogue, see what he's got and maybe see if I really can handle it. "Challenge accepted . . . Sir."

I feel his fists tighten in my hair, the sharp bite keeping me present, ready for whatever he says next. "Maggie." It's just my name, but it hangs in the air between us for a moment, meaning so much to both of us before he continues. "Maggie. I think you need to apologize for lying to me."

My mouth opens to argue but snaps shut at his look. This is Shane, yes, but this is a side of him he's never shown me before, a side that I've only seen hints of.

"Good girl," he says, smiling sternly. "Don't make this worse than it needs to be. Seems like I cleaned up your fingers for you rather well, I'd say."

I nod, head still cradled by his hands. "Yes, Sir."

His eyes flash again at the word, and he hums. "I think you need to clean me up too."

My eyes drop to his dick, straining against the cotton right in front of me. "Yes, Sir."

Heck yes, I'm in for this. I've been dying to get a look at Shane's dick after feeling it in his jeans and against my back.

I grip the waistband of his boxer briefs, slipping them over the head and down his legs, and his dick springs free, gorgeous and hard, with evidence of his earlier orgasm still covering him.

I lean forward, laying kisses and licks over the red head and along the velvety shaft, tasting the saltiness of his cum and moaning in delight.

I trace my fingertips along his length, wanting to drive him wild with the light touches all over, nothing aggressive enough to get him off, just enough to tease and torture him. I hear his growls above me, and I look up with what I hope is my most innocent look.

"Fuck, Maggie. Suck me already. You're killing me."

I pause, leaving my tongue out to lick at him like a lollipop as I look up through my lashes at him, smirking. "My apology, my way."

He groans, his hips pressing forward involuntarily, seeking more contact. I give in, sucking more of him into my mouth, but instead of his dick, I choose his balls, letting his length brush along my cheek as I swirl my tongue over one, then the other.

Finally, I lick one long line from the seam of his balls up the entirety of his shaft, and at the top, I swallow him to my throat in one smooth motion. "Oh, fuck. Right there."

Shane holds my head, using my hair as leverage to keep me deep-throating him. He gives tiny little pulses of thrusts, and I hum against him, already feeling him getting close to the edge. I start to gag, and he releases the pressure on my head, letting me catch my breath before he pulls out totally. He lets go of my hair to wrap a powerful hand to his shaft, squeezing himself to stay on the edge.

"Can you do it again?" he asks, looking at me with total adoration. "Fuck, I want to watch you swallow me down, cum and all."

I nod, diving back for more, and Shane's hands tangle in my hair again. He hits the back of my throat, pushing harder, and I hum, wanting desperately to taste him again. Shane pulls back, dragging the head of his cock over my tongue one last time before slamming deep into my mouth.

From above, I hear Shane cry out, roaring for a split second

LAUREN LANDISH

before I feel rope after rope of his warm cum shooting down my throat. I swallow, gulping deeply and not wanting to lose a drop as Shane jerks and shudders, holding me tight the whole time. As he tapers off, I lick along his length, getting every last drop before I sag, all the energy wiped from my body.

Shane pulls back, cupping my face and running his thumb along my cheekbone. The sweet oxygen is like a gift, and I look up at him, knowing my victory is written clearly on my face. But his eyes are serious, something more than I'd expected hidden in their depths. "Maggie. Apology fucking accepted."

I smile shyly, pleased with his response. "Thank you, Sir." And then because I'm a dork and can't help myself, I wink at him sassily. And I'm not one of those cute gum-commercial winkers, so it probably looks like I've got something in my eye.

He laughs, kneeling down to cup my face and lay a soft kiss on my cheek. "Fuck, I really want to throw you on this bed and spend all night buried in you, but we really do need to go. It's getting late and we've got miles to roll."

I have a thought, wiggling to the surface from deep inside, that my name isn't the only thing I'm hiding from him. He might've accepted my name with relative ease, considering it's not too uncommon at strip clubs to use a fake one. But if he finds out the real depth of my lies, I'm scared that no number of apologies, verbal or on my knees, will make that okay to a man like Shane.

CHAPTER 14

SHANE

*I*t takes us a little longer to get going than I thought. Besides Meg—Maggie and me crossing a line that I never thought we'd cross, it took me a while to locate a safe location for us to crash.

It's nearly sunset by the time I say fuck it and we hit the road, knowing that I need to get us out of the area so no one loyal to Dominick or Sal reports seeing us. I still haven't located a safe place for the medium term, but there are plenty of no-tell motels along the highways heading west.

The hardest part is that I don't know how Dominick will react to our running. Or if we show back up. He might understand us laying low until the smoke clears. Or we could be kidnapped and taken to him or Sal. Or worst case scenario, shot on sight. I'm sure that if Dom's innocent of the hit, he'd let Maggie go. Well, mostly sure.

I'm just not one-hundred percent, and that's the problem. As desperate as the situation is, or might be, I don't want to freak Maggie out too much.

Maggie. It makes me shake my head a little as we roll along the highway, the dim light hiding my movements.

I can't believe she lied about her name. Well, I can. I just can't believe I couldn't tell.

One thing I know without a doubt is that I can read people, but she somehow slipped right under my radar. In more ways than one. Without raising a single flag, she's slipped past all of my defenses.

That both irritates and intrigues me, making me want to know more, even if only so that she couldn't possibly hide anything else because I already know it all.

Know her inside and out. My cock jerks at that thought, but I talk it down, wanting to use the road time for a better purpose. I look over at Maggie, her feet in the seat, her knees pulled up to her chest. Yesterday, I thought that position was a sign of her shock, her curling into herself, but I'm starting to realize it's just her.

It's as if she's trying to be small, non-intrusive, or even over-looked. It's as good a place as any to start with the things I want to know.

"Why do you sit like that?"

Maggie startles a little before looking at me, confusion on her face. "Like what?"

I gesture at her feet, appreciating the way it folds her up and the curve it gives her pert little ass before refocusing on the road. "All curled up. I don't think I've ever seen you sit down with your feet on the floor."

Maggie grins, shrugging dismissively. "I don't know, just always have." She pauses, her eyes flicking up and to the left as though she's remembering something. "Even when I was a kid, my mom would tell me to 'sit like a lady' and try to get me to sit up straight and cross my legs. It never worked, mostly because at my house, all the chairs were so short compared to the tables. I had to sit on my knees or something just to be able to eat dinner for a long time. Later, in school, kids were sometimes cruel."

My hands tighten on the steering wheel, even though I know what she's talking about was years ago. "Kids can be motherfuckers."

"Making myself invisible helped to keep their sights off me. Eventually, I guess it just became habit, along with being invisible. It lets me watch from the sidelines, learn things about people because they don't perceive me as a threat even if they notice me."

It's a deeper answer than I expected, and that she shared makes me happier than it should. "Angel, nothing about you is invisible, and if you ever thought you were, you were fucking mistaken. I saw you the moment you walked into Petals and have been mesmerized by you every fucking day since."

She blushes, seeming pleased, but laughs lightly. "I don't think for a second that you were watching me sling beer when there are nearly-naked women swinging on poles right in front of your face."

I laugh and glance over. "Day one—a pink backpack with a daisy hanging on it. You wore your hair down, curled, and had too much makeup. We shook hands, and I remember that you had hands that were baby smooth."

"You notice and remember a lot," Maggie says quietly. "What else?"

I smile, remembering. "You wobbled on your high heels, and the first night you were nervous, never looking at the stage once but doing a surprisingly decent job waiting tables. By the end of the first weekend, you learned to pull your hair up. It shows off your neck and makes me want to bite it, but I'm guessing it's more to do with how hard you work. You lightened up on the makeup, playing up your big eyes and assuming a young bubblegum airhead persona that is complete bullshit. The customers didn't know, but we all knew you were a smart girl. Innocent, sure, but smart as a fucking whip. And you learned how to strut in your heels perfectly, your ass swishing this way and that. Yeah, I've been watching you every damn day, Angel."

"Oh." Her voice is softly high-pitched, surprise written clearly on her face as her eyebrows raise high on her forehead. "I had no idea. I mean, I noticed you too, hard not to with your whole . . . *you* going on," she says as she moves her hands about, encompassing my whole body, "But I knew the rules and figured if you were going to break them, it wouldn't be for someone like me."

I reach across the console, grabbing a handful of her thigh and squeeze gently. "If I'm gonna break the rules, it's only gonna be for someone like you."

She bites her lip, like she's not sure what to do with that answer, the glimpse of white making me want her teeth on me, marking my chest and neck. "So, what's your story?" she finally asks, trying to get her balance back. "You usually go around playing hero? I know you don't have any tights on underneath those jeans, and there's no S on your chest."

There's interest in her lightly playful tone, but also a bit of worry, and I know she's thinking about our situation. Happy to distract her, I try to give her an edited version of my life, one that won't cause us more problems.

"Well, I guess I do have some hero tendencies, but not usually to this extreme, admittedly. My dad was a real hero. He went to Vietnam right before the US pulled out, and when he got back, he became a cop in the small town I was born in."

"Vietnam?" Maggie asks. "What, are you the youngest of the kids or something?"

"No, it took him awhile after he got back to feel he was ready to have kids. He was older than Mom too. He was almost forty and she was only twenty-six when they got married. Still, he was a good role model, taught me right from wrong, and I grew up always wanting to make him proud."

She lays her hand on mine where it rests on her thigh, holding it tenderly. "I'm sure he would be. You're definitely my hero. Maybe after all this is over, you can tell him how you saved me from a mob hit and the resulting war?" She says it jokingly, like she's trying to make the monster less scary by laughing at how ridiculous it sounds, but the underlying fear is obvious. "I'm sure he would love this story, on the run but not sure yet exactly who we're running from."

I sigh wistfully, shaking my head. "He died about five years ago. He would have liked the story, and I know he would have liked you. I tell myself he's my guardian angel now."

Without thinking, I salute the way I always do, lifting my hand from her leg to bring two fingers to my lips and then raising them toward the sky. "Thanks, Pop."

My hand goes right back to Maggie's thigh and hers goes right back on top of mine. It's comfortable, and I ponder just how strange it feels that a gesture that's only been in my life for about three or four minutes feels like I couldn't go the rest of my life without it.

"I'm sorry for your loss," she says softly, with genuine regret that she won't get to meet him. "He sounds like a great dad. What about your mom?"

I smile, keeping my eyes on the road. "She's great too. After Pop died, she didn't let it get her down. They talked about that, and they agreed that she should do what makes her happy. So she sold the house and bought a little condo in a nice building. She works as a secretary at an elementary school. She says the kids keep her young, even though she's not all that old, really. I'm one of the lucky ones." Feeling like the storyline of my history might be getting into dangerous territory, like how the son of a war vet police officer ended up working door security in a mob-owned strip club, I turn the questions back to Maggie. "What about you? What's your family like?"

Maggie's lips screw up a bit, and she hums quietly before answering. "Well, not as picturesque as yours, but they're good. My parents divorced when I was little, so I bounced back and forth between their houses, but it was an amicable divorce at least, not some made-for-TV drama deal. I see them both regularly, talk to my mom almost every Sunday on the phone."

"How'd you end up waitressing at Petals?"

I can feel her retreat, like a physical removal of her warmth even though she hasn't moved. "Oh, I've done a lot of moving around, this job and that. Waitressing is something I did when I was younger, so it seemed like a good way to make some money."

She's lying. I can tell this time, but I can't put my finger on how I know. Her tone doesn't change, her face is neutral, her body relaxed. And that worries me. This girl, innocent as she may seem, is lying, and she's good at it. Really fucking good at it.

Wanting to tease out what she's lying about, I pick at her answer, keeping it casual and teasing her a little. "This and that? Tell me, what has an Angel like you done before becoming a strip club waitress?"

She smiles, but it's her fake one, too much teeth and not enough eyes. It's a dazzling smile still, but I guess when you've made a woman come and then made her deep-throat you, you get to see a lot of what her eyes can reveal. "Well, I've been a barista, a secretary, a copy girl, a waitress, a nanny, and a personal assistant. It's not quite the Village People, but finding a construction job is really difficult at my size."

Her list sounds real and honest, and I wonder where the lie was in her previous response, thinking maybe it was something else she was lying about. Maybe it was the moving? Or the money? A lie of omission, maybe?

Before I can ask more follow-ups, she redirects us to the current problem at hand. "What do you think is going on back at the club?"

I know pressing her more isn't going to get any results, so I decide to go with the flow. "I don't know. I've got a guy looking into it for us. I'll check in with him in the morning, see what he's heard."

"You've 'got a guy'?" Maggie asks, lifting an eyebrow. "Seriously? That even sounds like we've jumped into the middle of a mob movie. How in the heck did we end up here? I mean, how'd you get in touch with this guy?"

"Burner phone in my bag," I admit. "The phone's off for now, just in case. But I'll check in, and we'll see what he's hearing back home."

She looks at me with calculating eyes, and I'm reminded once again just how smart she is and how careful I need to be with her. "So, on a moment's notice, you snatched me up, switched vehicles to a nondescript sedan that you knew would be waiting in that lot, have a duffle bag packed with at least one day's worth of clothes, cash, and a burner phone, took us to a no-tell motel, and now we're headed to another safe location, and you 'have a guy'? That about sum it up?"

Fuck. She's putting a bunch of shit together pretty damn fast, and it does sound like a fucking action movie script. Scrambling, I try to stay calm and put her on the defensive, a tactic that usually works on most folks. I laugh heartily, not taking my eyes off the road as if I'm not concerned. "Well, when you put it all together like that . . . you're welcome, Angel. You planning to say thank you on your knees too? Because that was a damn fine apology this morning."

She doesn't take the bait, sidestepping the crude, and honestly rude, comment. "Who are you, Shane? You said you're not one of Dominick's guys, not in the mob. But it sounds like . . . are you tied up in all of this?"

I grit my teeth, growling as I clench the steering wheel a little tighter and hoping it'll scare her into backing the fuck off. "All you need to know is that you're safe."

As we've talked, her curled knees had fallen loosely to her left, toward me, but at my harsh words, she pulls away. Her knees are once again clenched tight to her chest in a protective posture. She half turns away, her back mostly to me as she faces the window, her eyes unfocused as the scenery flies by.

It hurts, honestly. I was enjoying talking to her, but I need to keep her from probing in areas that she shouldn't. I realize I likely hurt her feelings, and that despite her brains and sass, she's got a vulnerable side too. Unable to reach her thigh, I rest my hand on the back of her neck, squeezing lightly, comforting and not threatening, I hope. "Maggie, you're safe, and I promise to keep you that way. That's all you need to know right now."

She doesn't answer, doesn't even acknowledge that I've spoken. I turn my attention back to the road, knowing I should give her space. Hell, I should give myself some space to figure out how to handle this, handle her. Fuck, that doesn't even sound right. Maggie's a grown ass woman with her own mind. She shouldn't be 'handled'. She should be respected, but the situation makes my caveman instincts come out and all I want to do is protect her.

As my thoughts swirl, I leave my hand where it is, drawing small lines up and down her neck with my thumb, soothing her anger, her fear, even if some of it is my fault.

If I'm honest with myself, having her satin skin under my palm calms me too, and that's a fucking problem.

CHAPTER 15

*W*e drive for hours, only stopping for a bathroom break at a truck stop with a burger joint attached to it. We take the burgers and fries to go, along with some snacks and an odd assortment of cheap undies, a pack of socks, and some souvenir T-shirts so that I can have clothes, and keep driving. It's quiet for a long time, neither of us willing to give in to the stalemate.

He hurt me, and he knows it. I can feel his remorse, but I'm not ready to forgive and he hasn't apologized. Eventually, Shane turns on the radio and music fills the car. It's nothing much, just the regular late-night stuff you get on Top 40 stations, some slow songs mixed in with oldies and a few tunes for the young lovers who might want some mood music. After a bit, I hear him humming along with an old Green Day song, even singing softly under his breath. It's nice. I can tell he has a good voice, deep and mellow with a raw emotion to it that tells me he actually knows this song.

As the chorus begins, he gets louder, and I look over at him, enjoying the mindless way he's getting into it. It feels like a peek into the real him somehow. Without saying anything, I join in, singing along with the radio and Shane, a trio of voices filling the car.

"I've never heard anyone out-sing the original," I say as the guitar music fades and I wonder if September ever really is going to end for us. "You're pretty good." It's an olive branch, making the first move to break the silence between us and I'm curious if he'll take it or shut me out again."

Shane looks over at me, a small smile tilting the corners of his lips. "Dad loved this song. He always thought that even though it wasn't written about the 9/11 bombings or the Iraq war, that it spoke to him. He never was into what we did there."

"But he was a cop."

Shane nods, shrugging. "Dad was more *Andy Griffith* than *Criminal Minds*. He was the cop people came to for advice, the cop who'd walk into a domestic disturbance without his gun and get everyone calmed down. He always told me that he saw too much of the evil men could do to each other in Vietnam and he didn't want to add to it. So the first time he heard that song, it stuck with him."

It's not a truce. There are too many questions unanswered for that. But it's a pause on the inquisition, a recognition that whatever is going on and whoever he is, we can sing along as we run. And that there's something between us, something building. It doesn't have to be adversarial. Goodness knows, we've all got secrets, and maybe I shouldn't judge him too harshly considering the one I'm still holding close to my heart.

By dawn, we pull over to check into another sketchy motel. Shane apologizes for the seedy accommodations as we pull in, explaining why. "Folks around here aren't as likely to remember us and definitely aren't as likely to talk. They don't want anyone or anything putting attention on their own lives."

"Whatever. I just need a clean bed, not a five-star fancy place," I reply, trying to put a positive spin on things. "So, I guess no free continental breakfast?"

Shane laughs. "We'll be in bed during breakfast hours anyway."

My thoughts flash back to this morning in bed and how Shane and I had sex . . . kind of. Wow, was that just this morning? It seems so long ago, time both speeding by like a rocket and dragging like my ass after an all-nighter.

Once we're in the room, Shane pulls the curtains closed and then plops on the bed, lying back and closing his eyes as he stretches out. "You can take a shower first. I gotta work this tightness out of my back before I do anything."

He looks yummy as a bowl of peanut butter fudge, and I long to lick the sliver of his abdomen that shows where his shirt rides up. But I haven't forgotten his earlier words, even if we have ridden in relative civility for the last few hours. "Call your guy."

He opens one eye, giving me a semi-amused, semi-angry look. "No."

I cross my arms over my chest, giving him all the glare that I can muster. Which, considering the difference in our sizes, probably isn't much, but by gosh, I'm gonna try. "Call. Your. Guy. Find out what's happening back home."

I can see that he's trying to think of an argument to get out of this, some way to reason with me, but he settles on being an ass.

"No. Take a shower. I'll call, and we'll see what he says."

Knowing that sometimes, retreat is the finest form of strategy, I acquiesce. "Fine."

Grabbing the micro-sliver of cheap soap off the vanity and missing even the luxury of tiny bottles of cheap shampoo and conditioner, I stomp into the bathroom, closing and locking the door before turning on the water. Instead of stripping off my clothes, though, I put my skills and my strategy to use, listening intently at the door.

I hear Shane dig around in his bag, and then an unmistakable start-up song as he turns the burner phone on. I can only hear his side of the conversation, but it's enough for now. "Hey, Chucky. What do you got for me?"

There's silence for a moment, and I assume Chucky must be giving Shane some type of update. "So, he's a ghost? Probably wishful thinking to hope he left town straight from the job. What about us? Heard anything about my girl, Ma—Meghan?"

A zing goes to my heart when he calls me that. His girl. I like that, even if I know there's more to him than meets the eye. He's hiding something, but at his core, he's a good guy. I'm sure of it.

His girl. It makes me smile.

My sweet musings are abruptly stopped when I hear Shane start cursing. "Fuck. What the hell should we do then? She's got people who are gonna fucking notice if she goes missing."

Missing? I think back to our conversation in the car and

wonder again if Shane is a mob guy. I try to think it through. Is he lying about being Dominick's guy?

If so, why would he run with me? Or maybe he's not running *with* me? Maybe he's kidnapped me for Dominick and is making it seem like I need to run so that I'm a cooperative and stupid victim?

But to what end? If Dominick wanted me dead, Shane could've done that multiple times already. We've been driving on some lonely stretches of highway, and he could've dumped my body along any of them and I likely wouldn't have even been found.

Or he could be Sal's guy? Protecting his boss, or heck, maybe taking me *to* his boss?

But Shane has been protective. I at least know that and truly believe that's real. He wants to keep me safe, not turn me over to a mob boss to be handled like a witness in some B-grade movie. He's even bordered on the near-obsessive sometimes, not allowing me to go into the convenience stores at gas stops without him escorting me, even if it's just to pee.

No, I don't think Shane's a gangster, even if he's worked for gangsters. There's more going on, and I'm going to have to stay on my toes since Shane is hiding what that is, but I trust him. Lord help me, I'm listening to my gut and heart more than my brain, but that's what I'm going with.

I hear him wrap up the call with Chucky and quickly hop in the shower, wetting my hair and scrubbing my body as fast as possible. Luckily, the soap is barely better than rubbing sand all over my skin and I've got plenty of reasons to hurry it up. As I emerge from the steamy bathroom, Shane walks past me, his face hard, jaw clenched.

I open my mouth to say something, not even sure what, but he simply shuts the door in my face and I hear the water start back up again for his shower. I pull on the same tank from last night and clean panties and sit down on the bed, fighting the urge to lie back on the scratchy sheets. "Not this time," I promise myself softly. "I have to stay awake. We have to talk. There are too many questions that need to be answered."

It takes Shane awhile, though, and I'm lying down by the time the bathroom door opens. Shane is quiet, tip-toeing to put his clothes over the chair before carefully sliding into bed behind me. Still, he can sense the tension in my body as he lies down, and he props himself up to whisper, "You awake?"

I turn to face him, curling up on my side as he lies on his back. "Yes. What did Chucky say?"

He looks down at me, his smirk visible even in the low light, that amused glint back in his eyes. "Who?"

"Stop jerking me around," I reply. "You know who."

"Were you eavesdropping, Maggie?"

I growl at him, sounding more like a kitten than the tiger I'd prefer. "Well, what did you expect? You're not telling me anything. Two days ago, I was a waitress minding her own business. Today, I'm on the run from the fudging mob—oh, excuse me, *mobs*. Or what is the proper term?" I say, emphasizing the 's' to illustrate just how crazy my life has become in the last forty-eight hours. "And you're hiding stuff from me. Yeah, I eavesdropped. I'm furious. I'm . . . scared."

My voice cracks, the fire snuffed out by the cold fear in my heart. Shane grimaces, like my anger and fear physically hurt him. "Come here, Angel."

He pulls me to him, pressing my head to his chest as he wraps his arms around me, holding me tight, grounding me to him. "Don't be scared. I've got you, and I'll keep you safe."

"You keep saying that, but I don't even know what or who you're keeping me safe from," I reply, even as my body says it doesn't care about all that, the comfort of having Shane hold me telling my traitorous body everything it needs to hear to relax. But I still talk, demanding even. "Tell me what Chucky said."

Shane lays a light kiss to the top of my head. "Not too much, actually. Hitman is in the wind. They figured out who it was without your input. Dominick knows we're gone, and he's pissed and is trying to track us down. But Chucky doesn't know if it's because he wants to protect us or kill us. Dom's playing this very, very close to the vest, which is his style."

I fall silent, trying to take it all in. I know there are more questions to be asked, and I want to be strong and fierce, but this is so far above anything I've ever experienced it's crazy. My brain's being overwhelmed. I just want to go back to the way things were. My boring life was safe. Secure.

I break down, tears trekking silently down my cheeks, pooling on Shane's chest. He rolls us, my back hitting the bed as he holds himself on his elbow beside me, his thigh on top of mine, splitting my legs.

He swipes at my tears with a gentle thumb, his voice soft but still strong. "Don't cry, Angel. I know this is a lot, but it's gonna be okay."

I know my eyes are glossy with tears, my face flushing as I try to stop the torrent. "Ugh, I'm sorry for crying. I swear I'm not such a baby. Usually I never cry, but this is all so . . ."

"It's fine, Angel. It's your emotions needing an escape. The fear, the nerves, the . . ." He stops and I wonder what other emotion he was going to list because I've got a few in mind. Desire. Need. Hope.

Instead of continuing his list, Shane leans down, catching a tear with his tongue as it streaks down my face before kissing the trail away.

He lays more kisses along my cheeks, moving down to gently kiss my jawline and then my neck. I can feel the shift in him, going from comforting caresses to heated desire, and it awakens the same lust in me.

He talks into the curve of my neck, sending warm shivers through my chest and down my spine. "Your tears are salty, but here . . ." His tongue sneaks out for a lapping touch of my skin. "Here, you're sweet. So very sweet, Angel. It makes me wonder what you taste like all over."

I whimper, his words amping up my desire, bringing my focus to him and him alone, the rest of the world and my fears fading away. I need this, this release from the fear, release from the worries. For that, I need him. The wolves are out there, hunting us, and we don't even know why.

Shane isn't telling me everything I should know about him, and I haven't been honest with him either.

But right now, I don't care. Secrets, lies, risks, fear . . . they all slip away in his arms.

CHAPTER 16

SHANE

*F*eeling Maggie whimper under my tongue, the sound echoing in my ear, is pure liquid desire and heat being poured into my body. If I were a car, it's a shot of nitro and my engine's ready to tear up the pavement, but I hold back. I want more of those throaty sounds from her, want to make her moan and scream my name.

I know that we shouldn't, not in the middle of this shitstorm. She's going to regret this later, regret me and probably hate me. But I'm a fucking selfish man, and if she wants this now, wants me to make her forget everything else for a little while, I'm going to fucking make her forget it all.

It's cheap medicine for reality, but it'll work. The side effect is that I'm going to make it so that even after this is all done, she is mine, marked body and soul. Then again, I'm pretty sure that the reverse is true, that I'm going to be marked by her as well. A small price to pay for having an honest to God Angel.

I roll onto her, forcing her legs wide around my hips as I

press my cock to her pussy and cage her in with my arms. I can feel the heat from her pussy, the thin cotton the only thing between us as I kiss her neck and tug at her ear with my teeth.

She reaches up, her little nails leaving pink lines where she scrapes my arms, tugging me toward her. I lower my body, covering her lips in a searing kiss that leaves us both panting. She looks at me, her eyes full of want and fear and pain and more.

Grabbing her hands, I push them to the bed above her head, her back arching beautifully to press her full tits toward me. "Angel, tell me to stop and God help me, I will. But if you'll let me, I'll make it all better, even if only for a minute. Let me make you forget."

Her eyes are sparkly, the tears replaced with heat, lust, and need. Her voice is breathy, but I hear her clearly regardless. "Yes, Shane. Yes."

That's all I need to unleash the last of my personal restraints, knowing that I'm going to give her everything she wants. I kiss her again, fast and hard, my mouth claiming her perfect lips hungrily before I move along her neck, dipping down to her chest.

Her nipples are hard beneath her tank top, and I take advantage, taking one then the other into my mouth through the thin cotton to suck and bite at her. This poor shirt's going to have to go in the trash. I've stretched it out so much, but that's okay. I'll tear the damn thing to rags if it makes her happy.

She gasps, arching into me once again. I release her hands, yanking the straps of her tank down her arms, freeing her tits to my hungry eyes before pinning both of her tiny hands with one of my larger ones.

"Fuck, Maggie," I rasp, taking in the sight. I hadn't seen them yesterday, only felt their soft weight in my hand as we dry-humped, but they're perfect, soft and full and delicious looking. "Look at these pretty nipples, all pink like candy, making me want to eat you up."

"Please, do . . . all you want," Maggie says, and I remind myself again that maybe she knows, but she may not, just how intense her words are to me.

I lower my head to take her nipple into my mouth, swirling my tongue around again and again to drive her wild before finally sucking her deep, swallowing and feasting on her succulent body.

She cries out, begging for more. I keep suckling her, back and forth between her right and left, as her hips buck beneath me, asking desperately for attention and rubbing along my hard cock.

But her moans are getting sharper, and I lift my head up to look into her unfocused eyes, challenging her. "Are you gonna come just from me sucking on your tits?"

She shakes her head, lifting her hips to grind against me. "More," she begs, but now that I know how close she is, I want to see this up close. "Please."

I lower myself down, but this time, I keep my eyes on her face as I swirl my tongue around her nipple and she picks up her head to watch me.

"You like watching me lick you?" I ask, teasing her nipple lightly. "A voyeur?"

Her eyebrows pull together, her eyes locked on my mouth. "Or maybe . . ." I murmur before I grab her nipple between my teeth, biting just hard enough to keep it in my mouth as I pull, blending a sharpness with the pleasure to see how rough she likes it.

"Ahhh!" she cries out as her head falls back. I know she's on the edge, needing just a bit more to get there.

"Or maybe if I suck hard enough, the pleasure will shoot right down to your empty pussy, clenching on nothing and wanting my cock so damn bad that you can't help but come. Let's see."

At the same time, I pinch her left nipple between my finger-tips and suck her whole right areola and as much pale skin as I can into my mouth, drawing hard and deep. I grind against her soaked pussy, thrusting my hard cock to slide over her clit through her panties, pushing her over.

Maggie bucks wildly, crying out as her orgasm washes through her, and I have an up-close view of her face as the bliss overtakes her.

It's the most beautiful thing I've ever seen. Her fingers clench on my arms before going totally straight, her body shaking uncontrollably like a guitar string. She's still shuddering, her eyes closed as I release her hands, moving down her body. I pull the tank over her hips and off, tossing it to the floor before focusing on the soaked mess of her panties.

I trace a light touch through the moisture, pleased that it's because of me, that I did that to her. "God, I'm hungry for your taste again. So sweet, and so dirty for me. Lift your ass for me, Angel."

The meaning of my words hits her hard, and she stops, fresh

heat in her eyes as she lifts her ass just like I commanded. I pull her panties down and off too, my cock surging so hard I nearly come just from the evidence of her first orgasm and the anticipation of what I'm going to get when I lick every drop of it until she coats my mouth with her second.

I press her thighs open wide, hovering so she feels my breath, and look up at her, my voice a throaty growl of need. "Tell me, Angel. Tell me what you want."

She squirms beneath me, wordlessly lifting her hips toward me. I shake my head, pinning her hips with my hands, and blow a hot, open-mouth breath across her lips, knowing she's watching me tease her. "Say it."

"Lick me, Shane," Maggie says, spreading her knees out wider and mewling her need. "Please."

I raise an eyebrow at her, moving toward her inner thigh, right on the crease of her center, and licking a slow line with the flat of my tongue, watching as she jumps. "Here?" I ask before doing the same thing to the other side. "Or maybe here?"

She groans in frustration, and I have mercy, giving her the words. I trace her lips with the tip of my tongue before looking up again. "Tell me, *'Lick my pussy, Shane'* or maybe, *'Suck my clit.'* Tell me what you want, Angel. Unleash the dirty side of you, and I'll give you everything."

Her voice is stronger than I would've thought, need giving her power as she mimics my words, looking at me with a sexual energy that has me breathless. "Lick my pussy. Suck my clit, Shane. Make me come all over your mouth. Make me your Angel."

Fuck me, hearing those dirty words come out of my sweet

LAUREN LANDISH

girl's mouth is almost enough to make shoot my load into the bed I'm grinding against, but I manage to fight it off, needing to give all I have to her.

I growl, diving in and running a flat tongue from her entrance up to her clit, repeating it again and again as I watch her. I pay attention, stroking her pussy just the way she likes, switching when she needs it, and giving her everything she wants. She's frozen, her body rigid, hands full of the bedsheet, and her mouth dropped open in an 'O' of pleasure as her tongue curls up in her mouth.

When I focus on her clit, I thrash my tongue across it, fast as a fluttering hummingbird's wing, and she squeals, her voice high and tight, she's so close again. "Oh, God. Shane, don't stop! I'm coming."

I pause just long enough to look up at her, demanding. "Give it to me, Angel. Come all over my mouth so I can drink down your sweetness."

I press her hips down, not letting her move an inch and ravishing her clit with my tongue. It's only seconds before she shatters, crying out above me as her body shudders, her pussy getting wetter with each spasm. I clamp my lips over hers, drinking her honey and swallowing every delicious drop. She's heady, a liquor that I've never imagined before. It makes the world disappear, leaving me with just her while at the same time energizing me. My cock strains even more with every moan of satisfaction Maggie gives me as I sweep over her sensitive skin.

She collapses against the bed, spent as I pull away and sit up. I consider for a second that she might be done, not able to take more after coming twice so hard.

Instead, she inhales deeply, smiling and opening her eyes.

She looks hazy, satisfied, but at the same time playful. Somehow, I've tapped into an inner well of sexual energy that maybe nobody's ever seen, and here's the innocent vixen that I've known she's had inside her all this time.

Maggie sees the need on my face and sits up, kissing my lips tenderly. "Now it's your turn . . ." she murmurs as she reaches for my boxer briefs, pulling them down to let my cock free.

"Oh, fuck, Angel," I gasp as she wraps a soft hand around me. "See what you do to me?"

Maggie looks down, gasping softly and looking surprised at my size, like she hasn't already sucked me off. "Oh, Shane," she says breathily.

I help her lie back before drawing my head through her folds as I squeeze tight at the base my shaft, staving off the orgasm that's already drawing too close. I rub the tip of my cock over her clit before pausing at the entrance to her pussy. "I'll try to be gentle, Maggie. I don't want to hurt you, but I'm on the fucking edge."

"Don't you dare," Maggie says, grabbing my forearms. "I'm not that fragile, remember? You won't break me."

"I might," I rasp. There's more honesty in those words than I'd like to admit, but if she wants to take me, I can't hold back. I drive into her with one thrust, balls-deep, and she cries out as I grab her thighs, pulling her hard to me. It takes all of my willpower to freeze, letting her adjust and trying not to come from the tight grasp she has on me. "Fuck, Maggie. You're so damn tight."

She smiles, her voice cracking as the pain and pleasure mix for her. "Or you're just big. Really . . . big."

"You okay?" I ask, giving her a few tiny thrusts, testing to see if she can relax a bit but bottoming out deep inside her.

She moans, biting her lip as her head drops back, and I can feel her pussy walls already quivering around me.

"Damn, Angel," I half tease, my cock throbbing as she clenches me hard, her body massaging my cock even though I'm not moving. "Are you coming on my cock already?"

She nods, crying out as she begins to squirm on the bed, moving back and forth and fucking herself on my cock. I hold myself still, looming between her thighs, watching as she takes my cock, disappearing inside her and coming back out coated in her cream. It's the sexiest thing I've ever seen.

Her energy gives out, the orgasm depleting her, and I take over. Rolling her legs up until I can wrap my hands under her arms, I grab her shoulders for leverage.

I pound into her, pulling and pushing her tiny body under mine and using her pussy to jack myself off as I bury my face in the curve of her neck.

Sucking the tender skin into my mouth, I mark her, needing proof that she's mine, even if only for this moment. Maggie's crying out, holding onto my neck as I drive her harder and harder, my hips slamming against her and shaking the whole bed.

"Shane! Please, come. I need you to come," she begs. Her voice drops off. Her brain's so overloaded that all she can do is moan wordlessly even as her pussy squeezes me even tighter.

Anything my Angel wants, I'll give her. With a roar, I explode, my cock pumping jet after jet of hot cum deep inside her, triggering her once again, and her walls flutter, milking me. She cries, no words possible for either of us as we're both destroyed and remade in the energy of this bonding.

We ride out the waves together, finally crashing to the bed spent. I lift up, not wanting to crush her small frame with my heavy ass, but she pulls me back down, snuggling beneath me.

I chuckle lightly, not wanting to move, not wanting to disturb my still semi-hard cock inside her. "You sure I'm not smothering you? Can you even breathe?"

In response, she takes an audible breath and blows a weak raspberry against my neck. "Yes, I can breathe. It smells like you, manly and salty and sexy."

I bury my face in her hair, feeling a wide smile overtake my face. "Well, you smell like cupcakes and sugar. Is that just you? Or do you buy special soap that makes me want to eat you all the time?"

I move to nibble at her earlobe and she giggles. "A lady has to keep some secrets to maintain an air of mystery."

She says it lightly, teasing, but a beat later, even as we're still connected as one, the reality of the secrets we are both keeping presses down heavily. We both pause, and I pull back to look at her face.

She lied to me about her name. She's probably lying to me about why she's working at Petals, and fuck knows, I'm lying about shit.

But for a moment, we escaped. Just the two of us . . . until reality crashed back in like it always does. We release each other, both of us needing a moment now, and I quietly roll off her to grab a washcloth from the bathroom. Running it under the warm water, I clean myself before coming back with another fresh cloth for Maggie.

I wipe her down, letting her know that while I've still got issues, there's something that I don't want to let go of between us. She watches me silently, her face promising me things I'm not ready to trust just yet, but I want to. When she's all clean, I toss the rag toward the bathroom door before lying down. I feel like that rag, wrung out and used, and I imagine Maggie feels the same way.

"Come here, Angel."

She scoots closer to my open arm, curling against my side like a kitten and placing her head on my chest as I hug her to me. We might be hiding things, but right now, we both need comfort. And I can give that to her. I'll give her anything.

Her voice is a whisper, but there's steel in it, her bravery shining through, even in the face of a problem she never imagined she'd face. "Shane? What are we going to do?"

I squeeze her tighter and kiss her temple softly. "Right now, we're going to sleep. We'll figure out the next step this afternoon."

She sighs softly, and in moments, I feel her relax, drifting to sleep. I lie awake, though, mentally running through every scenario, every possible outcome, the risks of each making me tense.

We're going to have to trust someone, but if we choose wrong, it'll likely be the death of both of us.

CHAPTER 17

MAGGIE

*I*n what's starting to feel habitual, I wake up curled against Shane's side, my leg slung over his and my head nestled on his chest and shoulder. It feels right, comfortable. Safe. I snuggle in deeper, and he stirs, pulling me tight and lifting my hand to his mouth to lightly kiss my fingertips. "Morning, Angel. Well, evening, I guess."

I lower my hand to rub his chest. "What are we thinking today? Drive all night, eat crap food, and then sexercise ourselves to sleep?"

Shane cups my chin in his hand, lifting it toward him. "Sounds like fun, but we'll have to see. First, a kiss. Second, we need to hit the road. We slept in, so just a kiss."

He winks at me. I know a kiss between us could easily turn passionate and keep us in this bed all night, but we likely do need to get a move on. I don't know if Shane's burner phone could be tracked, but sitting around probably isn't the best idea.

I scoot up the bed slightly to reach him with puckered lips, but he pulls me astride him in one quick swoop instead. I gasp, laughing a little. "Whoa . . . hey! You said a quick kiss."

My center brushes against his washboard abs, and I can't help but circle my hips a little, the warm prodding of his morning wood standing proud behind me giving me naughty thoughts, even if it is late afternoon. "This does not feel like a quick kiss."

Shane mock-growls, pressing his hips up into me and adding to the sensation as his stiffy nestles between my cheeks and we both hum happily. "I didn't say quick. I said a kiss."

He's teasing, but the gravel in his voice sends jolts to my core. I swirl my hips again, letting him feel the heat and wetness he's building in me, and the tingle runs up my body to make me whimper. Shane grabs behind my neck, pulling me down to meet his mouth in a punishing kiss, his tongue licking along the seam of my lips, demanding entry.

With a moan, I grant him access, twisting my tongue with his, needing more. Forget the time. Forget the miles we need to roll. Fifty miles or whatever aren't going to make a huge difference. What is going to make a difference is the huge hardness pressing against my butt that I need inside me again. I lift my hips, trying to impale myself on his dick, but he stills my movements with strong hands on my thighs.

Breaking our kiss, he looks up, his chest heaving in the space between us. "Fuck, Angel. You're killing me. We really do need to leave. Tonight, I promise."

I whimper, hips pumping in the air as I try to push back. I can nearly feel the heat of his head against my lips. "We can be fast."

His dick jumps at my words, the tip touching my soaked lips, and we both groan. "Shane."

I'm pleading, something I would swear I'd never do, but right now, I need him filling me more than I've ever wanted anything.

With a growled curse, he pulls me down hard, sliding into my wet core easily and pumping fast and deep. "You want my cock, Maggie?" he asks in between each hard thrust. "We're in fucking danger. You get that, right? But all you want is my cock, isn't it?"

I throw my head back, my nails digging into his chest leaving little half-moons where I grab for purchase. I drop my hips in time with him, our bodies meeting in slaps that shake me to the very center of my body. "God, yes. Shane, fill me up. I want it."

I want it . . . and I want so much more. I know we're not being logical, and I'm normally a very safe girl.

But any concerns I might have are obliterated as Shane smacks my ass hard, the sound ringing out in the quiet room. "Such a bad girl. I said a kiss and look what you've done to me, Angel. I can't help but give you everything you want."

I cry out, the thickness inside me and the heat on my ass getting me so close to the edge. "I love being bad. With you. *For* you. You just feel so good inside me . . ."

The honesty in my words make Shane surge even harder, thicker. He thrusts powerfully, slamming deep in my core and I cry out. "Ahhh . . . Yesss . . ."

Shane groans. "That's it. Show me how your good girl pussy can take me like a bad girl. *My* bad girl."

It doesn't take long, my cries mixing with Shane's continued dirty words until I scream, clamping down around his hips. "I'm coming . . . God . . . Shane!"

Shane jackhammers into me, holding my hips still and forcing me to take his punishing thrusts as I spasm in his hands, the waves washing over me. "That's right, come on my cock. Squeeze that tight pussy and milk me. I'll give you everything you want."

I tense my muscles in time to his strokes, and he groans, losing the rhythm as I feel his hot cum filling me. I take over, slowly rolling my hips up and down to take him, coating him with a mixture of our orgasms and pulling every last drop from him as he shudders. It's warm, intense, and I feel emotions bubbling up inside me even as I feel the first drop of his cum squeeze out of my pussy to roll back down his shaft.

I lean forward, pressing our chests together, and Shane surprises me with another smack, to my other cheek this time. I wail in surprise, my muscles clenching against him once more.

Shane chuckles darkly, his eyes sparkling. "Mmm, I'll have to remember how tightly you squeeze me when I spank you, but we really do need to go."

I grin down at him, happy I got my way and knowing he got his way too. I give him a soft kiss, stroking his face and nodding. "Okay, let me rinse off and we'll go."

He grabs a handful of my mess of hair. "Oh, no, Angel. Bad girls don't have time to take a shower. You're gonna ride in that car all night, feeling me between your legs, knowing that cum you so desperately wanted is deep inside you. That you're marked by me."

He runs his thumb along my neck, and though I haven't looked in a mirror since our session last night, I can feel that there's a heck of a hickie glowing on the pale skin there. It makes me tingly inside, proud that he wanted such a visible sign of what we did.

I smirk, running my fingertips along the claw marks on his chest, knowing I'm not the only one marked. "All right, Bad Boy. But then that goes for you too. You're gonna have my scent all over you tonight too."

He grins, wiggling his hips and sending another little tingle through me. "Maggie, I would happily smell like your sugar anytime you'll let me."

The sweetness of the moment is short-lived because as we head out to the car in the golden setting light, I see a familiar face heading our way. Pulling hard on Shane's hand, I point. "Shane, that's the hitman."

Shane follows my finger, seeing the large guy who has already spotted us. We duck and try to make our way through the cars in the lot, shuffle-running toward ours as fast as we can.

No luck, though, as the window in the car next to us shatters violently. "Get down!" Shane yells, shoving me to the ground. The rough pebbles bite against my palms and against my cheek, but that's nothing compared to the fright racing through my body as I scramble behind a tire, hoping I've got enough to protect me.

Seeing that I'm listening, Shane pulls a gun out of his waist-band at his back. *What the 'fridgerator?* I didn't even know he had a gun! Has he been carrying that thing this entire time and I just didn't notice?

Popping his head up from between the cars, Shane aims toward the hitman and fires, his shot much louder than the first. Shane fires off three more shots and I hear glass breaking again. "C'mon!" Shane growls, grabbing my hand and pulling me up, placing it on his waistband at his back, right where the gun had been.

He starts to walk carefully but quickly, leading me toward our silver sedan as his head stays on a swivel, scanning in the direction of where he shot. *Pffzt . . . pffzt . . .* two shots whizz by us from behind, more air whooshing than a bang, and somewhere in my head, I realize the hitman has a silencer on his gun while Shane's is ringing loudly as he fires back again.

We sprint, reaching the car in a second that feels like an eternity. Shane yanks the passenger door open and shoves me in, still looking for the hitman. "Stay down."

It's silent for a few seconds that feels like forever, until the driver's door opens and I see Shane again. I start to sit up when I hear the *pffzt* sound once again and Shane grunts. "Fuckfuckfuck."

"What happened?" I ask, but Shane just slams his door, jamming the keys in the ignition before peeling out.

From the floorboard, I stare at Shane, who seems angry, but in control, nowhere near the basketcase-in-shock that I currently am. "Shane?"

His eyes cut from the rearview mirror to the road in front of him twice more before he looks down at me. "You okay? Are you hit?"

I shake my head, wanting to get up but afraid to move from my protected little hole. "No. I'm okay, but what—"

He takes a turn fast, throwing me toward the door, and then

another, throwing me forward into the seat, where I plant my hands. His eyes flick their circle again, rearview mirror, front windshield, then me. "You can get in your seat now. Buckle up."

I quickly do as he says, immediately looking out the side mirror behind us. "Is he following us?"

"No, I don't think so. Not right now, at least. But we need to ditch this car."

I've been undercover for stories before and have experienced a lot of stuff, but nothing like this. I feel like I'm in a freakin' action movie, like somewhere along the way, I got mixed up in something way above my pay grade. But I refuse to be the too stupid to live girl who always ends up dead or causing the hero to die because she's running around like a chicken with her head cut off, panicking at every turn.

I take a deep breath, letting my brain click into the reality my life has become. On the run from the mob, with a hitman chasing us down. Heck, I think I've even seen this movie before. The joke falls flat, even in my own brain. With another breath, I realize . . . okay, I can do this.

"Ditch the car? That means we need another one. Do you happen to have another one hidden around here?"

I say it without humor, totally serious and honestly curious considering I don't know how well-prepared Shane was for all this, but Shane laughs bitterly. "No. Don't have another handily stashed unfortunately."

"Okay, we need a shopping center," I reply, thinking quickly back to a stakeout I did once for a story. "An old one where the security won't have been updated. We can steal a car from the lot and not be caught on camera."

LAUREN LANDISH

Shane looks at me, lifting an eyebrow. "Done this before, have you? Got a juvenile record you don't like to tell people about?"

"No, but it stands to reason," I reply, trying to sound nonchalant about it. I look up and down the streets around us. We're not on the highway but close enough that there are plenty of little strip malls nearby. "There. Turn around."

Shane hangs a U-ey in the street, turning where I indicate, and we pull into the parking lot of a strip mall that looks like it might be on its last legs. There's a bail bonds shop, a Greyhound bus station, a tattoo parlor, a pizza delivery place, and four empty storefronts that look like gaps in teeth. Down the street, I see a newer, fancier looking mall that's probably the reason for this mall's downfall.

He drives across the back row, parking the sedan and turning to me. "Okay, the blue truck beside you," he says, nodding toward a twenty-year-old Dodge that's got a 'For Sale' sign in one window but not too much dirt otherwise. "I'll come around, bump it, and then you're going from this car, through the driver seat of the truck to the passenger side. Put your backpack on and I'll take the duffel bag. Got it?"

I nod.

Shane gets out, and I see a smear of dark wetness on the seat where he was sitting. If it was a white seat, I'm sure it'd be red. Oh, my gosh, he's hit, and he didn't say anything. Anger and fear war in my gut, but I know that leaving his blood here is a bad idea, especially so visible to anyone passing by the car. I reach over, wiping it off with the sleeve of my shirt. It's not much, but at least it turns into a sort of icky streak that'll dry to a dark black soon enough.

Shane knocks once on the window, and I open the door,

hopping into the truck. Thankfully, the truck has a bench seat and I slide over easily, buckling up as he does the same. He leans over, hissing only slightly under his breath as he fiddles around with the wires for a moment while I try to keep myself unseen.

"Come on, you son of a bitch," Shane grunts, and a moment later, the engine turns over. It's sluggish at first before catching, and Shane sits up, letting out a hum of satisfaction, but there's a hint of pain mixed in from the movement. "Okay. Let's go."

It's a little surprising when we pull out of the lot casually, not speeding to draw attention, and merge back with traffic. After a little bit, I reach up and grab the 'For Sale' tag and toss it in the back.

"Thanks," Shane grunts, his tone reminding me of his security guard grumpiness. I can feel my body calming, the adrenaline starting to wear off, and suddenly I'm feeling like a nap.

But I know Shane's hurt, and I force myself to pay attention. As soon as we're on the highway, I turn to him, crossing my arms over my chest. "You're hit. How bad is it?"

He looks at me, then turns his attention back to the road, his lips tight as he speaks. "Just a flesh wound. Bullet nicked me. I'm fine."

I give him an appraising look, then shake my head. "Don't lie to me, Shane. I can see it on your face. We're in deep trouble here. If you're hurt, we need to address that first."

Shane reaches over, weaving his fingers into my hair, holding my head in his palm and looking over with affection. "I'm okay. But I need to report in. See if Chucky has found out anything new, because the hitman tracking us shouldn't have been fucking news. Also, I need to know if the hitman is cleaning up loose ends on his own, or if someone sent him after us."

"What's the chances of each?" I ask, and Shane shrugs.

"About fifty-fifty. But whether the hitman is using his own network to find us or one of the bosses, the result is the same. We're the loose end he's hunting. But if one of the families is helping him, we'd know who the risk is and who the safety might be. Then we could decide if we should try to outrun this, lay low, or maybe even go back. Hopefully, Chucky will have some intel."

CHAPTER 18

I pull over at a large truck stop, parking in the middle of the lot mixed in with the other cars, knowing they'll disguise the truck a bit since there's a chance it's been reported stolen by now. Best guess, the truck was put out there by one of the workers at the strip mall, and if so, they'll notice as soon as they get off shift.

Maggie digs in my duffel, handing me the burner phone. I remind myself to buy a new SIM card for it, but one or two more calls shouldn't be a problem. I turn it on, and before I can even speed-dial Chucky, it rings, and I recognize his number on the display.

Shit, that's not good. I answer, putting it on speaker and staying silent as we always do as he jumps in. "Shane? You okay?"

"Yeah, Chucky. Fine and fucking dandy, except for the hitman who took us by surprise at the fucking motel," I reply, holding a finger up for Maggie to stay silent. "What the fuck's going on?"

Chucky hisses through the phone, sounding upset. "Yeah, I've been watching for you to turn the damn phone back on so I could warn you. Got word earlier today that he's looking for your girl because she saw his face. Loose ends, you know. He wants to disappear."

I reach across and take Maggie's hand, her face remarkably stoic for having confirmation that she's on a hitman's shit list. "Well, he found us already. Got a few shots off, hit me too. Took a nick to the left bicep, but nothing serious. Meghan's fine."

Chucky's voice drops to a whisper, and I can hear him lean into his mic, the wheeze unmistakable. "We need to talk about her, Shane. Your girl is in some deep shit, not just with the hit."

Maggie pales slightly, squeezing my hand, and Chucky continues. "You had me check out all the employees at Petals, and I did. I checked out Meghan Postland and she was clean. But when the shit hit the fan, I ran a wider search, and found a Maggie Postland . . ."

Maggie suddenly yanks her hand back, her knees pulling to her chest in a position I know all too well and was happy to see go.

She's mouthing, "I'm sorry, I'm so sorry," silently, and I can see the fear in her eyes. This isn't good.

My voice is hard as I answer Chucky. "What about Maggie Postland?"

I hear a few clicks, like he's typing on his end, and then he reads. "Maggie Postland, 289 Westminster Drive, Apartment 175."

I nod my head, knowing that's where I'd taken Maggie the night I drove her home. This is nothing new. "Yeah, and . . .?"

"She works for *The Daily Spot*, Shane. That online tabloid rag that reports on celebrities and shit."

Still hoping I'm wrong about where this is going, even as Maggie's head falls and she hugs her knees, I sigh. "You sure? I'm not saying it might not be Meghan, but maybe she answers their phones or something? She told me she'd done some office work before."

Chucky makes a tsking noise, and I can imagine him leaning back and giving me a sarcastic look. "I'm looking at her articles, Shane. She's a reporter. She was the one who sprang that expose on the basketball player. And if I know, they might know—all of them. Dominick, Sal, the hitman."

I nod, and I know I need to have a private conversation. "I gotta go, Chucky. Give me a minute and I'll call back in. Stand by."

I click the *End* button before staring across at Maggie. A reporter. A fucking reporter? My voice is icy, the anger turning my heart cold. "Were you ever going to tell me?"

She doesn't respond, doesn't even move, just sits there, small and curled around herself. She's so scared, so afraid . . . and right now, she should be. Not from me, but from what her presence and digital footprint brings down on us.

"Maggie!"

My voice rings out sharply in the truck, and she flinches but raises her head. Her eyes are red-rimmed, tears tracking down her face. "Yes! I wanted to tell you, but then everything went all to crap and I didn't know how to!"

179

"Well, do it now. Tell me what the fuck is going on with you," I demand, my voice hard. "If there's even a snowball's chance in hell of keeping you safe, you need to tell me everything. Omit fucking nothing."

She swipes her tears, her eyes flashing fire as she sits up a little, cobbling together the remnants of her courage from deep inside her soul. "Yes, I work for *The Daily Spot* as a reporter. I got a job at Petals a few months ago because we had reports there were a lot of celebrities going there for side action. I was undercover, reporting on that, like when Jimmy Keys came in."

I mentally recall our hallway conversation where she'd been taking pictures of the basketball star and claiming to be a fan. I'd been duped . . . that almost never happens to me. And this girl has done it several times without me even suspecting. If we were in any other situation, I'd be impressed. "I see."

"But I like the job, the people . . . like you, Allie, and Marco. Even Dominick didn't seem like that bad of a guy. I had no idea about how deep things went. I mean, who would expect this? This is for the movies. I just thought it was a popular strip club, exclusive VIP kinda stuff for the celebrities and businessmen. And then people started shooting, and Allie had blood all over her . . . and we started running."

Her eyes look to the left like she's remembering the scene at the club, and she shivers. I have to force the next words out through clenched lips, but I have to know, even if it hurts to ask.

"Is that it? You lied about your name and you lied about why you were there. Is there anything else you need to tell me? Now's your chance."

My voice is a bit softer than before, but still harsh and

commanding. Maggie notices and looks at me squarely, still so brave I want to pull her across and cuddle her to my chest.

"I did lie about those things. But nothing else. The things I've said to you, done with you . . . those were all real, all true."

Her eyes are soft, wide and open, letting me see into her soul. She's being honest. I can tell this time because the emotions I see are mirrored in my own heart too. I give a curt nod and turn away. "Okay, let me call Chucky back."

I reach for the phone, but Maggie lays a staying hand on mine. "Now, it's your turn." Her voice is laced with steel. "You've been hiding things from me too."

I look at her, a look of question in my eyes, but her expression is calculating now, the softness gone as she looks at me with a coldness I've never seen before. "*Shane*, is that really your name?"

"Have I given you any reason to doubt that it isn't?" I ask, trying to deflect.

Maggie's eyebrows lift, and she's not going to give up that easily. "I'm not stupid. You seem pretty intertwined in a mob-owned strip club. You had a bugout bag, a stashed getaway car, and you apparently carry a gun that you're skilled with. Those are all things a mobster would have, and I bet somewhere in that duffel of yours are some pretty good fake IDs. But there's also Chucky."

"What about Chucky?" I ask, scared but at the same time impressed. She's seeing a lot. No wonder she's a good reporter. I thought she was smart before. Now I *know* she's smart. And has probably been putting things together all along, just biding her time until the moment was right.

"Earlier, you didn't say you *needed* to call him. You said you needed to 'report in' and see if he had any 'intel'. It made me think back. You weren't close with Dominick, not any moreso than the rest of the employees. He trusted you, I could tell that much, but you were just professional with him. Same with Marco and all of the girls . . . and me, at first. I've been undercover for stories a lot. I can blend into the background easily, being small and underestimated. But that's not how you play it when you go undercover, is it? And I'm betting you've been undercover a time or two before too. So, what are you, Shane? ATF? DEA?"

Fuck. I need to get her on another track real damn fast. Even if it hurts. I make my voice harsh, glaring at her. "Maggie, you're seeing zebras instead of horses when you hear hoof beats. Just because you lied about everything from the moment you walked into Petals doesn't mean I did. I'm a security guard. That's why I know how to shoot a gun. Dom wasn't going to hire some idiot to head his club security team who didn't know how to do anything but use his fists. And Chucky's a buddy who helps me out. That's it."

Maggie jerks when I mention her lies, but she doesn't back down. "FBI?"

I'm a pro, so I know there's no reaction on my face, but that lack of response must be what solidifies it for her. She narrows her eyes, nodding almost to herself. "So that's a yes to the FBI then."

It's quiet in the truck, the gravity of the situation sinking in like a fog of heaviness. It's hard, and I feel my facade of sternness crumbling under her soft but unrelenting eyes. "Maggie."

She lifts a finger at me, silencing me like I did to her earlier. "So, to recap, I'm an undercover reporter for what is mostly a two-bit gossip rag. You're an undercover FBI agent working in a mob-controlled strip club. I'm guessing you're there to investigate Dominick. And now a hitman is chasing us because I'm the only witness to a hit. And we're in a stolen truck with a guy named Chucky as our only backup. That about right? Anything I missed?"

I nod. "Yeah, close enough. My name really is Shane, but my last name isn't Nelson. It's Guthrie. Special Agent Shane Guthrie, Federal Bureau of Investigation."

I hold my hand out, offering her a shake even though we're way beyond that now. Still, it's the only thing that seems appropriate, and she returns the shake, smirking a little. "Maggie Postland. Journalist with *The Daily Spot.*"

We eye each other, so much unsaid between us but neither of us knowing where to start with this tangled web that's quickly unraveling. Finally, she clears her throat and looks at me expectantly.

Maggie hums. "So now what?"

"Now," I reply, "we call Chucky back to see what else he knows. By the way, that's not his real name, but he always says his work is child's play, and he can be an evil son of a bitch when he wants to be . . . so the nickname was pretty natural."

She nods, and I reach for my phone once again. The line connects quickly, silence on Chucky's end.

"Hey, Chucky. So, we're transparent on all fronts on this end."

Chucky's voice is hesitant through the speaker. He's not used to this type of communication. "Just how clear are we talking?"

"Crystal, man. Say hi, Maggie."

Maggie grins and puts on her 'club voice.' "Hi, Maggie."

Chucky doesn't find it funny though. "Fuck, Shane. You can't do shit like that. She's a fucking civilian."

Chucky keeps babbling, but I don't have time for his shit. "It's already done, Chucky. Just be glad she doesn't know your real name. Now what's going on back there?"

Chucky sighs, still wanting to speak his piece about Maggie knowing I'm FBI, but we need to move on, figure out the next step. "Okay, so it's looking like Sal sent Carlos into Petals. Told him it was a power play or some shit, just to go in and see how things were looking, not make waves if he got recognized but to lie low, observe, and report back. Later on, he would use the fact that his son was able to penetrate Dom's HQ as leverage."

What a crock of shit. I know too much about Sal Rivaldi to buy that. "It was a setup then. But Carlos was his own son. That's pretty fucked up, even for Sal Rivaldi."

Chucky's hum tells me he's thinking the same thing. "Yeah, apparently, Carlos was sowing some dissension among the lower lieutenants and Sal decided he needed to clean house. On the down low. He contracted the hitman himself, but he's selling that Dominick killed Carlos for being in his club. Sal's wanted to declare war on the Angeline's for a while, and this way, he's getting a two-for-one . . . rid of his asshole son and riding into battle like some sort of avenging father."

"We can't let that war happen," I growl. "Those two kick off, and the streets are going to turn to rivers of blood."

"No shit," Chucky replies. "You're the one working with the guy. What's he like?"

184

I shrug, looking over at Maggie. "He's careful, methodical, and strategic. More businessman than loose cannon, even if he is a crime lord. He's scary, but it's like a controlled burn with him. If we let the Rivaldi's get even a small foothold on more power, Sal will destroy the city and everyone in it with his crazy power plays. He's more like a wildfire . . . it'll be chaos."

"That's what I'm seeing too. You want to call it in?"

"Not yet, that's a lot of bureaucratic red tape I'm not ready to jump into," I reply.

Chucky understands and laughs softly. "I gotcha. I've looked at this from every angle to see what the best move is and to be honest, I'm not sure, man. It's your call."

I tap my fingers on the steering wheel, doing the same analysis Chucky says he's done and coming up with the same results.

Maggie clears her throat. "I have an idea."

CHAPTER 19

MAGGIE

The tension hums in the air as Shane turns to look at me and Chucky goes silent across the phone line. Shane's looking at me with both respect and anticipation, while Chucky . . . well, he's at least not talking. "Whatcha thinking, Angel?"

"You said Dominick is the better choice for the city, and Sal Rivaldi used his own son as a pawn to incite war," I reply, trying to put words to the thoughts that have been tumbling in my head for only a few moments. I'm trying to put it together with what I know about Dominick, the city . . . everything I've learned in my career in journalism. "We have to appeal to Dominick to prevent the war. The FBI can't exactly go in officially and tell Dominick he's their pick as crime lord . . ."

"That's an understatement," Chucky says, interrupting. "But . . . they might be willing to work under the table if necessary."

"Exactly. He's the best option we've got," I add as Shane gives me a pondering look. "And he can help with the hitman, might be the only one who can."

Shane taps his hands on the dash, his head nodding quickly as he thinks. "You want us to go back to Petals? To Dominick?" he asks before his nods change to shakes. "That's a suicide mission, Maggie. No."

I want to challenge Shane, but Chucky interrupts before the stare-off can reach ridiculous levels. "Actually, I'm thinking she's on to something. You could go back, maintain your cover, share the intel, and nudge Dominick the right way."

"Almost right, Chucky," I interject. "If we go back, we go back honestly. We have to come completely clean with Dominick. If we hold back anything, he'll know and doubt the rest of the information. Besides, having a waitress and a security guy going back doesn't carry weight. A reporter and an FBI agent . . . if we go in and show all our cards, he's more likely to believe us and not go after the Rivaldis. It's risky, but it's the best play."

Shane looks at me incredulously. "You want me to tell Dominick Angeline, head of the Angeline crime family, that I've been undercover with him as an FBI agent for a year and that he's had a fucking reporter working as a waitress in his club, and expect to walk out of that room alive?"

I bite my lip, thinking it through. "Yes. Besides, we can offer Dom things that he would want to take advantage of."

"Like what?" Shane asks, and for the first time, I feel like grinning. "What's going on in your head?"

"Dominick's going to be surprised, and angry, that the FBI has infiltrated his organization," I say, knowing the description is kind at best, stupid at worst. "But if the FBI gives him a tacit agreement for some breathing room, a willingness to back him, even if it's under the table . . . he might be willing to help."

I know I'm pushing it, but Shane needs to understand that I'm all in on this, and I need him to be too.

He nods, obviously thinking through what I've said. "We'd need a safety mechanism, something that will make Dominick talk first and hopefully, *not* shoot later." He pauses, thinking for a moment before grinning. "Not a safety mechanism, but a safety *person*. Allie. We use her as a liaison, make sure she's there for the meeting. I don't think Dominick will kill us in front of her."

He's right. I hate to get Allie involved in this mess. She's my friend, and I don't want her to be in any more danger. But I think Shane might have found the only way to insure we get in and out alive and with any chance at securing Dominick's help with the hitman.

"Okay. We'll talk to Allie."

Shane reaches over, taking my hand and giving it a supportive squeeze. "All right, Chucky, you got all that? I'm going back offline. I'll text you the meet info when it's set."

We hang up, and then it's just Shane and me in the truck. The lies, the hiding, and the stress of the crazy situation melt away as we look at each other, our hands touching, leaving just the chemistry, the connection we've had even when we knew we shouldn't, couldn't pursue it.

I feel naked, vulnerable under his gaze like never before. Unconsciously, my knees pull up to my chest, but I don't drop my gaze. His dark eyes stare back at me, and he gives my hand another little squeeze. "Don't do that, Angel. Don't try to hide now, not when I can finally see you. And you can see me."

I let my knees fall to the side, facing him. My voice is quiet but steady as I meet his eyes, needing to see every nuance of his reaction. "Is this real for you? Because it's real for me. And as scared as I am about all this crazy mob stuff . . ." I wave my hand around, gesturing outside the truck, then place my hand on my heart. "I think I'm more scared that this is some pretend piece of the character you're playing and that you're going to walk away from me when it's all done, leave me alone, broken, and not knowing real from pretend."

Shane grabs my arms, pulling me across the seat and into his lap. Wrapping his arms around my waist, he looks into my eyes, his voice raspy and intense. "It's real for me too, Maggie. So fucking real, and I'm terrified that I'm taking you into the lion's den and won't be able to keep my promise to keep you safe. And I can't stand the thought of that. I need you. I love you."

The doubts in my heart burn to ash as he kisses me, the truth of his words resonating through me. Yes, we've only been intimate for a few days, but I don't care. For months, I've been watching him, dreaming of him, needing him. "Shane, I love you too."

He kisses me again, leaning me back in his arms to lay along the bench seat before covering me with his body.

Shane kisses down my neck, and I lift my head to give him greater access. He groans into the soft skin at the curve, sucking to refresh the mark he's already given me as he grinds the ridge of his dick against my core. "I want to take my time with you, Maggie. Worship every inch of your skin, but I don't want to risk anyone seeing us here. Let me get you somewhere safe for the night so I can make love to you."

I look up at him and pout, wanting more, wanting him now. But he's right. We're too exposed here and I feel like I just found the real Shane. I can't lose him.

With one last fiery kiss, I nod and we wiggle back into our seats, buckling up. "First thing, though. We're getting that arm bandaged."

Shane looks at his arm, chuckling before nodding. "Okay. We'll find a pharmacy or something. Just . . . I love you, Maggie. I promise to keep you safe, no matter what happens."

I take his hand, interlocking our fingers, my tiny hand engulfed by his giant one. "I love you too. I know you'll keep me safe. We'll do this together."

He dips his head, handing me the phone. "Call Allie. Don't answer any questions or give her any indication about where we are. Tell her to set up a meeting tomorrow at noon at the club. She needs to meet us at the front door with one guard of Dominick's choosing. Once we're inside, it's Dominick's show. Whatever he feels is warranted, as long as he listens to us."

I bite my lip, suddenly nervous as we're at the point where the poop hits the fan. "Is that smart? Shouldn't we try to limit the guards, give us a fighting chance if things go awry?"

Shane shakes his head, sighing. "If he wants to kill us, it won't matter if there are two guards or ten. Better to let him feel in control about as much as possible, because we're going in with a big favor to ask and demanding that he put the one weakness he has, Allie, at risk at the same time."

I take a steadying breath, turning the phone on and dialing

Allie's number, glad I have it memorized. Allie's voice is hesitant when she answers the unknown number. "Hello?"

Good, she's not dancing yet, or maybe she's not dancing at all after the shooting. "Allie, it's me, Meghan."

It feels strange to use my fake name again, but it's all Allie's ever known, and it's like a firecracker to her. "Oh, my God, Meghan! Are you okay? What the fuck happened to you? Where are you? Are you with Shane?"

She's shooting questions rapid-fire style, and I can't even answer one before the next starts. I try to reassure her. "I'm fine. I'm with Shane. Are you okay?"

Her voice is calmer now, but still tight and probably a little worried. "I'm fine too. I was freaked out for a bit, but I'm okay now. The club just went on like business as usual. I don't think the customers on the floor even realized what happened."

I don't think I realized how scared I was that Allie wasn't okay until I heard her voice, getting stronger and steadier as she speaks. Tears of relief fill my eyes, and I lean my head forward, holding in the sniffle as best I can. "Good, I'm so glad you're okay."

Shane waves his hand in a circle at me, indicating I should wrap this up. I guess it's got something to do with tracing the call, or maybe just because we need to get going. His arm has to be burning like fire. "Listen, I need your help with something."

"Of course, anything," Allie says immediately. "I've been worried about you."

"Look, there's a lot going on here that you don't know," I say, wishing I could tell her. "It's sort of safer if you don't for now. I need you to trust me and do exactly as I say, okay?"

Allie's voice tightens, and I can hear her tapping her phone with a thumbnail. "You're scaring me. What's going on?"

"I need you to set up a meeting with Dominick for us. Tomorrow at noon, at the club. There's stuff that Shane and I need to talk to him about."

"Why not just call—" Allie says, but I cut her off, needing to rush this.

"You need to be there to meet us at the front door. A guard's fine if Dominick feels it's warranted, and he can have as many guys there as he wants. We're coming in to talk, and he needs to hear what we have to say, for everyone's sake. If he asks, tell him it has to do with Sal. Got all that?"

Allie sounds confused, but still sort of put together. "Yeah, tomorrow at noon with security. But what's going on?"

"We'll explain everything tomorrow. I need you to be there, so you'll hear everything," I tell her, instantly hoping she'll want to still be my friend after my lies are laid out for her. "This is important, Allie. Please, tell Dominick he needs to listen."

"I'll set it up. Whatever you need," Allie says. "But you promise me, you're not doing anything stupid?"

I have to laugh. We're light years past stupid. "You know me, Allie. I just take after you, my friend."

"That's what worries me," Allie says, laughing a little herself. "Okay, well . . . see you tomorrow?"

"I'll see you tomorrow," I promise, my voice cracking a little. "Check ya later, babe."

I have to hang up before she can reply, the knot in my belly cinching tight. I'm scared now, and it's not the primal, instinctual fear that I've felt for the past few days. This is deeper, both body and mind, and part of it is that, of all the silly shiz, I'm going to disappoint my friend.

Shane wraps a hand around the back of my neck, pulling me toward him and laying a soft kiss on my forehead. He understands, and he'll be here for me. "Good girl, Angel. Let's roll some miles."

CHAPTER 20

SHANE

*T*he house isn't exactly a mansion in Bel-Air, but compared to the past two nights, it's a glorious luxury. A two-bedroom house in a nice suburban subdivision. It's an FBI safe house, and it feels good in a lot of ways to use it. It means that all our cards are on the table and that I don't need to hide from her any longer.

She might've semi-accepted the car switch without an interrogation, but having a random house stocked with all the goodies we could need would've raised too many questions I couldn't answer.

I'm glad we're being totally honest with each other now, because beyond all this craziness, I really have fallen in love with this brilliant, tiny, innocent woman.

It didn't take sex, or looking back, even a single kiss to start falling in love with her. It was in the snippets of conversation, in the looks that we've shared. It happened when I was willing to go as far as needed to protect her. It was when I was willing to beat a man within an inch of his life for threatening her, and when I was willing to defy a mob boss to keep her safe.

Sex? Oh, I'm not turning that down with my naughty little Angel—never will. It's been more intense, more satisfying, more meaningful than any I've had before. But I loved her even before that, and I think she loved me before that too.

I pull the truck into the garage, dropping the mechanical door and locking it tight behind us before we enter the house. Inside, it's small and tidy, neatly decorated in stuff that's used but clean and kept prepped and ready. I know without even looking that in the kitchen will be a freezer of basic frozen stuff and some microwave meals, and the pantry will have boxed goods. Nothing fancy, but we'll be able to eat.

"Won't the neighbors wonder about us?" Maggie asks, looking around. "I mean, that there are lights on and stuff?"

I do a routine full sweep of the interior, tossing our bags into the bedroom. "Safe houses are set up with a cover story for any nosy neighbors. In the old days, we'd say it was owned by a pilot who'd let flight crew crash during layovers. Nowadays, we tell people it's an AirBnB to make it easier. People usually accept what they're told at face value, and not many would suspect something as wild as an FBI safe house in their family neighborhood."

Maggie nods, looking around. "I never thought you were FBI, that's for sure. You seem like too much of a bad boy to be one of the good guys."

She says it with a teasing note, so I know that she's pleased with both sides of my personality. I grin. "Uh, you hungry? They keep the house stocked, so there's usually some Hungry Mans around here."

Maggie nods, stepping closer. "I am hungry . . . for *my* man. Forget the fried chicken."

Her words hang in the air, heavy with need as she looks up at me with pleading eyes. I cover the remaining space between us in two steps, sweeping her into my arms and lifting her by the backs of her thighs. "I think I can satisfy your hunger."

She wraps her arms around my neck and legs around my waist, her tiny body climbing my larger one like a tree. I devour her, my tongue meeting her hungry one and the two of us invading each other. Faintly, I can taste the sugary coffee she had earlier at a truck stop, the bitterness making the sweetness even more of a treat.

"Lock your ankles around me," I command her, kissing to her ear. "I want to see you fly."

I feel her feet shift behind me and hold her shoulders, dipping her back parallel to the floor. "Let go. I've got you."

Her hands let go of my neck, and she spreads her arms as she closes her eyes. She weaves her fingers into my hair as I kiss down her neck. "Mmm, Shane. I feel like I'm floating. Your kisses are the only thing anchoring me here."

She sounds dreamy, and I smile against her neck, proud that I'm the one making her hazy. No one has given me this much pleasure, and nobody has ever given her what I've given her.

"I want to anchor you to this moment, to me . . . mark every inch of you with my tongue and my teeth so no one doubts that you are mine. Not even you."

Her head lifts, eyes clear as she meets my dark gaze, and her fingers dig into the back of my neck. "Do it. Make me yours."

I return to her neck, leaving sucking kisses along her pulse,

LAUREN LANDISH

feeling it jump under my tongue as the bruise raises brightly against her pale skin. I know these are going to fade in a few hours, but I'm just getting started.

Fuck. I need all of her. I turn, tossing her to the bed and watching as she bounces on the surface, grinning the whole time. "Take your shirt off. Bra too. Now, Angel."

I rip my t-shirt over my head, a ripping sound coming from the exhausted cotton as my muscles tear the fabric off me. I'm covering her before she even tosses her bra to the floor. I'm so ravenous for her and for what she promises me.

Her palms cup my cheeks, lips puckered for a kiss, and I grant it to her quickly before returning my attentions lower. Moving down her body, I lick, kiss, suck, and nibble her upper body, tracing every inch with my tongue and lips and leaving more marks along her breasts as I find the spots that tickle her . . . that tease her . . . that drive her wild.

"Shane . . . ohh," Maggie cries out as I suck on her pink nipples, her nails clawing at my arms as she pulls me tighter. I love that my sweet girl turns into a wildcat in bed, her need making her desperate . . . for me.

I push off, standing by the bed and grabbing at her shorts, pulling them down and off, along with her gas-station wannabe Crocs.

I place her feet on my shoulders, needing to bend down a bit so her short legs can reach, even with her hips raised high, and begin to worship her shapely legs with little kisses on her toes before moving up inch by inch. "These legs have been in my dreams for months, Maggie. Wanting to slide my hands up your thighs every time you bent over a table, wondering how silky your skin would be under my palms, knowing they led to fucking heaven."

"I've been dreaming of the same thing. Just like this," Maggie whispers as I suck on her soft skin. "You make me feel alive."

My mouth makes its way from her ankles . . . to her knees . . . to her inner thighs, where I force myself to pause, knowing I want to indulge but also knowing I want to take my time. I nibble and suck still, leaving no doubt that this pussy is mine, her cheap panties framed by the signature of my marks.

"Did you know?" I ask as I look into her eyes. "Did you know how much I wanted you? That I wanted to risk it all, my career, my cover . . . my life?"

Maggie's breath catches, and she nods "Yes, and no. We were flirting, and I wanted you so much, but I thought I'd never have you. So I flirted back harder, bending over those tables with my ass toward you on purpose, hoping to tempt you into wanting me. You were like a predator, powerful and dominant, and I felt in my dreams that you could be the man I would spend the rest of my life with."

Her words ignite me, my hands finding the edge of her panties. I tug them to the side to gaze upon her pussy before using my thumbs to massage her outer lips, the softness under my rough hands the perfect symbolism for the two of us. Soft and rough, innocent and jaded, but somehow fitting together perfectly. I can see her juices coating her as she gets wetter and wetter. "Fuck, Maggie. I need to taste you."

"Yes, my love," she gasps, but it turns into a giggling rush as I scoop her up the rest of the way and stand, her thighs over my shoulders and her pussy right in front of my mouth. "Whoa. Holy Shitzu!" Maggie exclaims as her hands grab at my head for balance, but I'm holding her solidly in my palms, my fingertips dimpling her luscious ass as I hold her tight.

"I've got you and I'm just getting started," I promise, dipping my tongue into her folds. I groan at her taste, my cock still trapped in my jeans but straining for freedom. "Fuck, you're so damn delicious. All I want is to eat you up."

I lick her entrance, sucking at her clit, delighting at her whimpers above me. I want to drown in her, suffocate in her sweetness. She's gasping, her voice getting thick as she moans.

Gently, I lower her back to the bed, quickly kicking off my shoes and jeans to lay down naked beside her. I watch her pink face as she blinks, grinning at me. "Two more strokes and I would've come. Not sure you could hold me up if I was squirming through that."

"I wouldn't have dropped you, I would've pulled you in even tighter to get every drop." I reply, patting my chest. "Now get up here, you naughty Angel. Straddle me. Sit on my face and let me feast on that pussy."

She blushes a deep rose shade of pink but does it, stripping off her panties before turning so that she's facing my body. She looks down, and I can just see the naughty twinkle in her eyes before she lowers down. "I want to suck you too."

My cock jumps at her words, trying to get closer to her mouth for the pleasure of her murmured words. She chuckles and lowers her pussy slowly, teasing me. It's not nearly enough for what I want to do to her. I grab her hips in a hard grip, forcing her down to my mouth and immediately thrashing my tongue all along her pussy. Immediately, I'm covered in her sweet juices, my tongue in heaven as my nose presses lower and my eyes are covered in the soft weight of her ass. Heaven.

Above me, I feel Maggie lean forward and then her soft touch along my shaft as her fingers explore me delicately. I groan, my knees falling to the sides to give her total access. My tongue speeds up, finding the button of her clit and stroking it quickly, circling around it before sucking softly. I want to mark her, but not here. I'll never hurt her.

She cries out at my attentions to her clit, and I feel the wet heat of her breath just before she takes my head into her mouth, swirling her tongue along the slit to taste my precum. It shifts her hips down—she's so small compared to me—and I lift my hips while burying my tongue deeper in her pussy, my nose pressed between her ass cheeks, but I never stop.

She moans at my flavor, like it's a treat she savors, and the buzz of her moan zings through me. I pull back, smacking her ass playfully. "That's it, Angel. Suck my cock down your pretty little throat. I'm gonna lick this sweet pussy and make you moan around my cock. Moan on me, Maggie."

I dive back into her pussy, thrusting my tongue in and out of her. She's close, grinding her pussy on my hungry mouth and moaning around my cock as she keeps sucking me down. The feeling drives me wild, making me growl against her pussy. "Fuck, that's so good."

"You too," Maggie gasps breathlessly, her hips bucking, wanting more. "Let me feel how much you like me sucking you."

We become louder, our grunts and groans echoing against each other in a cycle that renews with each sound until Maggie freezes, my cock deep in her throat as she cries out her release.

I pull her tighter, burying my face in her so deeply I can't even breathe, but I don't care because all I need is her and the sweet nectar she's pumping against my tongue.

As soon as her spasms stop, I push her off me, pinning her underneath me and slamming my cock into her.

I don't give her time to stretch, wanting to feel those last orgasmic quivers of her pussy, but I slide in and out slowly, needing to feel every bit of her silky walls against my cock. She moans, wiggling her hips as she squeezes me with her pussy, wanting more.

I gather her hands above her head, holding them with one hand and cupping her jaw with the other so that our eyes meet.

"You and me, Angel. I don't know what's going to happen tomorrow, but it's you and me. Together. And if this is all we have, then I'm spending the rest of my life with the woman I want by my side until the end. I love you, Maggie."

Her eyes shine with tears, but her voice is strong. "I love you too, Shane. Tomorrow is tomorrow. You said you were anchoring me to this moment, but I need you here with me. Right now, just be here with me. My man. Forever."

I look over her body, my marks visible along her neck, her chest and tits, her hips, and though I can't see them, I know she's claimed on her thighs and above her mound too. "You are mine, always."

Maggie smiles, nodding and biting her lip. "Yours. And you're mine too."

I thrust into her, harder and more powerfully, my strokes getting rougher as I demand more and more from her small body, but she takes me, fiercer than I'd ever imagined my Angel to be.

Our eyes stay locked the whole time, never leaving each other for a moment, even as we both come hard. We don't even cry out. The whole time, we're nearly silent as our eyes say everything that needs to be said, the only sound the rush of our breath and the slap of our hips.

My cum creams out of her as I pull out and we collapse in each other's arms. Maggie curls against me, falling asleep fitfully in my arms, but I stay on alert.

I'm dreading tomorrow's meeting, knowing it's potentially a suicide mission. But I'm hoping that we can make Dominick see reason.

CHAPTER 21

MAGGIE

*E*ven after an entire morning of Shane's constant coaching about what to do in every possible scenario he foresees for the meeting, I'm still nervous. Noon comes faster than I expected, and my stomach is grumbling as I sit in the passenger seat and watch the streets. "I should have eaten."

"I offered," Shane reminds me. "Nothing better to start your day than frozen breakfast sandwiches."

I laugh, looking over. He's wearing just a tank top, the bright white of the bandage over the taut skin of his arm taunting me. It really was just a nick, didn't even need stitches or glue, but still . . . it's a bullet wound. I nod, "I know, I know."

Shane chuckles and flexes his arm. "You know what I want to do when we get some normalcy again?" he remarks. "I want to go to the gym again. Gotta stay in shape. You wear me out."

I smile, knowing he's just trying to relax me. "I could be enticed into watching you get your buff on."

Our conversation tapers off as we drive up and down the street three times before Shane pulls the old blue truck up outside Petal's front door.

He does a full scan, and then with one last quick kiss, we get out and approach cautiously. Shane knocks twice on the door, and it opens a crack, Nick peeking out. He looks wary and confused at the same time, like he shouldn't be this concerned about people he knows.

"Shane? Meghan? You alone?"

Shane nods "Yeah, Nick. Alone and unarmed. You know Dom's got three cameras on us right now. It'd be stupid not to be. Allie here?"

The door swings open wider, and I can see Allie, her face a mask of confused fear, but when she sees me, she squeals and runs for me. Her long arms surround me in a tight hug even as she starts demanding answers. "What the fuck is going on?"

Her hug has pulled me away from Shane a step or two, and with a quick jerk, he pulls me back to his side and out of Allie's reach. Allie's jaw drops in surprise at his move, and then she narrows her eyes, taking in the visible marks along my neck and the upper swells of my breasts. "Ooh, it's like that?"

She's teasing, giving me a thumbs-up, and I almost even feel like smiling. Until I realize Nick is leering at me like he never has before.

Before he can say anything, though, Shane steps between us, blocking his view. "Nick, we need to see Dominick. Now."

Nick nods once, moving to pat down Shane, looking a little embarrassed by it. "Protocol, man."

Shane allows it but barely manages to hold himself in check as Nick does a more thorough check on me, like I'd be hiding a gun in these shorts. I knock Nick's hands away when he gets a little high on the inner thigh, though. "I'm clear and you know it, pervert. This ain't the airport, and I'm pretty sure that 'don't touch' rule still applies."

He smirks but turns and leads us into the main room. It's well-lit, more like it is when we clean after closing each night than the usual dim ambiance I'd expected.

But it lets me see the room and its inhabitants more clearly. Dominick is sitting alone at a table near the edge of the stage, right in front of the big pole that dominates the middle of the room, a glass filled with amber liquid on the polished wood beside him.

As Nick takes his place, I can see that there's a guard in every corner. Dominick doesn't bother standing, just gestures to the chairs opposite him, and we sit.

It'd almost feel like a double-date, Dominick and Allie on one side, and Shane and I on the other, if it weren't for the pesky fact that things are about to go more than a bit sideways. Well, that and the guards in every corner.

Dominick picks up his glass and takes a sip before setting it down and studying us curiously. "So you asked for this meeting. What is so important?"

Shane looks at Allie, then back to Dominick. "I appreciate your agreeing to meet with us. And I apologize for asking that Allie be present. I know that would not be your preference, but I feel it affords us a certain amount of safety, considering the information I'm about to share."

Dominick's face tightens slightly, just at the corners of his eyes, belying his anger, but he keeps his cool. I can see it now, the aura of power, the comfort in his place in the hierarchy. I'd been fooled that it was just about him being the boss of such a hot club, but there's so much more. Not to mention, I think he has ice in his veins considering the cool tone as he speaks. "There is always risk to sharing information. I hope that you have not set either of us up for any . . . safety issues."

The pause in his speaking makes his threat crystal clear. I don't need to look to know that each of the guards are on high alert, ready to handle us if there's a problem. Or just at Dominick's say-so.

Shane and Dominick stare each other down for a moment, the testosterone and dominance contest drawing out between the two of them for too long, so I break in, hoping to deter the two alpha males from locking horns until one of them's dead. "Dominick, I would like to apologize for lying to you."

My words aren't totally unplanned. It was one of the many different scenarios that Shane and I went over, a way to keep Dominick off balance and willing to listen.

The shock of my admitting to lying does exactly what we hoped, and Dominick's attention diverts solely to me, his eyes now boring into mine with his eyebrows raised in question. "Meghan, you lied to me? Explain."

I start rambling, trying to get out the whole prepared speech at once. "My name is not Meghan. It's Maggie Postland. In certain circles, Petals has a reputation. Apparently, it has several. But I was only aware of one . . . I didn't know what Petals was, what *you* are. I just knew that celebrities of a certain caliber frequent the club for a bit of fun. I work as a tabloid reporter, writing stories strictly about celebrities. I began my job at Petals as a way of investigating these stories and wrote articles a few times."

My eyes tick to Allie, who looks like I just slapped her across the face. I focus on her, the next words not important to Dom, but I insisted on them with Shane. "But while I worked here, I found friends and a place of belonging, a family that worked together, day-by-day and shift-by-shift, to look out for one another. I found a self-confidence and power I never knew I possessed. It hurt every day to lie to them, because I care about them very much."

I look back to Dominick, who's leaning forward a little, interested now. "I didn't know exactly how deep the rabbit hole runs around here, and honestly, right now, I don't care. My concern now is the trouble chasing me, trouble brought because I'm a part of the Petals family."

Dominick's eyes have gotten colder as I've spoken, and I can see the muscle in his jaw working as he clenches his teeth. His voice is a deadly whisper, but at least he's not yelling as he looks around at the guards. "A fucking reporter? How the fuck did you get past the background check?"

I shrug, downplaying my awesomeness because it doesn't seem the time to brag about how many times I've success-fully gone undercover. "I'm good at my job. Please feel free to take a moment to Google me. I promise, you'll see I've only written a couple of stories that relate to celebrities attending strip clubs, and I never mention Petals by name."

He holds up a finger, reaching into his vest pocket with his other hand and fishing out his phone. He clicks around for a moment, and I speak up helpfully. "The only one that prob-ably would've caught your attention is the Jimmy Keys story."

Dominick laughs, setting his phone down. "You broke that

story? That guy's a total douchebag, tried to stiff me on the bill too. I was glad he got busted . . . but not in my damn club."

His voice is hard again by the end, and my momentary hope that maybe he wouldn't be too mad, at least about that part of our revelations, are crushed.

I lower my eyes, unable to help it because I know there's worse news coming. "Dominick, please. There's more."

He huffs, sitting up as Allie lays a hand on his shoulder, helping to calm him. He glances at her and nods, waving a hand at me. "It's your show, apparently. Tell me."

I glance at Shane, but he gives me a reassuring nod. I'm doing fine. Keep going. "So, the night of the shooting . . ."

I see Allie flinch and give her a soft smile of apology for bringing up something that must be scary for her to think about. "That night, I was in the hallway after delivering the scotch, so I saw the hitman. I don't think he even registered me at the time. I'm just kinda invisible to most folks."

I shrug because it's the truth, but Shane squeezes my hand, and I know he sees me. He always sees me, and it gives me the strength to continue.

"But yesterday, when Shane and I were lying low, the hitman found us. He's tracking me, tying up loose ends because somewhere along the way, he realized I'd seen him and could recognize him."

Dominick steeples his hands, fingertips pressing together under his chin. "And this hitman chasing you, you want me to do something about it, I take it?"

I nod, the plea in my eyes. "Please, Dominick. Help us."

"Tell me, Maggie Postland," Dominick says, leaning forward again and studying the both of us. "The suit with the scotch. Do you know who he was?"

"I didn't then, but I do now," I admit. "Carlos Rivaldi. This is where Shane comes in, I think."

Dominick looks to Shane, annoyance and anger clearly written on his face. "It appears you've been tagged. You're *it*."

Shane holds Dominick's glare with steady eyes before beginning. "Dominick, I want you to take a minute and think back on the time I've been working for you . . . the things I've done, the things I've seen, the things I've told you."

Dominick smiles, but it feels threatening, not friendly. "Yes, we have done some rather interesting things in your time here. And until this little incident, I thought you were a fine *employee*, one of the best I had. But what's that got to do with this?"

"Have the guys step out for this. Just you and me, and the girls. Trust me. Please."

They seem to be communicating with their eyes, taking each other's measure, but I think it's the 'please' that does it.

Dominick turns, his voice clear and sharp as he looks at the guards. "Leave us. Secure the building perimeter."

The security guys disappear at once, and I hear both the front and back doors open, then close. Dominick waits, then looks back at Shane. "Okay, we're alone. Out of respect for what you've done and the honor you've shown toward all the ladies who work here, I did that. Don't make me regret it. Now tell me what's so important."

Shane nods and leans forward, his elbows wide on the table

as he looks at Dominick. "Approximately twelve months ago, word on the street was that Sal Rivaldi was making progress, increasing the size of his operation, but doing it quietly and in small pocket areas that are only loosely in your control. The way things were looking, he was positioning himself to divide East Robinsville, or maybe take over the whole city."

Dominick leans forward, his eyes intense. "And you know this how?"

Shane looks Dominick in the eye. There is no fear, no hesitancy, no apology on Shane's face. "Because I'm FBI."

Dominick explodes, standing so fast his chair clatters to the floor behind him as he slams his hands to the table. Allie and I jump at the sharp sound.

Shane stands too, holding his ground as Dominick stalks around the table to grab him by the shirt. Dominick rears back for a punch and Shane doesn't try to block him, just keeps his voice level. "There's more . . ."

Dominick pauses, and I think for a second that he's not going to punch Shane in the face. But he redirects the punch to Shane's gut, the powerful hit echoing in the empty room.

Allie cries out as Dom rears back again, and I can't sit here and let this happen, so I yell, "Dominick, Sal's declaring war! You have to listen!"

Dominick's head whips to me, one fist cocked back and frozen. "I thought you didn't know anything about that side of the business? Hmm, Miss Postland?" he sneers. "Or is that another lie?"

I'm trying to be strong, but I know my voice sounds weaker than I'd like as I stand up to him. "I didn't before. I do now.

I've spent the past twenty-four hours learning so I can try to stay alive. Please listen."

He shoves Shane back, letting go of his shirt, and both men slowly sit, wary of each other.

"That's your freebie because I respect the fuck out of you, Dominick," Shane says as he smooths his hair. "Next time, I'll fight back."

Dominick's eyes narrow, the coldness intimidating as frick even when it's not directed at me, but Shane doesn't flinch. "If you get a chance. But say your piece."

"I was sent in undercover in your operation, another agent in Rivaldi's," Shane says, leaning back in his chair. "It took some time to get that agent's information, but I'm giving you all I have. Carlos was giving Sal shit, and you know there's no love lost between the two of them. Sal decided he needed to stop the coup Carlos was stirring up, but for Sal, that's not enough. If he's going to kill his own son, why not use it as a power play? He knew that if he could pin Carlos's death on you, he'd have the Colombians with him when he wanted to go hot around here. So he sent Carlos to Petals on a fool's errand and secretly hired out the hit so it'd take place on your territory. Sal's telling his whole crew you killed Carlos, and now he has the best justification ever to start a war . . . to avenge his son."

"The Colombians do go for family," Dominick concedes. "Never hired a Colombian dancer for just that reason. Too likely to have some bloodthirsty cousin on my doorstep."

"But Sal set it all up—set *you* up. He's making a play for more control, and he's ready to war with you to get it."

I can see Dominick taking in everything, the calculations and strategies running through his mind as he plays out scenario after scenario. He reaches down, picking up his seemingly forgotten drink and draining the rest of it in one swallow.

"That is a lot to think about, many things to consider. But tell me this, FBI agent. Why are you telling me all this? You wouldn't be trying to entrap me into something, would you?"

Shane chuckles darkly, crossing his legs almost casually. "No, Dominick. I'm not trying to entrap you. What you do with this information is your choice—war with the Rivaldis or don't war with them. My thinking is this. There are devils in every world, some more evil, some perhaps less. But they're necessary, to balance out the angels."

Shane takes my hand and looks lovingly at me before turning back to Dominick. "Sometimes, you help the devil you know is the lesser evil in the hopes that they will help you too."

Dominick looks from Shane to me and back. "Ah, so this is where the help comes in. You've given me information in the hopes that I will do something for you too. What is it you want?"

Shane lets go of my hand and leans forward again. "The hitman. I've got a name. I've seen his face now too. He's seen us and is hunting us still. I'm slightly worried about how he's getting his information, but that's a fight for another day, and likely solved if he's dealt with the way I'd prefer. Right now, I need him to stop. Means and methods are yours to decide, of course. If you do us this favor."

Dominick nods thoughtfully and rubs his chin in consideration. "I do not like people who choose to do their dirty work inside my own place of business. It's disrespectful and bad for my reputation, you see? It's in *my* best interest to punish the hitman for his transgression, but I will say that it's for your benefit and hold that over you. Agreed?"

Shane nods. "One more thing . . ."

Dominick smirks, the smug arrogance obvious on his face. "I thought there might be."

"We walk. Maggie and I walk away from all of this safely. Forever. No outstanding threats, no looking over our shoulders. You will never see either of us again."

That hurts, and I glance at Allie, knowing that if Dominick agrees, it means our friendship's over too. But it has to be.

"Agreed. You may both walk away safely, but I will not promise you will never see me again. Having friends in certain positions can be an excellent resource, so while I will not use you frequently, I will keep you available if the need comes up. And . . . Mr. FBI Agent, your East Robinsville privileges are revoked. Permanently. You don't set foot in this town again. Unless it is by my invitation."

There's a carefulness to his phrasing, the details somehow in the words he's not saying. I can see the methodical strategic mind Shane said Dominick possesses, making contingencies until the end.

I feel like we're all pawns in Dominick's chess game, but we're still on move three and he's already planned out his game to the checkmate move.

Shane nods and offers his hand. "Agreed, with one caveat. You will not use either of us in a way that would endanger us, especially Maggie."

Dominick bows his head and offers his own hand. "I wouldn't threaten a man's family. That's how cockroaches operate, and while I may be a devil in your eyes, I'm no cockroach."

They shake, and the agreement's made.

CHAPTER 22

SHANE

"Oh, my goodness, I can't believe Dominick's going to help us!" Maggie exclaims happily, falling ungracefully to the couch. We're upstairs at the club, in the private apartment Dominick keeps. I've been up here before, mostly on days when Dom's stayed over himself. It's a cush place, small but fancier than anything I've ever had for damn sure. And it's not even his real home, just a crash pad.

After reaching our agreement, Dominick 'offered' us the protection of the club and the use of the place. It wasn't so much an offer as a demand. We're definitely more prisoner than guest, but his protection comes with his rules, so here we are.

I sit down beside her on the couch, pulling her legs into my lap and slipping off her shoes to rub her feet. "He's helping, but we can't get too comfortable in this gilded cage. I'm not certain he won't flip on us. And we still don't know what he plans to do about Sal."

Maggie looks thoughtful, smiling as she wiggles her toes

217

for me. "Honestly, I'm not sure I care. All this mob stuff was happening before, right under my nose, and I was oblivious. If I wasn't in the middle of it this time, I probably still wouldn't know about this potential threat to the city. Maybe I'd be better off, happier in my blissful ignorance."

I run my hand along her calf up to her thigh, marveling at the power in her muscles and tracing the fading marks from last night. "Maybe so. But the power structure that directs the city, from politics, to businesses, to the streets, it's all intertwined, and if things are running smoothly, you don't notice them."

"Kinda like the sewer company?" Maggie asks. "As long as the toilets are working right, you never notice them."

I nod, thinking Maggie's found a pretty good analogy. "You haven't noticed things here because Dominick does a damn fine job of keeping himself seamless. If Sal were running things, you'd know the difference. You'd see it on the news, you'd feel it when you walked around your neighborhood. To be a part of the solution, you have to be aware of the problems . . . all of them, even the scary ones."

Maggie's eyes bore into me even as she leans back against the couch cushion. "Is that why you do it, why you're an FBI agent? To be part of the solution?"

My hands still. I've known this was coming. We dropped these big bombs of who we are on each other but then had to let the issues lie while we got to safety.

Now that we've got the semblance of protection, the tenuous pause on our questions drops away. "Remember how I told you about my dad?"

Maggie's chin dips as she whispers quietly. "Yeah. Barney Fife, more or less."

"Well, Barney Fife, who was about the same size as me, but yeah. He's why I do this. I grew up seeing him help people, sometimes by being a big, powerful guy with a badge, but more often, it was by being an ear to listen to people's problems and help them find a way out of whatever trouble they were having. When I was a kid, it was normal to come downstairs and find that Dad had taken in a stray overnight . . . sometimes a kid, sometimes a whole family, and a few times, a recently released felon who needed guidance to see the better path available to him. We had a couple of tents that Dad would let them use, or if the weather was bad, he'd let them crash on the porch or even inside in winter. I always knew I wanted to be a police officer like him, to help people."

"So, how'd you end up in the FBI?"

"I knew I wanted to be more than a street cop," I reply honestly. "Dad always said that the real criminals were the ones he could never touch, and I thought I could make a difference. So I went to college for criminal justice, and my grades and performance were good enough to catch the attention of the right people. I was given a few scholarships and cranked my way through a four-year degree in three years before reporting straight to Quantico for the FBI Academy. They broke me down and molded me the way they wanted, taught me how to go undercover, that creative problem-solving is an asset, not a rule-bending problem, and so much more. I don't think my dad fully realized the extent of what I'd gotten into, but he knew I was an agent before he died, and he was proud of me. My mom kinda lives in denial about my job, but she's proud too. She just can't handle the constant anxiety when I disappear for long assignments."

Maggie bites her lip, worry written on her face. "So, when this is all over, what will you do then? Will you leave for another assignment? Leave me behind?"

I pull her into my lap, cupping her face and laying a sweet kiss to the tip of her nose. Leaving no doubt as to the truthfulness of my words as I lay my heart open for her, I look in her eyes, my voice quaking with intensity. "Angel, I honestly don't know what happens after this. All I know is that I love you. I want to be with you, know every thought that runs through that brilliant mind of yours, watch you drink coffee ice cream for breakfast every day, and hold you while you sleep every night. I want to grow old with you, have a family with you, and claim not just your body," I rumble as my eyes rove across her skin, peppered with my love, "but also claim your heart. Forever."

Maggie is smiling, the hope shining in her eyes as she takes my hands and holds them in hers, almost like we're praying together. "I want that too, Shane. God, I want that too, to be your haven when you're protecting everyone else, to fill your heart when you've given more than you should, to create a life with you that you want to come back to reality for after a long time pretending to be someone else. I love you so much. I never thought something like this would happen to someone like me."

Our words feel like vows, promises for a future we may not get. There's no preacher, no ring, nobody to even witness them, but none of that matters. I kiss her fiercely, putting every bit of my heart and soul into the breath I give to her and demanding every bit of hers in return. Nothing less than pure honesty between us will ever be enough again.

My body responds, my cock surging inside my jeans as we

part lips, panting, and I want to slip inside her sweet pussy once again, be one with her.

But I need to be inside her mind even more, know everything there is to know about my sweet Maggie, so I still her squirming hips, holding her tightly against my thickening cock. "Tell me, Angel. What did you think would happen to someone like you? What did little Maggie Postland think her life would be like?"

She smiles softly, suddenly shy. "Don't laugh, okay?"

My face is calm, more curious than anything, and after she's sure I'm listening, she continues. "I wanted to be Barbara Walters. She's like this spitfire you don't expect. Early in her career, she was seen as this blonde woman who couldn't possibly do a man's job and interview these powerful leaders. But she did, and she used her charm to get insights no one else could, without selling herself short. Nobody imagined she'd accomplish so much, but she never doubted her ability to get the scoop, verbally wiggling and manipulating her way into the interview of the decade, all the while making it seem like it was just a friendly chat. And it gave little me, blonde, sweet, kinda nerdy little Maggie hope that I could do that someday and make a difference."

I take a moment, studying her face before nodding. "I can see it, *Interviews by Maggie Postland*. You sitting in a chair, sipping coffee, and smiling that sweet smile. Maybe not Barbara style, but more like Oprah, maybe, or like one of the late-night hosts?"

"But more serious," Maggie says, and I nod.

"Right. The people you interview would never see it coming until you hit them like a fucking heat-seeking missile and started asking the tough questions. Hell, they probably wouldn't even know they'd spilled government secrets until it was too late, mesmerized by your sweet girl goodness."

Maggie lays two fingers over my lips and then lifts them high, blowing a puff of air across her fingertips. "From your lips to the universe's ears."

I smile, knowing that she's being silly but at the same time, very serious. "What about now? What about your job?"

Maggie scrunches her nose up like a bunny before making a disgusted sound. "Ugh. I'm pretty sure that I'm fired by now. My boss is strict and demanding, and considering I haven't submitted a story in over a week and haven't even called into the office in days, she'll have already started paperwork to fire me. And I'm guessing Dominick won't let me wait tables here anymore, so currently, I'm unemployed."

"And how does that feel?" I ask because she doesn't seem all that upset, which surprises me because I've seen how hard this girl works. If someone could figure out a way to generate electricity from her, she could power half the city.

Maggie grins, sighing happily. "Honestly, I feel free. You have to understand. *The Daily Spot* isn't like working for *CNN* or even *TMZ*. Sure, it was a job, but everyone there—well, nearly everyone—was either trying to scramble their way up the ladder or was bitterly hanging on so they didn't fall down to *Weekly World News* level. It was dog-eat-dog, and not even about important things. Just an overarching sense of desperation and disrespect. And here with you, even though we're basically being held hostage and everything's going to hell right now . . . I feel free."

She smiles, and I'm struck stupid once again at her beauty. I don't know how, or why, but I do think I've freed her of something she's been carrying around for a very long time.

Although I bet if I were to dig deep enough, I'd find out that all I did was help her free herself.

From there, we spend the rest of the afternoon and well into the night talking about our lives, our hopes and dreams, books, TV, and everything in between. It's like we're taking our courtship, the little things that most people learn over the course of weeks or even months of dating, and compressing them into a hyper-speed conversation.

But I don't feel rushed at all. Instead, with every revelation from the mundane to the philosophical, I fall deeper in love with this girl, storing away every tidbit she gives me in my heart.

The heat builds between us, embers always burning just below the surface but spark-flashing into flames, and we pause our conversation to make love or fuck, sometimes both. The pulsing music from the club below occasionally gives us a new tempo to match, leaving us both laughing at times afterward.

With Maggie, even when I'm slamming into her from behind, her hair wrapped in my fist as she cries out, her ass pink from my hand and my marks all over her smooth skin . . . even then, it's a hundred percent love.

Finally, we fall into bed together, happily exhausted.

"Well, at least we've done one thing right," Maggie says as she giggles and lays a naked thigh across my leg.

"What's that?" I ask. "I think we've done a lot of things right today."

"Oh, no doubt. But what I meant was that everyone goes to a strip club to indulge in a sexual fantasy, but it's only that, a fantasy. We get to do the real thing."

"Good point. Now we just need to get a pole up here and—"

Maggie tickles me in the ribs, making me laugh. "And I'll make you dance for me!"

I don't answer, but the reality is if she asked, I damn well might do it.

CHAPTER 23

MAGGIE

*B*y late that night, or technically early the next morning, Shane and I finally lift our heads from being lost in each other and the hopes that there's any way this is going to be okay.

Okay, okay . . . we lift our heads from a nap, but as I told Shane, I'm unemployed.

Soon after the club closes, we carefully head downstairs, as Shane says he wants to check in with Dominick. I sneak backstage and find Allie alone in the locker room.

She's dressed in her silky robe, sitting at a mirrored table to remove the layers of makeup she wears for the stage. "Hey, Allie. How was the show tonight?"

She looks up, meeting my eyes in the mirror, and I can tell she's still mad. Guess I can understand. I mean, I did drop a grenade into the middle of her world.

"No, don't do that," Allie replies, barbs in every word that sting as they hit my eardrums. "Don't ask me shit like how my dancing went or how my night was. Like you care when your whole gig here was fake."

Ouch. I step into the dressing room, really trying. Allie's important to me. "I do care. And it wasn't all fake. Yeah, the job, calling myself Meghan . . . but I meant what I said about feeling like I belonged here and that I found a family."

Allie snorts, her eyes glued to the mirror as she peels her fake lashes off. "I don't know if I should believe that. I mean, you're obviously a good liar, so how can I ever believe what you say?"

I sigh, hugging myself and knowing she's got a point. "You're right, but I swear, Allie. You're one of my best friends, not just in *this* life," I say, indicating the club around us, "but in my whole life. You think I didn't want to let you in all the way? I'm sorry I didn't tell you the truth and that it hurt you."

Allie finally turns around to face me. "This is some really fucked up shit you've gotten me into. I didn't know all that stuff from yesterday."

My eyebrows jump as my jaw drops, and I try to keep my voice to a whisper. "You didn't know about Dominick, about the mob?"

Allie shakes her head, whispering back just in case we're overheard. "No! I mean, I knew Dom was a bigwig, but I thought it was just . . . here, as the owner of a fancy strip club. I didn't know he was *big*, like in charge of the city. Who wants to work in a mob-owned strip club?"

I nod, knowing that especially with Allie's background, that's the last place she ever imagined she'd end up. "So, what happened?"

Allie turns back to her table and starts working on her

makeup again. "That guy's blood was all over me. Dominick carried me into his office and helped me get cleaned up. He was furious, the anger buzzing around him like a force field, but he was gentle with me. Tucked me in on the couch in his office and went out to talk to the guys."

"That was about the time Shane was hustling me out of the club," I reply. "He was so worried about me. Looking back, it was touching."

Allie finally gives me a ghost of a smile, looking into the mirror. "I bet. I don't know what Dom told the guys. I guess I just avoided thinking about it because I was in shock. He gave me a couple of days off, even offered to let me stay upstairs in the apartment you're in, but I just wanted to go home and hide in my own bed, you know? So he drove me there himself and came by morning and night to make sure I ate and was okay. He took care of me, and when he wasn't there, Nick or Logan was downstairs, making sure I was safe. And then you called with the whole meeting thing, and he said he needed me to be there, for him and for you. And the three of you just sat there and spouted off all this big scary shit like it was normal conversation."

I realize that while everyone always teases me about my innocence, this time, it's Allie whose bubble of innocence was burst. "I'm sorry you found out like that. I didn't know what you knew, but we needed you there because we thought Dominick wouldn't hurt us in front of you."

Allie smiles sadly, turning around to face me. "You used me. I figured out that part, at least, and I guess I can see why. I just wish I could go back to being blind to all of this around me. I mean, Dominick's a great guy who's been taking care of me, a good boss who makes it feel safe here, considering it's a strip club. But now, I'm just . . . lost."

Her words break my heart, and I step closer, putting my hands on her shoulders. "You're not lost, Allie. Nothing here has changed. You're still you, Dominick is still Dominick, and I'm still me. Now, the veil is just lifted and you're seeing behind the curtain a bit. It's shocking, but it's better to know the truth, even if it's ugly, than a pretty lie."

Allie puts a hand over mine and looks over her shoulder. "That's me, the pretty tragedy. Don't worry, I'm just still adjusting. I don't know what to think about all of this. Tonight was the first night I've performed since the shooting. I was just in total mind dump mode, not thinking at all. Although I practiced so much at home that I finally got that spinning death-drop move perfected. It was flawless."

I grin, even as her eyebrows pull together. "I might need to rename the move though. Seems a bit dark, considering what's been happening."

I rub her shoulders gently. "Call it whatever you want. Allie, what's awesome about you is how even in the deepest of valleys, you've never given up. You keep working until you find a hilltop, and that's where you make your stand for the next journey. You sort of helped me, too. So many times over the past couple of months, I kept telling myself, 'be like Allie. She'd keep going.' And it was true."

Allie takes a deep breath, nodding. "I like that. So . . . Shane? Is that where you're standing for your next journey?"

I smile, feeling the mood shift to some semblance of before, when we'd dish about how hot the security guys are and lament Dominick's no-fraternizing policy. Even as she cheered me on, she also thought it'd never happen. Guess we were both wrong.

Grabbing a chair, I sit down next to her, grinning foolishly as she raises an eyebrow. "What can I say except . . . he's amazing, even better than what you used to tease me about. The last few days have been scary, especially when we had to explain the huge web of lies and get everything untangled. But he's been there for me, kept me safe."

I sigh, not fully able to put into words everything I feel about Shane.

But Allie seems to understand, grinning mischievously. "I can see he's been there . . . and there, and oh, over there too, twice, by the looks of it," she says cheekily as she indicates the various marks visible on my body. "Is there any part of you he *hasn't* been?"

I blush furiously, proud of Shane's claiming of me but feeling shy that she's pointing them out so . . . individually. "Yeah, he's a little . . . mouthy . . . and possessive. I, uh . . . I like it."

I can feel my face burning even brighter, and Allie smiles.

"Well, that's what matters. And good God, a mouthy man. Bet he gives the best oral! Lucky girl."

She winks at me, and things feel like they're okay, or at least like they might be okay someday. "Hey, you wanna see my spinning death-drop?"

Eager to get the focus off me and Shane and our bedroom activities, I nod. "Yes! Let me see, girl! But only if you're not too tired after your performances tonight."

"Never too tired for you," Allie replies with a snort. "I could use a few more practice spins too. Come on!"

We go onto the floor, where everyone but Marco has already left, and Allie takes her place on stage while I sit at the front row center table. In the background, I can hear Marco working downstairs, probably still cleaning up.

She does a few warmups, and within minutes, she's twirling around the pole, high above the stage floor. There's no music, so it has a different feel. Gone is the sexy sway. It's just the quiet intensity and small grunts as Allie *works* the pole. No wonder they do pole dance fitness classes.

Allie does some kick trick that I couldn't describe even if I tried because it happens so fast, my brain can't even register it. All I see is her stilettoed foot kick out, and then Allie is speeding upside down toward the floor in a spiral with her arms spread wide in a T, and I gasp. "Allie!"

Right before her head smacks into the stage, she grabs the pole and rolls it along her shoulder, her legs straddling open for a moment before she settles to the floor in the splits.

As if she didn't just cheat death and defy gravity, she pulls her feet back under and rises gracefully. "So, what do you think?"

My mouth is still hanging wide open, but I manage to yell out, "Mother trucking smurfin' yeah, biz-nitch!" as I clap loudly. "You're my hero!"

Allie smiles, and I can see the pride on her face, even as she downplays it. "Yeah, it's not ballet, for damn sure, but it sure is fun!"

From the side of the stage, I hear a door open and close, and both our eyes snap that direction. But it's only Marco coming up from the stockroom, boxes of beer in his hands.

He sees me and immediately sets them down. "Holy fuck, Meghan! Where have you been? You okay?"

I run over and give him a hug, and Allie joins in. The three of us hug like it's been years instead of days, and even though Marco called me by the wrong name, I feel at home.

It doesn't matter that it's a strip club or that there's more to the story than we planned.

I'm home with these people.

Guess Shane's right. There is a bit of bad girl inside me.

CHAPTER 24

SHANE

I stand on Dominick's left, Nick to the right as we knock once on the door of the large brownstone near downtown. That we're even here is just shy of batshit crazy, but it's Dom's show. I'm just the muscle who may or may not have to pull out his FBI badge along with a gun at some point.

"You sure?" Nick, who doesn't know the full story, asks. "I mean, this place—"

"If you don't have the balls, Nick, I suggest you leave," Dom says, not turning his eyes from the door. "I'd rather go in with just Shane having my back than someone who doesn't have balls."

Nick swallows but stands his ground. The door opens, and though the muscled man who answers doesn't say it, his surprise is written clear as day on his face.

Dominick doesn't pause or look at all worried as he adjusts the cuffs on his perfectly tailored suit. In a tasteful black, of course, befitting the occasion. "Good afternoon. We're here to pay our respects for the loss."

You can tell the goon wants to object, or at a minimum wants to pat us all down, but what's the use when we're all obviously carrying weapons at our sides? Instead, he steps to the side, giving a respectful nod. "Please come in, Mr. Angeline."

We enter as a group, both for security and to make sure that we can't get separated. Inside, the wake is loud and boisterous, more of a party than the somber affair of a man who just lost his son unexpectedly and tragically. Actually, considering that I hear what seems to be Latin music playing, it sounds like a damn graduation party.

Still, when Dominick enters the room, a hush falls over the gathering and eyes dart left and right, obviously confused about his appearance. The music stops, and the only sound is one kid who's in the corner and obviously doesn't quite understand what's happening as he keeps doing some lame ass jig until someone pops him in the shoulder.

Fortunately, no one pulls a weapon. From an armchair in the center of the room, a man with slicked back ebony hair and large thick-framed glasses stands up. I've never met him, but for the past year plus some, I've made sure I'm intimately aware of his face. He's old enough to be Dominick's father, and considerably larger, but there's no mistaking who the real alpha male in the room is.

Sal Rivaldi might try and push his way into East Robinsville, but Dominick isn't going to let that happen with a breath in his body. Even in his thirties, Dominick is the king of this city and wears his invisible crown like a man with experience and the balls to back whatever play he has deemed correct.

It matters not if the battle is physical or mental. I'd bet on Dominick to win every time.

Looking as if he were standing in his own church instead of the wake of his biggest rival's son, Dominick extends his hand toward the older man. "Don Rivaldi, I wish to extend my most sincere apologies on the loss of your son. Word of his character had spread throughout the city, and you must be devastated."

Damn, he is a slick son of a bitch. Not many men could make an expression of sympathy include a backhanded comment about what a shitstain your son was, while also letting it be known that nothing happens in your city without your knowledge. And the use of the term 'Don'. Very smooth, in that it both gives Sal respect, while at the same time saying he's behind the times. Dominick's never insisted on being called Don. In fact, I've never heard anyone under the age of sixty use the term with him.

Rivaldi dips his chin in acknowledgement but keeps his eyes on Dominick the whole time. "Please, we are past all these niceties. You can call me Sal."

I hide a smirk. Dad used to listen to an old song that sounded a lot like that. Dominick looks genuinely pleased, although probably because in the subtle game of mob bosses, he was just elevated in the Rivaldi family's eyes. "Of course, Sal. And you may call me Dominick."

Everyone notices the infinitesimal put-down. Sal said that Dominick could use his casual name, while Dominick insisted on his full first name. Nearly, but not quite the same level, and Sal knows it. They eye each other for a moment, the tension in the room building, but Dominick stays cool as a cucumber, no tension in his body even though I know he could snap into asskicking mode in an instant. "Sal, the timing may be indelicate, but I wondered if we could speak?"

Sal looks like he might start something but then relents. "Yes, of course." He gestures to the chair next to the one he just vacated. Sal moves to a bar in the corner, lifting a decanter of what's either scotch or something similar. "Drink?"

My training says to never, ever accept a drink from an enemy. Especially alcohol. It's too easy to hide shit in there. But Dom operates by his own rules and instead nods easily, confident that Sal wouldn't be stupid enough to try something. "That would be lovely. Thank you."

Dominick takes the amber liquid from Sal and swirls it in the glass before resting it on the arm of the chair. Sal sits, the excitement obvious in his eyes. He thinks he's gotten one over, that he's actually going to take over the city from a man clearly his better in every way.

I'm reminded of the saying, *'Pride goeth before the fall.'* because Sal has no idea the precipice he's standing on. I take station behind Dominick, while Nick stands a few feet away, his eyes scanning the rest of the group as quiet, tense conversation begins anew.

"I wanted to discuss some things with you," Dominick leads off, still swirling his drink as he looks Sal in the eye. "Some rather troubling things I've heard about your organization."

Sal doesn't move, but the light in his eyes turns more suspicious and the tension in the room pulls even tighter. The room is silent, with only an occasional whispered comment as everyone keeps their eyes on the two bosses. I scan, noting the guy to my left who just unbuttoned his jacket, a sure sign he's getting twitchy.

"What things have you heard?" Sal asks, sipping his drink. Dominick, though, keeps his glass swirling, almost maddeningly. The liquid never stops moving and Dom's gaze never wavers. Motion and stillness, attack and patience . . . both Dominick's strong suits, and something everyone in the room is well aware of.

"Word on the street is that you'd like to expand your stronghold, which I can, of course, understand," Dominick says casually, as if he's discussing the weather. "I can even appreciate your ambition. But you forget your position of power is in *my* city simply because I allow it to be. And your growth, or lack thereof, is also at my discretion."

Sal sneers, his fingers tightening on his glass. "I'm sure you'd like to think that, wouldn't you? But I own parts of this city because I work them when you don't. The people there fear me, not you. They need my drugs, my protection, not yours."

Dominick nods, still unruffled. "Perhaps. But that is because I've let you have the scraps from my table, the areas that are too troublesome for the meager dollars I could wring out of them. Do not think that I've not kept my fingers on the pulse of those areas, nor that I could not cut off that pulse with a single twitch of my fingers if I wished. I haven't concerned myself with your actions. Until now."

Sal feigns a look of surprise, trying to regain his balance. "My actions? I've done nothing but continue my business as usual. Yet, here we are, mourning my son. Dead in your club, let us not forget."

Sal is playing up the sympathy card with the audience.

Dominick chuckles, playing to the audience as well as he turns away from Sal to look around the room, speaking to those watching. "Ah, yes, Carlos Rivaldi. The bastard son who shows up out of the blue, full of ego and demanding his birthright. Must have put you in an uncomfortable position, not able to deny your blood-son, but he was just so . . ." Dominick pauses dramatically before locking eyes with Sal, "*weak*. And ungrateful for the scraps you gave him. I dare say, he was much like his father. And how did you handle this?"

Sal stammers, his voice quaking with rage and an undercurrent of worry that tells me he's scared of what Dominick might say. "I gave him every chance, and then he gets killed on a simple mission."

Dominick smirks, knowing he's totally in control of the conversation and where it's heading. "No, I don't think you gave him every chance. You knew he was weak, ungrateful, and power-hungry, so *you* had him killed. On my territory. Such disrespect and ugliness. Especially the part where you've been blaming me for his death to anyone who'd listen."

The reaction to Dominick's revelation is instant, the crowd of men all murmuring and looking at one another. Sal rears up, finding indignation in Dominick's accusation. "I would never! He was my *son*!"

"Perhaps so," Dominick says before dropping the bomb I know he's had planned this whole time. "In which case you should know that I am also hunting the *hitman* who conducted his business on my grounds. I will have revenge for that insult, and it will be slow and painful. I'll make sure that he tells me *everything* I wish to know. But beyond that, I would say that having a son who is such a disappointment, who even in a sacrificial death was not able to serve your ends, is punishment enough. Although his mother's Colombian family may not feel the same way." Dominick locks eyes with the dark-haired man we all know is the Colombian's representative at the wake.

Dominick lets that sink in for a moment, silently watching Sal's face for any response as he realizes that his plan is backfiring in his face. With shaking fingers, he downs the rest of his drink, the ice in the tumbler chattering when he sets it down. "So you're not here to discuss war."

Dominick looks amused again and chuckles lightly. "I'm merely here to extend my apologies for your son, and perhaps to share some advice with a fellow businessman."

"Oh, and what's that?"

Dominick stops his swirling scotch and tosses it back in one practiced movement, not reacting at all as it burns its way down his throat to explode in his stomach. He sets the empty glass on the table in front of him pointedly, commanding every eye in the room with his presence. "When you are being allowed to scurry and play like mice, it is best to not draw the attention of the cat. Because once the cat has set his sights on you, it's difficult to circumvent his instincts. His instincts to hunt, to destroy, to own. In the scheme of life, the cat worries not about the mice. They are inconsequential until they become a nuisance. Then, the cat takes delight in playing with them, until eventually, he kills them."

Sal looks a bit flushed, the tip of his olive nose and cheeks ruddy with fury, and maybe alcohol, but he manages to keep it together, trying to save face with the room full of his men who are now looking at him with new eyes. "Excellent advice, I'm sure. Thank you."

Dominick rises, indicating the conversation is over. As he nears the door, Nick and I still shadowing him, he turns around. "Oh, Sal. I was discussing the shooting with my team when a curious thing occurred to me."

Sal, who's whispering furiously to an underling, looks up. "Oh?"

"In watching the security feeds, it seems the hitman never entered the club through the front door," Dominick reveals. "In fact, it seems he entered through a back door and completed the hit during an irregular blip in our surveillance. Most unusual, wouldn't you agree?"

Sal nods, a smarmy smile crossing his face. "Yes, must've been his lucky day."

Bad move, and Dom just won the war without even firing a single shot. With his words, Sal just unintentionally confirmed Dominick's version of events in front of his entire crew. The men look angry . . . at Sal.

Dominick nods, letting things play out with just one more nudge in the right direction to let Sal destroy himself. "I don't particularly believe in luck myself. I believe in planning and strategy. And I asked myself, what would be my plan for a job like this? It took me a moment to come to terms with my answer, admittedly because I wanted to refuse the truth, but truth is apathetic, neither caring whether we want it or not. It simply is . . . true."

In a lightning-fast move that I can barely follow, Dominick turns and punches Nick square in the jaw, sending him crashing to the floor. I drop my foot back to steady my stance, keeping my eyes on everyone but Dominick, knowing he can handle himself with Nick on the floor. Everyone in the room is frozen, on high alert, but not getting involved . . . yet.

"*An inside man.* That's what he needed to get in and out unde-tected," Dominick growls, bending down to grab a handful of Nick's hair and slamming his face to the floor. "Someone in the club had to let him in the back door and mess with the security feed."

Dominick slams a heel on Nick's knee, the crack audible even as Nick cries out in agony. I see Rivaldi men tensing, but this isn't a matter they can involve themselves in. Dom is beating the shit out of his own man. Besides, they know I've got the drop on the whole room, my pistol in my hand but not drawn yet.

Dominick trusts that I'm watching the room, a huge move on his part, He ignores the gathered men, instead addressing Nick, his voice rising in anger. "Even once I admitted that someone in my organization had to have been in on it, I didn't want it to be you. You were the good soldier, I thought. But it lined up. It was you. Did you even try to catch him when you pursued him? I doubt it."

Nick is trying to crawl away, but Dominick stomps on his right hand, twisting his heel to get every finger. The bones sound like twigs being broken, and Nick collapses, rolling onto his back and cradling his ruined hand to his chest. "Dom—"

Dominick grabs Nick's shirt, pulling him face to face. "I trusted you, Nick. And you repaid me with betrayal, working for the little mice and their hired gun. For what? Money? Power? You think they'll trust you when you've already turned once?" Dominick sneers in disgust. His voice quiets, the amount of control scarier than if he was raging. "Not killing you today is a kindness for the years of service you did give me. But if I ever see you again, I *will* kill you."

And with the final threat, Dominick lands one last powerful punch to Nick's nose and blood splatters. Dominick drops him, reaching into his pocket with his clean hand to retrieve his handkerchief and meticulously wiping the blood away.

I reach down, taking Nick's gun while Dominick finishes up, turning back to Sal and sounding like nothing's happened. "I'll leave this trash for you. Not sure he'll be of any use to you with a bum knee, fucked trigger finger, and buyable loyalty. But he is *your* man after all. I trust there won't be a repeat of this issue."

Sal looks from Dominick's stone-cold eyes to Nick, groaning in agony on the floor, and seems to realize that he'd severely underestimated just how smart and how batshit-crazy Dominick really is. "No, Mr. Angeline."

Satisfied, Dominick walks out the door, stepping over Nick dismissively. I wish I could do the same, but the anger in me is too much to bear. Nick is part of the machine that put my Angel in danger.

I can't do anything about Sal right now. I can't get my hands on the hitman the way I'd like, but I trusted Nick and Maggie trusted Nick. He was the guy I thought was my most trusted coworker.

So I give in, kicking him as hard as I can in the gut with my steel-toed boot. Nick screams, curling protectively into a fetal position. He probably deserves more of a beatdown, but I'm done.

I follow Dominick out, getting behind the wheel to drive him back to Petals. Outside, we stay silent until we pull away. "Shane."

"Yes?" I ask, looking up into the rearview mirror. If he did want to kill me, this would be the best time. He could shoot me through the seat. He's buckled in, and we're not going that fast.

Dom's eyes meet mine in the mirror, icy grey and hard. "I wanted to handle that myself. It was necessary for an appearance of strength and knowledge," he explains, finally answering the question I'd asked in his office when I checked in with him last night. The conversation had led to some rather unsightly conclusions after I reviewed the remaining security video and we'd talked through different possibilities of what happened. "The hitman on the other hand . . . if you would like, you may have your turn. Or I can take care of that as well. Your choice. For now though, let's go back to the club."

Back to Maggie.

CHAPTER 25

MAGGIE

I pace back and forth in the apartment, trying my best not to get freaked out. When Shane told me last night that he was going with Dominick on a mission to hopefully prevent the war that could ruin the city, I begged him not to go. I was nearly paralyzed with terror that it was a setup by Dominick.

But Shane said that he and Dominick talked things through, and he felt like he needed to back Dom's play. He also promised he'd be safe before we made love and he left a few new souvenirs along my skin.

But since they left, I've been jittery with nerves that I'll never see him again. Knowing I need to keep busy, I give up pacing and decide to check in with my regular life . . . the one I had before everything went so haywire.

I can't believe that Dominick's let me have access to a computer, but he did. After our first night here, I gave Allie my keys, and she went to my apartment, coming back with some clothes and my laptop. Dominick didn't even ask to go through my files. "Maggie," he said, "anything you have that you've already published can't be pulled back, and anything you have in there that you could publish, I trust you won't." He said it kindly, but the threat was apparent in his simple words.

A quick run through my email deletes most of the spam, but there are several from Jeanine at work. She's left several voicemails on my phone that were forwarded to my email program too, but after two, I turn them off. It's best to go straight to the source.

I grab the burner phone Shane left me, dialing into the office and waiting for the receptionist to transfer me to Jeanine's office line. I get lucky. I'm not left hanging on hold for long.

"Jeanine Matthews."

"Hi, Jeanine. It's Maggie. I wanted to call to—"

Before I can even get my greeting out, Jeanine interrupts me, her voice crisp and hard. "You have some nerve calling in like this. You drop off the face of the Earth, don't return my calls or meet deadlines for nearly a week, and now you just call in? You should've just stayed gone."

She's mad. Still, some professional instinct guides me to try to patch things up so I'm not leaving under the pall of job abandonment. "Ma'am, I had an emergency and I couldn't call in or check emails for a while. I'm back now and trying to catch up."

Jeanine stops her rant, greed tingeing her voice. Toss her a sniff about a headline, and she'd let me get away with murder. "Anything story-worthy?"

If only she knew, but she thinks I'm just a strip-club waitress looking for celebrity gossip. She has no idea about the depth of how things go at Petals, who Dominick is, or any of the things I've learned over the last few days. And this is a story I wouldn't touch with a ten-foot pole. Dominick's shown me some trust. I'm not stupid enough to betray that.

"No, just a family emergency."

It's not really a lie because the people at Petals are my family now, and while it might take me awhile, I plan on regaining their trust, if that's possible.

Jeanine sighs, annoyance making her drag it out longer than usual. "Unacceptable, Miss Postland. We have standards, the least of which is that you turn in quality work on time. Abandoning your job and your duties cannot stand. You're fired," she jeers, obviously enjoying the opportunity to shut me down. "I wish you all the best in your future waitressing endeavors."

I'm not surprised. I figured this would be coming, even told Shane as much when we discussed it. But now that it's real and actually happening, I thought I might be upset. But all I feel is relief . . . free. And it's a bit funny that she thinks getting fired is such a big deal, considering I'm on the run from a hitman trying to kill me. Losing a crappy job is the least of my concerns.

Instead of laughing like I want, I clear my throat, but still, my voice is light, maybe even hinging on giggly when I respond. "I understand, Jeanine. If you could please have the HR department mail me my last check. My apologies. It's been *interesting* working for you."

It's as close as I can get to telling her that she's a shrew whom people mimic at the office. Hanging up, I let the laughter overtake me. "I'm fired!" I cheer as I throw my hands up and laugh uproariously. "Bwahahahaha, I'm actually fired!"

I'm still basically a prisoner for my own safety, but I truly feel free. No more lies—with Jeanine, with Dominick, with Allie, and most importantly, with Shane. Knowing I need to make one more call, I dial my mother, but only to tell her I'm fine, not filling her in on recent events.

Luckily, she wasn't worried about me, saying she figured I was just busy with work and stuff. It's hard to imagine, but it's really only been days since this whole debacle started. It feels like so much longer. So much has happened. So much might happen still. And Mom never has really asked about my job. I think she's still disappointed I didn't become an accountant or a lawyer or get some nice office job where I could meet a 'good man'.

Well, guess what, Mom? I've met, bedded, and laid claim to not just a good man, but an amazing man. And if I live another month, who knows where Shane and I will be? We're moving so fast already.

I feel the smile spread wide across my face, the happiness bubbling out unbidden. I turn the phone off and lay down on the couch, eyes on the door as I wait for Shane to get back.

I have to trust that he and Dominick are going to come back. That I'll be safe again. That I'll have a chance to figure out what to do from here. That Shane and I will figure out a way to be together.

I don't nap, but the time just sort of slips by. Still, when I hear the familiar heavy tread of his footsteps coming up the stairs, I'm waiting for him. "Angel, I'm—"

Shane doesn't have a chance to finish his greeting as I throw myself across the little apartment, laughing and leaping into his arms to smother his face in kisses. With each smooch, relief and happiness course through me. He wraps his arms around me, picking me up higher and using my momentum to spin us in a circle as we kiss.

It feels like I haven't seen him in forever, even though it's only been a few hours. I was just so scared.

Pulling back, Shane looks deep into my eyes. "Damn, Angel. That's a welcome home I could get used to."

I smile, kissing him again, softly this time. "I missed you today. I was worried."

Shane sets me down, cupping my face in his hands. "I told you, we're gonna be okay. Today was a step in the right direction, and Dominick handled Sal like a boss."

"A boss?" I ask, and Shane laughs.

"Well, more like The Boss. It went well, and I think we prevented the war. Sal's guys know what he did, how he tried to manipulate and lie and killed his own son. I don't imagine them charging into Dominick's territory after his display today. Hell, half of them probably want to work for Dominick now, and the other half pray they never have to see him again."

I smile, trying to imagine Dominick as a monster who would make grown men shake in their boots, but I just can't. Dominick is scary, no doubting that, but he's civilized and has a code of honor. I can't picture him getting rough and dirty.

"So, one crisis averted? One to go?"

Shane looks at me, then nods. "Yeah, Angel. For now, all we can do is stay here, wait for intel, and be safe. Dom even found a mole who let the hitman in. It was Nick."

"Nick? Really?" I ask, disappointed. "He seemed like a nice guy."

"Maybe he was, but it doesn't matter," Shane says, kissing my forehead once. "You're what matters. We can relax for a bit. Chucky and Dom are both looking into the hitman issue, so we should know something soon, but for now, all we can do is wait."

He lays his cheek against the top of my head, hugging me close. It's sweet and comforting, but that's not what I want. I don't want to be babied and kept like a fragile doll he's scared to break.

I want to celebrate that things are getting better—freedom from my job, hope that there won't be a war—to celebrate this moment as the gift it is.

My cheek pressed to his chest, I reach down, letting my hand roam closer and closer to his waistband. "Well, that's not *all* we can do . . ."

Shane looks down at me, and I bite my lip, waiting to see what he says, what he'll do. He's searching for something in my eyes, some sign that I'm really okay with everything that's happening.

I can't wait any longer for him to decide and force the issue by lifting up to my tiptoes and using his shoulders as leverage to press my mouth to his. I lick the seam of his lips, begging him to open for me as my free hand reaches down to cup him through his pants.

It's all it takes to wipe away the last of his worries, and it's the last moment I'm in charge. His tongue presses into my mouth, consuming me as he pulls my hair, tilting my face higher toward him.

A moan escapes me, and Shane answers with a growl. Holding me in his strong arms, he carries me across the room into the living room, but our mouths never break contact. Instead, he's guided by some form of internal radar or something until he reaches the middle of the room. He sets me down, immediately ripping my long T-shirt over my head and slipping my panties to the floor.

I stand there, naked and wanting as he pulls his clothes off with almost unnatural speed. His cock is hard, reaching toward his belly button, and I can see a drop of clear precum on the head. I want it and unconsciously, I lick my lips as my knees start to bend.

Shane notices and smirks. "You want to taste me again, Angel? It's yours. I'm yours."

I drop all the way to my knees and look up at Shane from the floor. "Then give it to me."

I stick my tongue out as Shane grasps his cock, guiding the tip to my outstretched tongue, and the flavor of the salty drop explodes across my tongue, making me whimper for more. I want to worship him, to show him that he's my everything.

Shane slides a hand into my hair, holding me still, and slips his tip along my tongue, teasing me, teasing himself as he reads my eyes, nodding. I cover his shaft in little butterfly kisses and lollipop licks until he shudders, his control stretched as far as he can take it. "Fuck, Maggie," he growls, pulling my hair tighter. "Suck me."

It's all the permission I need to take back a bit of control, and I close my lips around him, letting my tongue dance around his slit before bobbing up and down along his shaft, setting a fierce pace.

I hollow my cheeks, sucking him hard and delighting at the sounds I'm drawing from him. I reach up, my fingers digging into the dimples on his powerful ass muscles as I pull him in all the way. He's mine, and I'm his . . . his loving, worshipful woman who can take all he has.

All too soon, though, he pulls back, squeezing tight at the base of his shaft as he shakes his head. "Not yet. I want to come inside that sweet little pussy."

I nod, smiling as Shane offers me a hand, helping me rise from his feet and then immediately turning me so that my back is to his front. The entire skin of my back is pressed against him as I look over my shoulder while he cups my breasts. He guides me toward the couch near the wall. It's big, and when he pushes me over the high arm of the couch, my toes barely reach the floor while he gets me positioned the way he wants.

"Damn, Angel," Shane says, his voice raspy and heavy with need. "You look so pretty like this, ass up in the air so I can see your wet little pussy, so ready for my cock. Only one thing could make it better."

I'm squirming, needy, so when he bends down, I expect a nice lick to my soaked core. But that's not what Shane does, my mouthy, possessive man.

He swipes a thumb through my folds and bites low on my ass, right at the meaty part above my thighs, and the sharp prick of pain blends with the pleasure as he strokes me. I cry out, arching my back for more, but Shane stands, and I look over my shoulder.

He's licking his thumb, sucking my juices from his skin and moaning at the flavor. "Always so sweet . . . but I think I'm turning you into a dirty girl, Angel."

"A naughty angel for my devil with a heart of gold. I am a dirty girl, Shane . . . *your* dirty girl."

The words set him off, and with a growl, he slams into me balls-deep and immediately begins pumping in and out, hard and fast. I reach back, wanting to feel him piston into me, my nails scratching along the skin of his hips. I can't see them, but I know I'm marking him too, little pink lines proclaiming him as mine. I dream that maybe those marks will be permanent, maybe something that we can share.

Shane grabs one of my hands, pulling it to my lower back and locking it in place with a tight grip. His other hand twists tightly into my hair, and I'm at his mercy, pinned down and getting *fucked*. Even to myself, the word sounds filthy, and that turns me on even more. I mewl, whining as I beg him.

"Yes Shane . . . fuck me . . . please . . ."

He pulls me tighter, his voice a low, growling demand. "What did you say?"

I don't know if he likes it or hates it, and right now, I don't care because it's all I can manage to say. "Fuck me, Shane. Fuck. Me. Hard."

He leans over me, covering my back with his body and pressing me into the couch arm, one hand still trapped between us. "Mmm, my fucking *dirty* Angel." He strokes into me again and again, filling and stretching me as I whimper, begging for more. "Come for me."

He suckles the flesh along my shoulder into his mouth, marking me once again, and I feel pushed harder than ever. His cock is so deep, and I cry out in pleasure and pain.

The moment stretches, both of us on the precipice forever,

riding that edge before I fall off, crashing into my orgasm, and Shane comes too, ropes of his hot cum filling me. It drives me more, my pleasure drawing out like a rope too, going on and on as I scream hoarsely. I'm calling out his name and swearing that I'm his as his deep bellow accompanies my cries in a symphony as we finish together.

CHAPTER 26

SHANE

*W*e spend the rest of the evening in the apartment, relaxing. For several hours, we can hear the music booming below us as the club carries on business as usual. We'd done the same, continuing our rounds of talking and lovemaking, pausing to eat and chat before our passions overtake us again.

Around two in the morning, Maggie mentions going downstairs to see Allie, but after the run-in with the Rivaldis, I'm uneasy. "Angel, I know Dominick seems to think this is all handled, and I'm hopeful he's right, but sometimes, a cornered animal is the meanest, and I'm nervous Sal is going to be desperate enough to do something crazy."

"But what about Allie and Dom and . . . well, everyone downstairs?"

I nod, hugging her tightly. "I know. But I can't protect them all. I can protect you, though, and it'd make me feel a lot better if you had Allie come up here rather than us go downstairs."

She agrees, and Allie's actually willing to hang out a bit before she heads home so we can all grab some shut eye. Waking up at noon, Maggie and I eat a simple breakfast of Golden Grahams and tea before sneaking downstairs carefully to check in with Dominick.

I knock on his door, my usual two raps, and from inside, I hear him. "Come in, Shane."

We enter, and he turns around from his desk, smirking that he knew simply by my knock. "Please, sit."

He motions to the chairs sitting in front of his desk, and we sink into them. I notice Maggie has her knees pulled to her chest again, her arms wrapped around her legs. It makes me worry, but I know it'll take her awhile to feel comfortable in Dominick's presence now. "Thanks. Just wanted to check in."

Dom nods, stroking his chin. "So you've heard."

I furrow my brow, confused. I came down for a general check-in and to see if there was a way for Maggie and me to safely stretch our legs. "Heard? Heard what?"

Dominick leans back in his chair, relaxing. "Have you been in contact with . . ." He seems to be searching for a word, an uncommon occurrence for a man who uses words like sharp knives. "Your handlers?"

I look to Maggie and then shake my head. "I don't really have one. An unofficial contact, but making official contact is . . . dramatic."

Dominick smiles, seemingly laughing inside. "Perhaps you should check in with them. At least your unofficial contact."

He doesn't seem inclined to give me privacy for the call, so I reach into my pocket and speed-dial Chucky, putting the phone to my ear.

The line connects with silence, and I talk first, keeping Chucky's name out of it lest Dominick get curious for more information. It may be a nickname, but I wouldn't put it past Dom to find out Chucky's real name and entire history in less than forty-eight hours if he was motivated to do so. "Hey, man. It's Shane."

Chucky sounds excited, panting as he greets me. "Damn, dude, you must have balls of fucking steel! Everyone here is talking about how Dominick walked into Sal's house, in the middle of a fucking wake, told all his shit to the whole damn crew, including the Colombians, and then beat the shit out of a traitor. And you just stood there, sweet as you please, with no reaction."

Interesting. Guess they didn't hear about my kicking the shit out of Nick on my way out. Probably a good thing, considering everything else. I never actually met the man the FBI put in the Rivaldi family, but he must not have been present. The FBI wouldn't ignore my beating the fuck out of Nick like that. The boot to the gut on a downed man was definitely past 'appropriate use of force.'

"Yeah," I reply airily, though, trying to play it off. "That's pretty much what happened."

"Weren't you shitting your pants that Dominick was going to kill you?" Chucky asks, still panting a little. "I mean, I know you're in Dom's custody, but it would've been real fucking easy for him to say he was taking you to Sal's and then dump your body in the river. Probably even keep the girl for himself."

I look at Dominick, considering what happened in the car

yesterday, and make up my mind. "No, if he wanted me dead, I would be. He's a man of his word and said he'd help, so I trusted him to follow through."

Chucky whoops like a teenager at a pop concert, and I have to pull my phone away for a moment to wince. "That's some top-notch loyalty there, man. Not sure I'd trust anyone that that much, even if they were player one in the game."

"It's not a game, man. Any other updates? Word on the hitman?" I ask, getting irritated at Chucky's casualness considering this is my life. Maggie's life.

Chucky whistles, obviously surprised. "You haven't heard about the hitman?"

There's something to Chucky's tone, a weirdness I can't place. I look to Dominick, who's eyes are crinkling a bit . . . in amusement? "No, I haven't heard. What is it?"

"Sal Rivaldi woke up this morning to find the hitman dead . . . in his living room . . . sitting up in his fucking throne of a chair . . . and none of the guards saw a thing." Chucky delivers the details with dramatic pauses for effect, and it works.

"So, he's dead?" I ask, a little disappointed. The bastard almost killed my woman and put a groove in my left bicep that's going to leave a wicked scar. I wanted to at least get a little bit of a receipt on that.

Chucky laughs darkly, obviously pleased, although I know if he found a dead body in his living room, someone would need to call an ambulance for his heart attack. "Yeah, you could fucking say that. That's not even the best part, though." I wait, knowing Chucky will tell me when he's ready. Finally, he laughs. "The best part is that on the coffee table were a handful of bullet cases, presumed to be the brass from Carlos's shooting, and an invoice . . . for the repairs to Petals's private room!" Chucky is wheezing, laughter taking his breath away, and I can't help but smile. Dominick is a twisted, manipulative son of a bitch and a damn scary motherfucker.

I like him. Too bad we officially have to be enemies when this is all said and done.

Chucky is winding down, getting himself under control while I study Dom, who's openly grinning now. "You know, I gotta ask. Everyone knows Dominick either did it or had it done, but you're the inside guy. You know anything?"

I grin back at Dominick, who's watching me with interest, and lean back before forming a casual reply. "Nope, Dominick came back here after we went to the Rivaldis' and was here all night. It was business as usual at Petals."

"Yeah, figured he wouldn't have you in on any of the dirty work," Chucky says. There's a rustle on Chucky's end, and he seems to messing around with something on his computer from the clicking sounds. "The office thinks you're clear. Word I've got here is that you can make official contact, mission accomplished, and you can exfil now. Report in when you're out."

"Understood," I reply before hanging up the phone. I look over at Dominick, who's still watching me. "Seems the hitman has been taken care of, rather spectacularly. Better than anything I could've done for sure." Dominick tilts his head, a pleased smirk on his face as he accepts the compliment and understands that I'm thanking him while not saying that he actually did anything because that would be dangerous. "We're clear."

Maggie stutters, her voice a near-whisper. "Really? We're safe?"

And then she turns to Dominick, the question in her eyes, knowing he's really the one who decides if we're safe or not. He nods once, his face schooled back into tightly a controlled blankness. "Yes. "Yes, you're safe. But do not forget our agreement. If I have need of you, I will use you as a resource. Otherwise, you will not return."

Maggie nods, then opens and closes her mouth like she has something to say. Dominick waits patiently, not encouraging her but not dismissing her either.

"What about Allie?" she asks desperately. "Can I still talk to her?"

Dominick smiles, and I think I see a bit of melt in that frost behind his eyes. "If Allie wishes to speak with you, I would not prevent something that makes her happy. I personally think you two have had a good effect on each other and make good friends. However, if she doesn't want to talk, I will support her choice to cut you out of her life."

Maggie nods, still encouraged. "Thank you, sir."

Dominick smirks at the turn of phrase and gives me a knowing look. "Maggie," I say calmly, "can you wait outside for a second? I need to talk to Dominick."

She bites her lip, uncertain, but nods. "Yeah, I'll go backstage and see if Allie is here yet. Maybe she can show me her new move again."

She leaves, and both our eyes follow her out. When the door closes, Dominick turns back to me with a look I've not seen before. It's like he's showing me a glimpse behind his mask, to the real man he is underneath the mob boss persona. "She is an unusual find, Shane. I told you once that a man like you would break her, and then I'd be forced to break you as well. I find that perhaps I was wrong. She is stronger than I gave her credit for, although if you hurt her, I think I'd still find myself inclined to take the offense out on you."

"No need. If I hurt her, I'd punish myself more than you ever could," I reply honestly. "Even with your . . . creativity. I do appreciate the way you make a statement, that flair for the dramatic when warranted," I tell him, smiling as I envision the brass balls it must've taken to pull off a stunt like that.

Dominick inclines his head, smirking. "And I appreciated your company last night while I was at the club." The lie is crystal clear, but only because Dominick allows me to see it. He could lie to me easily, but he's telling me in just a few words that he's approving the lie I told, giving him an alibi.

"So, we can leave?" I ask, moving things along. "No offense. Your apartment is nice, but we've stopped the war, sent Sal scampering back to the dark, stopped the threat of the hitman, and you know the truth about everything. It seems our agreement has been met. And I'd like to be able to get some fresh air and sunlight with the woman I love."

Dominick nods, his mask coming back into place. "Yes, same as I told Miss . . . as I told Maggie. I'll reach out if I need you. However, for you in particular, Shane, there is something else. You mentioned that you were placed in my organization, and another FBI agent into Rivaldi's. Is that agent still in play?"

I nod, already seeing where this is going. "Yes, that agent is in place. I don't know his name, though. It's standard FBI procedure. That way, if one of us got outed, we couldn't be tortured to reveal the other."

Dominick nods in understanding. "I thought so. A policy I've used myself when I've had to send men . . . undercover. But, if any information comes up that would be either potentially beneficial or harmful to me, I trust that you will reach out to share?"

He's smiling, but there's an implied threat to his words, and I know that he would see a lack of information sharing as an insult. "Of course. I assume your phone number won't be changing?"

Dominick laughs softly. "Well, it might, but even if so, the number for Petals won't. I'm sure you'll keep that number around."

I nod, then rise and offer him a hand. "You are an interesting man, Dominick Angeline. Regardless of the initial reason for my placement, I have enjoyed working with you. I like you."

Dominick shakes my hand, pulling me closer to his desk. "I like you too, Shane Guthrie. Hope to *not* see you around my town."

I chuckle at his slickness, a compliment tied up in an 'I know who you are' threat with a bonus order to get out of dodge. He's one of a kind.

CHAPTER 27

MAGGIE

*I*t feels weird to walk through the quiet main room of Petals, knowing I'll likely never return. I look around the room, seeing the dinginess to everything in the light of day.

But somehow, it makes it feel comfortable. I like knowing that table nine is a little wobbly so you have to be careful setting the beers down or else you'll have slop to mop up, or that the fastest route from the bar to the private rooms is to take the outside loop even though it's twenty-five extra steps, but there are no grabby hands to get in your way. The biggest thing, though, is knowing that the people here are my friends.

I mean, what else can you say when Allie and a bunch of the dancers and waitresses are here to say goodbye? I have no idea what Allie told them to cover up the reason. But even Marco's here, looking slick as always, even as his practiced smirk looks a little faded at the edges..

I give Allie a big hug, still loving that she's promised we'll get together soon. "I think we'll have to get you a bright slutty red when we get together for mani-pedis next time," she teases, looking over my shoulder at Shane before giving me a wink. "And some sweet gel nails that are guaranteed not to break when you scratch someone's back."

The other dancers laugh along with me while I give hugs all around. When everyone's wished me well, I turn to Marco, who's talking quietly with Shane. The two shake hands, and Marco turns to me. "You know, it's not gonna be the same without you around."

"Oh, you'll just have to be more careful with those harassing comments," I joke, making Marco laugh. I give him a big hug, patting his back. "You make sure you stay out of trouble, you got me?"

"Never." Marco laughs, hugging me back and picking me up. Shane looks a little jealous, which makes Marco and I both laugh. "Relax, Dragon. I'm not gonna try and take a girl who settled for your ugly ass."

Shane laughs, flipping him off. "Fuck you, man."

I don't get the inside joke between them, but it seems good-natured as they bro-hug. Shane shakes hands with a few of the girls and gives a quick hug to Allie, and then we're done. As we approach the door, I look up, seeing Dominick watching us. He doesn't say a word, just stands in the doorway of his office, watching us, but I wave goodbye and smile anyway. Dominick had sent someone for Shane's truck days ago, so it's waiting in the parking lot for us.

I curl into the passenger seat, tears already starting to slip down my cheeks. Shane looks over and wipes them away with a gentle thumb. "Hey, what's wrong?"

I shake my head, kissing the ball of his thumb softly. "It just feels . . . final. Like I'm not going to see them again, you know?"

"Angel, you literally just made plans with Allie for this weekend," he reminds me. "You two are going to be thick as thieves, and I doubt I'm gonna get two minutes of you to myself. That's the definition of *not final*."

I smile through the tears, chuckling. "You're right. It just feels like I'm saying goodbye."

Shane is thoughtful, considering that for a moment, then puts his truck into drive and pulls away. "Well, you are saying goodbye to a lot of things. Your job at Petals, your job at the tabloid, your innocence at how the city runs. But you're starting a lot of new things, like this with me. It's not the end of things. It's the beginning of new things."

I lean across the seat to wrap my arms around his arm, laying my head on his shoulder. "You're right. Let's go home."

It doesn't occur to me that I didn't say 'my place' or 'your place' until Shane pulls into the parking lot of my apartment. "Oh, if you need to go to your house, we can. Sorry. I didn't mean—"

Shane puts a finger to my lips, shushing me. "Maggie, *you* are my home. My apartment in the city is a front, part of the assignment. For the past year, I've basically lived out of a duffel bag. My place is more of a pit stop than anything else. I like your apartment, it's like you, sweet, innocent, warm. If you don't mind, I could use a little more sweet innocence in my life."

I smile shyly, nodding. "Okay, then let's go home."

We walk up the stairs, and I feel like we're walking hand-in-hand to something bigger, better. At the landing, Shane swoops me up into his arms and carries me across the threshold like a bride. It makes me warm and bubbly inside.

He kicks the door closed and bends down for me to lock it, and then continues his trek to my bedroom. He sets me down gently on the edge of the bed before looking around. "Bathroom? I sorta forgot."

I point behind him, and he disappears for a minute. I can hear him digging around, looking for something, and I call out. "You okay? Need something?"

"Nope, got it," he says, then I hear the bathtub turn on, the water echoing out in the quiet apartment. "There, that's perfect."

Shane reappears, pulling me up from the bed. He begins stripping me, and my body responds instantly, knowing what it wants, and I try to kiss him.

Shane steps back, his eyes twinkling in amusement. "Nu-uh, Angel. I will always give you what you want, but trust me to know what you need too."

Confused, I let him undress me the rest of the way and then watch as he strips too. Once we're both naked, he leads me to the bathroom. I've always liked this bathroom. It's why I put up with the rest of the place. The big garden tub is full of steaming water and fluffy bubbles, and there are tea candles lit on the countertop.

The bubbles in my belly rise again, the happiness bursting out as I giggle and turn to Shane. "Are you giving me a bath?"

Shane holds me, our naked bodies pressed together as he kisses my temple. "Angel, we've had a rough few days. And tomorrow, I'm going to have to start the process of becoming Agent Guthrie again. But for now, I want to wash all the roughness away, start fresh and clean and honest with each other. Never lie to me, never hide from me. Give me all of you. And I'll do the same for you."

I nod, tracing a fingertip along the designs covering his chest. "I love you, Shane."

He presses his lips to mine, smiling. "I love you too, Maggie. Now let's get in."

He steps in first, holding my hand to help me in too. I grab a hair band from the tub edge and quickly twist my hair up into a messy bun on top of my head.

We sit, my back to his front with his legs spread wide around me. Settling in the hot water, the suds tickle and tease against my skin. Shane grabs my pouf and pours body wash on it, working it to a foam and inhaling the scent deeply, grinning. "Mmm. I figured it was a special soap that makes you smell so good. Makes me want to eat you up."

I smile, too dreamy to reply as he moves the pouf along my skin, covering my arms and my chest in the warm vanilla sugar scent of my body wash. "I'll make sure to buy another couple of bottles this weekend."

Shane nods, reaching down and motioning for my foot. "Give me a leg."

I raise a foot toward the ceiling, not as flexible as the dancers at Petals, but not too shabby, if I say so myself. I can feel Shane hardening against my back as he washes down the length of my calf to my thigh, where it disappears into the water. He repeats the move on the other leg, his forehead dotted with sweat, either from his arousal or the warm water, or both.

Once I'm curled back under the surface of the warm water, he shifts, pressing me forward so he can wash my back. The pouf drops into the water, and I feel Shane's rough palms tracing along my back, washing the bubbles away and massaging my soft skin. His lips follow the path of his hands, kissing and nibbling along my shoulder and up to my neck. "Angel . . . so sweet."

A moan rolls past my lips, and I feel like I could lie in his arms forever, but I want to do for him what he's done for me. I want to wash all the past, the lies, the fear away. I want him to know that I want to be by his side. Even if the FBI says that we have to move, or that he has to go man the office in Alaska or something, I'll be there with him. I sit up, breaking his embrace for a moment before turning to face him and sitting between his splayed legs.

I feel around for the pouf. Finding it, I use more body wash to work the lather back up as Shane watches me with hooded eyes. "Hope you don't mind smelling like me," I say flirtatiously as I start to swirl the pouf along Shane's chest. "I happen to love covering you in my . . . scent."

Shane growls, his hands resting on my hips and pulling me closer, bit by bit. "Pretty sure I told you I'd smell like you anytime you'd let me. I meant I liked your juices marking me, reminding me and everyone else that I've been between those sweet thighs. But I'll take any damn thing you want to give me, Angel. Although I am hoping that normally I can use some regular soap."

Having washed his thick chest, the bumps of his washboard abs, and along the length of his powerful arms, I move my hands lower. His cock jumps as I lick my lips, leaning in. "Good . . . because time for getting washed is over."

Under the water, I let the pouf go, wrapping my hands around his thickness and giving him a few strokes.

Shane groans, his fingers tightening on my hips. "Fuck, Maggie."

I keep the pace slow, wanting to control how fast he builds, but he bucks against me, fighting for more. I move to straddle one of his thighs, forcing him still, and lean forward, licking his earlobe. "Shane, let me love you. Let me jack you off, let me mark you the way you mark me. Let me . . . let me be your woman."

His body is strung tight, using all of his control to hold back and let me have this. I move down his neck, kissing and licking and nibbling the way he does to me.

I find a spot in the curve that makes him moan as his dick jumps in my hand, and I smile to myself. I latch onto the spot, sucking and nibbling just to the edge of pain before soothing it with a licking kiss.

All the while, I stroke him, every stroke up his shaft timed with a sucking draw on his neck. I'm mindlessly riding his thigh, letting the soft hairs tickle my lips and grinding my clit along his tight muscles. "That's it, my man. So hot and sexy," I purr in his ear. "So strong, you could break me, but you didn't. You woke me. I'm yours now, your sweet angel and your dirty girl. You like that, don't you?" I kiss back down, finding that sweet spot on his neck and suck again.

I can feel his balls pulling up tight, on the edge of letting go. "Fuck, yes," he groans. "I want you by my side, Angel."

I let go of his neck and lick his ear as I pump him quickly under the water. "You're *mine*, and I'm *yours*," I whisper.

It's enough to trigger him, and he bucks beneath me, raising his hips out of the water. His cock pulses in my hand as he comes, white cum coating my hand. The sight does me in, and I grind along his thigh, finding my own release as he holds me, keeping me steady as I shudder on him.

"Mmm, that was wonderful," I whisper, cuddling against him. "Thank you."

"Thank you," Shane whispers back, holding me close. "For everything."

Eventually, we get clean, and still naked, we walk into the bedroom. Shane throws the covers back, tossing pillows to the floor as he sees my carefully constructed arrangement.

He laughs as I scramble to pick up a few of them. "Why do you have so many fucking pillows? There's like a dozen of them here!"

I laugh, picking up one to swat him on the butt. "Because they're pretty and soft and I like to curl up in them."

Shane tosses me in the bed, climbing over me and caging me in. "You're pretty and soft. And you can curl up with me now."

He lies on his back, one arm stretched wide in invitation. "C'mere, Angel," he says, and I quickly snuggle into his side, throwing one leg over his before he pulls the blankets back over us.

It feels comfortable, right, just like always. "You'll be here when I wake up, right? This isn't all some dream?"

Shane kisses my forehead, tenderly stroking my arm with his

hand. "I'll always be here when you wake up. Sleep now, though. You've been through a lot."

I can feel sleep already overtaking me, but I manage to kiss his chin before yawning. "I love you."

Just as I drift off, I hear him reply softly, "I love you too."

CHAPTER 28

SHANE

For three days, after waking up and deciding that no, I don't need to formally exfiltrate myself from my assignment yet, we've camped out in Maggie's apartment. This time, not because we need to. There's no one chasing us, no monsters looming.

Instead, it's simply because we can. We've enjoyed every moment of being together, and we've had a wonderful vacation 'playing house,' but we have to be responsible too. I've put off the FBI as long as I can, but when Chucky sends me a text to *get to the office today or else*, I know I have to go.

But I'm taking Maggie with me. It's not protocol, but fuck if I care. I'm not letting her out of my sight. Not until we're one hundred percent sure that she's safe and we're settled in.

"Are you sure?" Maggie asks as we approach the Federal building. It's small. East Robinsville isn't exactly Los Angeles or New York for a field office, but that's okay. "I mean—"

"I don't give a damn what Uncle Sam has to say," I reply, holding her hand as we approach security. I watch her go through first before laughing as her jaw drops when I put my gun and badge in the bin to walk through the metal detectors. "Guess you haven't seen these yet."

"No," she admits, her eyes going even larger when I flash the badge in its black leather billfold at her. As I replace them, badge in my back pocket, gun in my holster, I realize she's watching me, biting her lip. I cup her chin, bringing her eyes up to look me in the face. "It's okay, Angel. Don't be scared. I'll never hurt you."

She shakes her head, looking left and right to make sure no one can hear her before whispering in my ear. "It doesn't make me nervous. You look hot and tasty as fresh French fries, all confident badass. Especially in that T-shirt."

I smirk, kissing her hard but keeping it fast. I don't want any of the fuckers around here seeing my woman turned on. That's fucking private, just for me and her. I groan, wishing I could shove her into a broom closet or empty office, but there's never anything private in this place.

I take her hand again and start to lead her to the elevators. "Come on, we'd better get this over with so we can get back home."

The ride up to the fourth floor is quiet but slightly tense. Maggie's probably never even been in a normal police station, except maybe to pay a parking ticket, and now she's going to an FBI office. I give her hand a squeeze as the door opens, and we head into the bullpen area. I'm surprised to see Chucky jump up immediately when he sees me.

"What the hell? When'd they let you out of the basement?" I ask, giving him a big hug, bro-patting him on the back. "Damn, Chucky, you lost weight! What the hell happened?"

He steps back, flexing and patting on his considerably flatter stomach. "Yep, Pokémon Go sucked nuts, but getting outside to catch the little fuckers did me some good. Got me away from my desk and even to the gym. Having to watch my diet now that I'm mostly playing Fortnight and my usual Call of Duty team."

I grin, shaking my head. He's a geek, but he's a good face to see. "Battle Royale?"

Chucky grins. "Fuck, yeah, anytime."

I glance at Maggie, who's wearing a half amused, half scared shitless look on her face. "Might be a bit, but soon, man."

Chucky sees Maggie, and he walks toward her, hand outstretched. "You must be Maggie. Nice to meet you. I'm Chucky. I sorta run the computers, you know."

Maggie smiles, shaking his hand. "I remember, and thank you. Nice to put a face to the voice on the phone."

Our reunion is cut short by the appearance of my boss, SSA Solomon. A tall woman in her early sixties with a no-nonsense brown helmet of hair that nobody in the office has the balls to fuck with, she's run the East Robinsville office for five years now. "Shane. How good of you to join us. You two come on in my office."

I look to Chucky for some read on the situation, but he shrugs. Keeping Maggie's hand, we go into the office.

I try to start on the right foot, with introductions. "Maggie, this is my boss, Maria Solomon. Maria, this is my . . . Maggie."

I didn't know what to call Maggie. Girlfriend doesn't seem remotely strong enough, and I can't just go around proclaiming her 'mine' like a caveman to other people. When it's the two of us, fuck, yeah. But in public, probably not exactly politically correct. Although, Maggie's still got a bit of pink tint to the delicate skin of her neck where my lips sucked a day or two ago, and she looks proud of it.

I knew this meeting was coming and at least tried to keep my marks to the skin that'd be covered by her clothes. I smirk a bit, knowing that she's got my claims on her tits, her belly, her thighs, her ass, and she was begging for me to *'fuck her'* just this morning.

It's those filthy words that do me in every time my sweet girl uses them, my dirty Angel who makes me hard as a rock in an instant.

But right now, she's sitting prim and proper. A lady by every appearance, except to me since I know what lays under those clothes and in her dirty mind. While I've been daydreaming, they've shaken hands, and we sit down, Maria behind her desk and Maggie and me in chairs in front of her.

"I haven't seen your report yet, Shane. But I've got Organized Crime calling for a quick and dirty update, so I need a rundown of everything verbally. And then you can start catching up on your far overdue paperwork. Time to be an agent again, Guthrie."

She's mad I haven't finished the job, but fuck it. I was busy. The hard work was done. The paperwork is always the part I hate anyway. It's part of why I'm better undercover than as a regular agent. I mean, undercover just has to get shit done. The paperwork's later.

Still, I do my best to give Maria a rundown even though she knows parts of it from my check-ins with Chucky. Starting with the shooting at Petals, I move on to the hitman, Maggie and me on the run, and I end with my conversation with Dominick as we left.

"I think we parted on respectful terms, all things considered. War averted, Dominick on alert to watch out for Sal a bit more carefully, and the hitman handled so Maggie is safe. My recommendation is to leave the agent in Sal's organization for a bit to make sure that licking his wounds doesn't turn ugly."

Maria looks at Maggie, and I know I'll have to answer a few hard questions later about the details of why Dominick just let me walk out with a handshake. "Anything you'd like to add, Miss Postland?"

Maggie looks at Maria for a moment, sizing her up, and nods. "I guess just that when I worked at Petals, I didn't know about the mob stuff. All I knew was that Dominick ran a tight ship, cared about his employees, and when the crap hit the fan, he helped us."

"That's his style," Maria replies. "But—"

"He didn't have to do all he did for us, but he did," Maggie continues, and for once, I see Maria actually shut up. "I don't know what the FBI's going to do about him. I just want you to know that he is a good man. It's not black and white, criminal or not, and I hope you'll take that into consideration for future operations regarding Dominick and his businesses."

Damn this woman. I'd half expected her to sit here, quiet and shy like she sometimes gets, and just nod along with the big scary FBI folks. But the other piece of her, the brilliant mind she keeps hidden behind blonde curls and innocent eyes, is a work of fucking art. Maria smiles, a predator who's seen her prey, and I'm not about to sit here while Maria skins Maggie with poisonous words.

"Maria, I think we should go. I'll type up the report at home and send it in ASAP."

Maria looks to me dismissively and then returns her eyes to Maggie. "You are quite something, aren't you?"

Maggie shrugs but doesn't break eye contact with Maria. "I do what I can."

Maria nods, an amused glint in her eyes. "When we figured out who you are, I had Chucky do some digging. You have quite the impressive resume, Miss Postland."

I'm confused. I know Maggie is a tabloid reporter, but that's not exactly something that would impress Maria. I look out of the office window to the bullpen, seeing Chucky watching our exchange. When he catches me looking, he startles and looks down, shuffling papers.

Before I can ask what's going on, Maria continues, ignoring me for the moment. "Your resume includes undercover work on a number of stories, everything from politics to celebrities. You've been . . . let's see, an intern for a state Senator, a candy striper—"

"Candy striper?" I ask, imagining my innocent Maggie in one of those uniforms. Maggie gives me a little smile, blushing as I'm sure she's thinking the same thing I am.

"As I was saying," Maria says testily. "A secretary, and a waitress in a mob-owned club. In none of those jobs have you ever been detected until after the story came out and sometimes not even then. You've written many articles about mostly frivolous fodder. The FBI doesn't really care who's sleeping with whom—"

"Most of the time," I say, earning a glare. "Sorry."

"But some of your work—the investigative part, the under-cover work—is well beyond your current situation at a tabloid," Maria finishes.

Maggie smiles but shakes her head. "Actually, I no longer work for the tabloid. Nor Petals. I've been fired by both."

There's delight in Maria's eyes, and she opens a manila folder on her desk, taking out a small packet and toying with it. "Ah, so sorry to hear that," she replies in a way that makes me suspect she's known that since Maggie walked in. "However, I do have something I'd like you to consider."

She looks at me, then back to Maggie. "Working undercover, finding ways to tell the truth while lying, and finding out people's secrets in subtle ways are skills that are very difficult to teach. Most field agents in the FBI will go through quite a few training courses and never be able to do them effectively. Wouldn't you agree, Shane?"

I nod, knowing that most FBI agents are products of their bureaucracy. They can grind, they can use the FBI like a bludgeon, but very few can do what I do. "Not many. Are you saying what I think you're saying?"

"Seeing possible solutions beyond the scope of the usual point-to-point way of thinking is also exceedingly rare," Maria says, turning her attention back to Maggie. "It seems you do well with both of these. In short, you impressed me, Miss Postland. And I don't impress easily."

Maggie gulps beside me, and I squeeze her hand. "See? I'm not the only one."

Maggie blushes more deeply, but smiles. "Thank you."

"The FBI has a very straightforward system for becoming an agent," Maria says, toying with the paper in her hands. "But, there is considerably more flexibility when it comes to being a consultant. Especially when you're a relatively minor field office like this one. So I'd like to offer you a job with my team. Very entry-level to see how you do, an internship, if you will. But an opportunity beyond anything you've ever considered before."

Maggie looks at me, shock clearly written across her face as Maria slides the paper across her desk. "Me? Working for the FBI?"

I smile, encouraging her. "It's your call, Maggie. You're free to do anything you want now. If this sounds interesting, go for it."

"Can I become an agent too?" she asks, looking at Maria. She picks up the paperwork, flipping through it for a moment. "I mean, what does a consultant do?"

"Basically, you'd be able to do all the grunt work, but you can't carry a gun or arrest people," Maria says. "But if you want, well, I could set you up on the path for that. I'd discourage it, though. Consultants don't have to worry about rank or getting reassigned away from their . . . significant others."

Maggie nods, then grins at me. It's so beautiful I want to kiss her, right here and now, but I manage to refrain.

For now.

"That does sound interesting," Maggie says, setting the papers back down on Maria's desk. "I accept, but can I have one request? That I work with Shane and Chucky as I get my feet wet. I trust them and want to learn from them."

Maria stands, offering her hand. "Already planned, although

you'll get some oversight and training from me too. See you two on Monday then. Get out of here for now."

Just as we reach the door, Maria speaks up again. "Oh, and Shane, I need that report. Today."

I grin, knowing that I can get it done and still be able to take Maggie out for a little celebration later. "Sure thing."

We walk out hand-in-hand, ready for the next beginning. Together.

EPILOGUE

MAGGIE

*W*alking into the apartment, I can immediately tell something is off and I go on high alert. Quietly opening my purse, I reach for my pistol. I scan the living room for anything amiss, keeping my back towards the door I just cleared.

Seeing nothing but trusting my instincts, I walk heel-toe further into the apartment, looking into the kitchen to make sure no one is ducked down to take advantage of the blind spot. Clear. Other than a couple of dirty dishes in the sink, everything looks just like it normally does.

Silently steadying my breath, I breach the bedroom doorway. Before I can fully scan, an arm pops down across mine, knocking my weapon to the floor and continuing the maneuver to twist my arms up behind me.

I'm yanked against a hard body, male, judging by the impressive bulge pressing against me, and a lot taller than me, considering the bulge is pressed to my back, not my ass.

"You forgot to check your blind spot first," a deep voice growls in my ear. "You know what happens now.

My training kicks in, and in one smooth motion, I pop my hips back to knock my attacker off-balance, pull forward in a twisting motion, and dive into a front roll to get space between us.

I grab my gun from the floor, standing in perfect stance with my attacker three feet away with his hands up in surrender. "On your knees."

My voice is hard, projecting power, something Maria's had me work on in training. He lowers to his knees, a smirk on his face as I step closer. "Usually, I'd prefer for you to be on your knees, sucking me off. But this works too. Come here and let me lick you, Angel."

The gig is up when he calls me that, and I laugh, letting the gun lower to my side. "Dang it, Shane! I was doing so well! And you ruined it with your sweet dirty talk."

Shane takes the empty training gun from my hands, setting it on the dresser behind him and grabs around my waist to pull me to him. "Allie even laughed at my training pistol today. She sent a pic to Dominick, who said he thought mine would be pink, not bright orange."

Shane smiles. "How was your shopping?" But before I can answer, he shakes his head, "Never mind, tell me later. But really, you did just fine clearing the rooms and even handling me. But fuck if you don't turn me on when you get all fierce and badass like that. Makes me want to earn your sweetness back, taste the innocence you only share with me."

As he talks, he's kneading my ass, his nose nudging along my belly and down to my core. More brave than shy these days, I begin unbuttoning my blouse, tossing it to the floor.

Shane sits back on his heels, watching me. "More," he demands.

Having learned a few tricks from Allie, I don't obey instantly. Instead, I tease him, tracing a finger along the swells of my breasts, which are almost eye-level with Shane. He growls, licking along the edge of my bra, and I decide maybe teasing can wait. I reach behind to unclasp my bra and shrug it off.

Shane cups my breasts, pressing them together and burying his face in their fullness, groaning as he begins licking my skin, sucking here and there to leave the marks he always wants to see on my body.

Finally, he takes my nipple into his mouth, and my hands tug on his hair, holding him there, wanting more. His fingers work at the waist of my pants, undoing them before he helps them slide down my legs.

I step out of my shoes and then the pants, standing before Shane in just my cotton panties. I asked him once if he wanted me to wear sexier lingerie, but he assured me with his words, his hands, and his cock that he liked my simple bikini briefs. He said they look sweet, like me.

Seems his opinion hasn't changed because he's using his thumbs to trace my lips through the soaked cotton, desire darkening his eyes.

"Lie down on the bed," he rasps. "On your stomach."

Like I need a reason to do as he says, feeling Shane's weight on the bed as he straddles me, his strong thighs supporting him so he doesn't squish me.

"Hold the headboard, Angel."

I look back at him over my shoulder, but his face is unreadable. I move my hands up, holding one of the slats in the headboard.

Shane leans forward, and before I realize what he's doing, he's handcuffed my hands around the slat.

He sits back, pleased with himself. "Good girl."

I laugh, half turning even as my body thrills. We've talked about this, but this is the first time we've taken the game this far. I love it. "Shane? What are you doing?"

I can feel his rough hands tracing my skin, and once in a while, he bends over to lay a sucking kiss or nibble to a spot that entices him. "Celebrating. The first night I came here, I drove you home after that asshole scared you at the club. Your keyring had a fluffy white pompom on it."

I smile, loving that he remembers details like that about me. "I still have it. And?"

"And as of today, you're officially field cleared," Shane says. "Maria texted me the news."

I've been working hard these last few months, both with Shane and at Maria's insistence. I've learned so much, including FBI procedures, hand-to-hand fighting, firearms, and more. And while I've been able to sit next to Chucky as he pores over his computers, learning the in-house intel side, I hate that Shane is out there, undercover without me.

After his last mission, we decided he was going to wait for me so we could do the next assignment together. He took some well-deserved vacation and requested that Maria let him oversee my training, to which she agreed.

Maria's actually excited to have a team available for under-cover work as a couple. Apparently, that's rare and makes us uniquely fit for a few different intel-seeking positions. I squeal in excitement at the news, kicking my feet behind Shane, but not dislodging him. "What's that got to do with handcuffing me to the bed?" I ask.

"Look at the handcuffs," Shane whispers, licking my earlobe and making me shiver. I look up to see white, fluffy hand-cuffs encircling my wrists and laugh. "They're a bit of the old you, soft and innocent, and a bit of the new you, badass. And best of all, they make you all mine."

Shane scoots back, sitting between my legs, and I arch my back, giving him access to my center. "Tell me, Angel."

I groan, more comfortable with the words now, but still only with him. Maria laughs at my cursing workarounds. "Lick my pussy, Shane. Suck my clit. Mark me up so everyone knows I'm yours."

He growls, lowering his face toward my pussy. Right before his tongue touches me, he whispers, "Give me your sugary sweetness, Angel. I want it all."

I'm already gasping from the heat of his breath, so when his tongue touches me, it's like fireworks exploding inside me, and I buck, fucking his face and chasing his tongue. Shane tortures me, his tongue and lips keeping me balanced on the edge, drawing it out until my stomach is quaking and my toes curling in frustrated desire, and I whimper.

"That's what I wanted, Angel," Shane says before sucking hard on my clit. Like a pistol shot, I'm released, my body spasming as I cry my relief.

"Yes! Shane, I'm coming!"

I didn't even hear him unbuckle his jeans, but as soon as I cry out, he's there, shoving his thick cock into me. It paralyzes me, my orgasm stopped almost mid-crash as he fills me like I dream, pushing me higher again already.

"Fuck, Maggie. Finish coming on my cock. Squeeze me with your sweet pussy, and I'll fill you up," Shane says as he starts pumping deeply in and out. "I'll give you what you want."

I tense my muscles, drawing out every drop of pleasure from my own orgasm as Shane thrusts into me. I push back, meeting him stroke for stroke, wanting his cum inside me, wanting him to lose control and experience this bliss. Knowing what will send him over, I look back, biting my lip. "Fuck me, Shane. I love you so much."

With a powerful thrust, Shane bottoms out deep inside me, grunting like an animal as the heat of his cum sears me. It pushes me to another toe-curling orgasm, and my eyes roll back, my mouth trapped open as I pull on the handcuffs. We're going to have to do it again this way. I like it.

Spent, he lies on top of me, keeping his weight off so he doesn't smush me. "That's my dirty fucking girl," he growls lightly in my ear, "and I love you too. In fact, I had a question."

I raise my head, and he meets my lips with his own, sealing our vows of love with a kiss. "What's that?" I ask as our lips part. "And can you unlock me now?"

"Of course . . . if you're willing to lock me up," Shane says, reaching into the bedside drawer and taking out a keyring with a small handcuff key. On the keyring is a golden circle, with a small, beautiful diamond on it. "Think you want to?"

"Is that what you call a proposal?" I tease, my heart racing.

"Because if it is, I'm gonna have to call Dominick to teach you some manners."

Shane laughs and unlocks my wrists, rubbing them gently even though the fuzzy trim cushioned my skin from the metal. I sit up, turning to face him and he moves to kneel in the floor beside the bed. "You know you've had the key to my heart for months now. This is just making it more . . . formal. You're my woman, I'm your man. Now . . . Maggie Postland, will you also be my wife?"

I smile, nodding like a bobblehead. "Yes!" I hold out my hand and Shane puts the ring on my finger. I look at it happily, then give him a huge kiss, a sloppy one because I can't stop smiling long enough to pucker properly.

Pulling back, I give him a serious look. "Oh, there's one condition . . ." I say, and his face sobers.

"You know I'll give you anything. What is it, Angel?"

I grin, not able to play serious any longer. "We do that again right now!" I say, nodding towards the handcuffs dangling from the headboard.

"Deal. You're a tough negotiator, future Mrs. Guthrie." He smirks, then tackles me and I squeal, rolling over and lifting my hands for him to cuff me again.

Our future is still full of unknown possibilities and opportunities, but one thing is for sure—us.

This is real. This is love. This is home.

Other books in the *Get Dirty* Series (Interconnecting standalones):
Dirty Talk
Dirty Laundry

Read on for a preview of Dirty Laundry, and bonus material from my Irresistible Bachelor series! At the end, there's a preview (prologue) of my current work in progress!

ABOUT THE AUTHOR

Other books by Lauren:

Get Dirty Series (Interconnecting standalones):

Dirty Talk

Dirty Laundry

Irresistible Bachelor Series (Interconnecting standalones):

Anaconda || Mr. Fiance || Heartstopper

Stud Muffin || Mr. Fixit || Matchmaker

Motorhead || Baby Daddy

Connect with Lauren Landish
www.laurenlandish.com
admin@laurenlandish.com

Join my mailing list (www.laurenlandish.com) and receive 2 FREE ebooks! You'll also be the first to know of new releases, sales, and giveaways. If you're on Facebook, come join my Reader Group!

Made in United States
North Haven, CT
22 June 2024

53935039R00163